THE WHISPER TRILOGY: PART III

Michael Bray

Voices by Michael Bray

Copyright © 2014 Michael Bray

The moral right of Michael Bray to be identified as the author of this work has been asserted in accordance with the Copyright, Designs and Patents Act, 1988.

All rights reserved. No part of this publication may be reproduced or transmitted in any form or by any means, electronic or mechanical, including photocopy, recording or any information storage and retrieval system, without permission in writing from the publisher.

This book is a work of fiction. Names, characters, businesses, organisations, places and events are either the product of the author's imagination or are used fictitiously. Any resemblance to actual persons, living or dead, events or locales is entirely coincidental.

WWW.MICHAELBRAYAUTHOR.NET

VOICES

Michael Bray

"What would your good do if evil didn't exist, and what would the earth look like if all the shadows disappeared?"

— Mikhail Bulgakov

"When I despair, I remember that all through history the way of truth and love have always won. There have been tyrants and murderers, and for a time, they can seem invincible, but in the end, they always fall. Think of it—always."

— Mahatma Gandhi

PART ONE:

AFTERMATH

CHAPTER 1

The tan Mercedes jostled down the rutted dirt road leading to the Hope House hotel, driving through a steady drizzle which had been falling all morning.

A thick mist hung in the air, held in place by the overhanging tree canopy which only added to the gloom. Detective Alex Petrov squinted through the windshield, wishing away the headache that had been present since he'd woken up.

At thirty-seven years old, the Russian born Californian was already missing the warmth of the sun. Standing an imposing six feet three inches tall, with chiseled features, blond hair and piercing blue eyes, he was one of the best, or at least, that's what he'd been told prior to being sent to work the Oakwell massacre case.

He slowed as he reached the checkpoint, manned by an officer in a rain poncho who looked just as miserable as Petrov felt. Recognizing the detective, the officer waved him through, and he made his way into the hotel car park. Huge lighting rigs had been erected, pushing back the gloom of the day and casting the hotel in an ugly artificial spotlight. His partner, Warren, stood under the entrance awning, shuffling his feet as he smoked.

Ten years older than Petrov and showing every one of the strains and stresses of an overworked detective, Warren Bush didn't look at all happy. Short and balding with dark eyes and skin that was losing the battle against the aging process, he was an acquired taste, and wasn't very well liked outside those he classed as his friends. Petrov brought the Mercedes to a stop, half wishing he had thought to bring a coat. He exited the car, expensive Italian shoes ruined by the mud as he strode toward the hotel.

"This better be good, Warren," he said, joining his partner under the covered entrance.

"I wouldn't have called you if it wasn't. Trust me; I don't like this place any more than you do."

Petrov nodded. He felt it too. There was a unique atmosphere here. An ominous sense of foreboding which he suspected was fueled by the stories that surrounded it.

"Sooner we crack this, the sooner we can get the hell out of here. Believe me, I miss the sun."

"Tell me about it. It's rained pretty much every fucking day since we came here. I don't know why they had to bring us in. This isn't our business. Local law enforcement should be handling their own shit," Warren grumbled.

"There *is* no local law enforcement. Closed down. This town is on its last legs. The military are moving in just as soon as we're done," Petrov said, shoving his hands in his pockets.

"The military? Why the hell would they get involved in this mess?"

"They have their feathers ruffled. Uncle Sam is worried about what happened here."

"Some guy went apeshit. Seems pretty cut

and dried to me."

"You think I don't know that? For all I know, one of the people involved could be on the terrorist watch list. Either way, we have no choice. They've already given us the hurry up."

Warren sighed and pulled his jacket closer around his body. "This is a bullshit case, Alex. Who the fuck did we piss off to be sent out here?"

"Didn't you hear? It's a reward for our hard work. Apparently we're the best."

Warren snorted, then took a last drag on his cigarette and tossed it out into the rain. "Yeah, well, I wouldn't expect to be out of here anytime soon. We found something new. You need to take a look at it."

"Oh yeah?"

"Yeah. Come on, I'll show you."

Warren led the way into the hotel. Lights blazed as the two detectives walked through the deserted foyer. For the last few weeks, the place had been a hive of activity as photographs were taken and evidence searched for and catalogued. Now, they were the only two left on site.

"The cleanup guys were up here last night finishing off before the military come in next week to close the place up. They found something we missed."

Warren ducked under the yellow police tape and pulled open the steel door in the central core of the hotel. Within stood the broken remains of Hope House. Intended by Henry Marshall as some kind of morbid tribute, it had been encased by the hotel, left in its own self-contained concrete cell.

Most of the structure had been destroyed in the fire, and only three of the outer walls and the staircase remained. Blackened wood littered the site, and a huge roof beam had half crushed the stairs. As had been the case outside, lighting rigs had been set up to illuminate the tableau. Petrov had only seen it once during the initial investigation of the murder scene, and liked it even less now.

"What's with the lights?" Petrov asked, eying the spotlights set into the roof of the chamber.

"Powers out in here. Some kind of surge fried the electrics."

"Yeah?"

"Yeah. One of the witnesses said there was a white flash just before Marshall was taken into custody. I'm guessing someone fucked up with the wiring."

Petrov grunted and followed Warren through the remains, old glass and wood crunching underfoot as they picked their way through the debris. There was no real way of guessing the previous layout. All Petrov could recognize, apart from the staircase, were the stone fireplace in what used to be the living room and the doorframes which led to other equally fire-damaged locations.

"Through here," Warren said, leading them into the kitchen. This room at least still bore a few recognizable features: pipes, a cracked porcelain sink and the frame of the rear door which would, at one point, have looked out over Oakwell forest but now had only a concrete wall of the house's tomb beyond it.

"There's nothing left here, Warren. We already searched the place," Petrov said irritably.

"Hang on, just bear with me."

Warren led Petrov over to one of the remaining walls and the hollow within. At one time it had been the kitchen pantry. Now, however, it was empty, its frame blackened with soot. Two of the three shelves inside were missing.

"Check it out," Warren said, stepping aside.

Petrov looked, taking everything in, allowing his brain to process the information.

"How the hell did we miss this?"

"Just look at the fucking place," Warren replied. "It looks like a damn bomb went off. Besides, the house wasn't ever our focus. It was only by chance that our cleanup guys stumbled upon it. It looks like even the people who used to live here didn't know about it. The room was full of junk from the previous tenants. If it wasn't for our guys clearing it out and kicking up the old carpet when we were trying to fix the electrics, we would never have known about it. Lucky break I guess."

Petrov nodded. On the ground inside the pantry was a wooden hatch with a circular brass ring pull.

"You're sure the previous owners didn't know about this?"

"No, this room was full of crap, most of it wasn't even theirs. You know how it is, all the shit you never get around to unpacking. Most of it was from before."

"Yeah, I know what you mean," Petrov

mumbled, distracted by the hatch set into the floor. He crouched and pulled it open, dust and cold air drifting out toward him. Petrov leaned closer. Below the door was a chamber with a rickety looking ladder leading below.

"Give me a torch or something."

"I don't have one."

"Well hand me your lighter then," Petrov snapped as he got down on all fours. Warren handed him a purple Bic disposable, and Petrov ducked his head and arm into the hole before flicking the lighter on. Although it barely illuminated anything, he could see there was a corridor cut into the foundations beneath the house. At first, he thought it was some kind of basement, but soon realized that it curved away from the foundations of the building. Something else caught Petrov's attention; a smell that in his line of work he was all too familiar with. It was the slightly sweet, putrid stench of death.

"Who else knows about this place?" Petrov asked, crawling back from the hatch.

"CSI are on their way. Apart from that, just you."

"What about the army?"

"No." Warren shook his head as he said it. "Like I said, I only called you."

"Good," Petrov said, walking toward the exit.

"Where the hell are you going?"

"To get a torch out of my car."

"You ain't going down there are you?" Warren said as he hurried after him.

"Damn right I am."

"Come on, Alex, you don't know what's down there. Let's just wait for crime scene to get here, okay?"

Petrov was already in the hotel foyer. He paused by the door, turning back to his partner as thunderous rain continued to fall. "I'm just going to take a look. Once crime scene get here, the military will get wind of it and we won't ever find out what's underneath the hotel."

"Why does it matter? We got our guy for this. What's the point?"

"Because something doesn't add up. We know what Henry Marshall did, but we don't know why. That bothers me."

"Let it go. Let's get out of this shithole town."

"You know that's not my way, Warren. It's only gonna eat at me otherwise."

"Alright, if that's what you want," Warren said, pulling out his cigarettes. "But for the record, I think you're a crazy son of a bitch. We already closed the case. We don't need to be doing this."

"Come on, you know me well enough by now. I'm curious," Petrov said, grinning. "Let's get this done, okay?"

"Whatever, let's just get this over with and get the hell out of here. This place gives me the creeps. Do I have time for a quick smoke?"

"No, Warren. Come on, let's do this."

"Goddamn it, Alex, why always me?" Warren grumbled as he put his cigarettes back into his pocket.

II

Torch in hand, Petrov stood over the hatch. He peered into the darkness below and wondered if Warren was right, that the best course of action would be to wait for the crime scene investigators to arrive. Even as he considered this, he knew he would never do it. He was too curious; too interested in discovering what had happened. He sat on the floor, his legs hanging over into the void. He eyed the ladder. Old rotten wood, rusty nails holding the rungs together, equally rusted hinges pinning it to the wall.

Warren followed his eyeline. "I wouldn't trust that thing to hold your weight."

"Yeah, I was just thinking the same thing."

"Want me to see if I can call one of the guys? See if we can get a ladder out here?"

"There's no time. I need to get in there and check it out. Just stay close and keep your eyes and ears open."

"There's nobody else here. Who are you expecting to find down there?" Warren asked. He had been trying to lighten the mood, but Petrov was too tense and too mentally in the zone to acknowledge it.

"Just keep your eyes open," he said, slipping the torch into his jacket pocket.

With nothing else left to say or do, Petrov lowered himself over the edge, testing the strength of the ladder's rungs. Although they groaned in protest, they held his weight.

"Okay, I'm heading down. Keep a look out for the crime scene guys. If they get here before I'm out, don't be afraid to yell."

"Fuck it, just do what you gotta do," Warren muttered with an exasperated sigh. He was more than used to Petrov bending the rules when he could sense a potential new lead. Hoping that the light, fuzzy feeling in his gut was just the vibe being given off by the house, he resigned himself to being a spectator, for the time being at least.

Petrov lowered himself down, taking each rung on the ladder carefully. He was desperately trying to concentrate on what he was doing while ignoring the idiocy of his actions at the same time. As his head dipped below floor level, he was enveloped in a cold shroud of air. The lights from above ground barely penetrated the darkness, and until he could reach the floor and take out his torch, he was entombed in pitch black. His every sense was alive, body tense, ears straining for the slightest sound. From floor level, the drop had appeared to be no more than eight feet, ten at most. Now, as he made his way deeper, he started to think his judgment may have been wrong. The small square of light over which his partner was peering seemed impossibly far away, and it took all of his will to continue his descent.

"You okay down there?" Warren shouted, the words echoing off the walls.

I'm fine.

That was what Petrov had intended to say as the rung of the ladder snapped under his weight. Gravity dragged him down, plunging him toward the ground as his stomach traveled in the opposite direction, feeling as if it were trying to leap out of his throat. He landed hard on the dirt floor, surrounded by broken pieces of the rotten ladder rung.

"Are you hurt?" Warren said as Petrov got to his feet, brushing dust and cobwebs from his clothes. He glanced up the shaft at his partner's smirking face.

"I'm alright, but I changed my mind about that ladder. See if you can get a hold of one so I don't break my neck when I need to come back up."

"Where the hell do you expect me to find a ladder?"

"There's a tow rope in my car. Grab that."

"You coming up now?"

"Soon. I just want to take a quick look around down here first."

"Alright, just don't do anything stupid."

"I'll be fine. Just go grab that rope."

Warren raised a hand in acknowledgement and disappeared, leaving Petrov alone. Without anyone nearby, the overwhelming silence was harder to ignore, as was the crushing psychological pressure of the weight of the hotel above him.

He took the torch out of his jacket and switched it on, wishing the beam was bigger so it would penetrate deeper as he swept it over the chamber. It was roughly square, and looked to have been cut directly into the earth.

Cobwebs hung from ancient beams which

had been set at regular intervals within the space, and to Petrov's reckoning, barely looked up to the task of keeping the roof from collapsing.

He inched into the darkness, swinging the torch beam from left to right as he went, unable to shake the overwhelming feeling of being watched despite knowing he was alone.

A doorway appeared in the wall, its black maw refusing to betray any of its secrets to the torch's light. He approached the opening, automatically drawing his weapon and holding it below the light so the two of them moved in unison as he made his way deeper into the chamber.

He tried to mentally map the surface area of the house, and was sure his geography must be off, as it seemed that, rather than staying within the foundations of the building, he had taken a path away from them. Indeed, as he approached, he noted that the ground sloped downwards toward where the river would be. His every sense was alert and focused on the darkness. He inched along slowly, shuffling his feet as he approached the makeshift underground door. Images of wet crawling things, slick and sightless, burrowing through the walls flickered into his mind, and for a moment, he was sure he was going to run and scramble back up the broken ladder, as unsafe as it was.

His training, however, asserted itself. He placed one foot in front of the other, aware of the thunder of blood pounding in his ears along with the wheezing of his own breathing. He directed the torch beam into the room, his eyes soaking up the information beyond, his mind struggling to process it.

He heard Warren calling from the hatch, warning him that the crime scene investigators had arrived. The sound of his partner's voice was different, distant, like it was coming from underwater. All of Petrov's focus was on the contents of the room, which was cut into a rough circular shape.

Large bricks formed the wall, and three doors were cut into the opposite side. In the center was an altar of some kind, a course stone table upon which stood a filthy, brass-framed mirror. Candles of various sizes lined the rear and sides of the altar's surface, their melted bodies awaiting the light of flame to bring them to life again. Beside the mirror was some kind of object which Petrov couldn't quite figure out. It looked like a domestic cat, or had been at some point; its withered, rotten body was displayed upright, standing on its hind legs. The wings of a blackbird had been stitched to the cat's back, pinned in the open position as if it were about to take flight.

In place of the cat's head was one from a human; brown and dry, skin cracked, lips pulled back from yellow teeth, hair stringy and wispy. In the light of Petrov's torch, the eye sockets were twin voids of absolute black, giving the illusion of something ancient staring in defiance at him for encroaching on its territory. Behind the macabre display, written on the wall in what looked like blood, was a statement, perhaps the philosophy of those who had created the room.

The Blood shall feed the earth so that the dead need not feast.

Petrov let his eyes take in the words, committing them to memory, before looking back to the despicable creation on the table, its form as shocking as it was disgusting. As more and more of the room was revealed under the sweeping light of the torch, symbols appeared, adorning the walls, accompanied by words which he didn't understand, written in a language he had no comprehension of.

Something snapped in him then, perhaps from a combination of the mental strain together with the visual horror in front of him, and Alex Petrov lost his nerve. He turned and almost fell, then ran back toward the hatch, grateful to see the rope waiting for him. He grasped it and climbed, unable to shake the feeling that those crawling things from the walls were burrowing into his skin, or the human-headed abomination from the table was half running and half flying as it gave chase.

He scrambled up the rope, dirty and breathless, as Warren and the crime scene officers looked on. Not content just to be out of the chamber, Petrov stumbled outside and into the car park, where he threw up by the wall, stomach lurching as his lunch hit the ground. Around him the trees groaned in the wind.

CHAPTER 2

A flash of silver as the blade touched the boy's throat. He could feel it, cold steel against his skin. As confused and afraid as he was, the boy couldn't take his eyes off his dead father, or the blood pooling on the ground around him. Isaac looked to his mother, who was sitting on the ground, and knew she couldn't help him. The man at his back pushed the blade a little harder, almost enough to split the soft, delicate skin. The knife didn't concern him, and the words being exchanged between his mother and the man went unheard. Isaac was instead listening to the other voices, the ones drifting in and out of his head. He couldn't understand the things they were saying, but was frightened nonetheless.

What happened next was a blur. A hazy flash of bright light and warmth after which the man was gone, leaving him standing alone. In his dream, the man at his back remained, and dragged the knife across his skin, severing nerves and arteries, spilling his precious blood onto the ground. It was at this point he always woke, screaming and thrashing in his bed, smothered and confused until he kicked the blankets off and gulped in fresh air.

Melody hurried into the room, hair a knotty tangle, eyes dark and tired. She sat beside her son and held him, stroking his sweaty, matted hair as she tried to calm him from the nightmare. He grew quiet, comforted by her presence. She stroked his head until he settled back down, drifting off to calmer waters. Soon enough, he was asleep, arms thrust out at his side, mouth open as he snored gently.

The routine was the same every night. She stood and picked up his duvet, untangling the Ninja Turtles on the material and covering her son. Going to the door, she paused at the threshold and looked at him for a moment. Her seven year old son meant everything to her, and yet she could no longer deny that he was having serious problems dealing with what had happened.

She closed the door gently and made her way to the kitchen, slippers padding softly on the wood floor. After grabbing a glass from the drainer, she lifted the bottle of whisky from the top shelf of the cupboard and headed back to the sitting room to try and figure out what she was going to do.

She set the glass and bottle down, and poured herself a generous shot, trying to ignore how much her hands were shaking, and how thin and leathery they'd become.

She perched on the edge of the sofa and glanced toward the empty chair. People said it would get easier, yet she knew well enough that it didn't. If anything, it became more difficult. It had been almost six months since the massacre at the hotel when she'd lost her husband. Although she'd been sure it would never happen, she had already started forgetting little things about Steve. The way he spoke; the way he laughed. She scanned the room, hating the fact that she had no photos of him.

Like everything else of their lives together, they'd been destroyed, and he had refused to take new ones after the fire, which she completely understood. Even so, she would have given anything to have just one picture, one memory of the time before they'd moved to Hope House and inadvertently changed their entire futures. Even though it was over, she still felt the intense burden; the guilt that she was still alive and healthy, while Steve had paid with his life in order to save her.

There was a knock at the door.

She didn't move at first. She never had visitors, especially so late. Memories of Donovan and his wide, white grin flashed in her mind, and she shrank against the seat. Knowing he was dead made no difference. He still lived within her, haunting her in death as much as he had in life.

Another knock, louder this time. She couldn't face having to put Isaac back to bed if he woke, so forced herself to get up, pausing to drain the glass of whisky, which simultaneously burned and soothed. She walked to the door and looked through the spyhole, feeling ridiculous for being so afraid. She slid back the deadbolts and unhooked the extra chains she'd had installed before turning the doorknob.

"Are you okay? I heard some commotion?"

Melody nodded. "I'm fine, Mrs. Richter. Isaac

was just having a bad dream."

The short, prune-like old woman glanced past Melody, her devious, sunken eyes scanning the apartment before coming back to rest on Melody, false smile in place.

"Are you sure everything is alright? I heard it loud and clear. Right through the walls. I wasn't eavesdropping, not at all. It's just that the walls are thin and…" her words dried up, faded away, leaving just the smug expression behind.

Mrs. Richter was one of those women who it was impossible to pin a specific age to. Broad at the shoulders with a flabby neck and wide, bulbous eyes, she was reminiscent of an ugly, wrinkly fish. She pursed her lips and looked past Melody to the apartment beyond again.

"Are you sure you haven't had too much to drink?" she asked.

"I haven't had *anything* to drink, not that it's any of your business."

"Are you sure? I can smell it on your breath. With that boy to look after, are you sure it's a good idea?"

"I'm not drunk, Mrs. Richter."

"And the boy? Is he okay too?"

The boy. She always referred to him as that. Never as Isaac. It was always just 'the boy' when she made her semi-regular visits to stick her nose into business that didn't concern her.

"Look, Mrs. Richter," Melody said, forcing herself to remain calm and friendly, "I appreciate you checking in on me. Isaac just had a nightmare, that's all. Everything is fine."

"Are you sure?" Richter said, still bobbing and weaving to see inside the apartment. Melody pulled the door closed and leaned on the doorframe to block her bug-eyed view.

"Everything is fine," Melody said, keeping her tone cold and sharp. Before Richter could say anything else, she closed the door and rested her head on the cool wood.

Out in the hall, Mrs. Richter waddled back to her own apartment next door. She closed the door, walked to the desk in the corner of the sitting room and powered up her computer. As much as she didn't want to interfere, she was worried about the child. Perhaps a quick word with child services would at least let her feel as if she had done something to help if things took a bad turn. She had already decided that she would make the call anonymously just as soon as she found the number.

CHAPTER 3

Dane Marshall strode through the corridors of the hospital, the cheap roses he'd purchased in the gift shop by the entrance swinging by his side. They were something of an afterthought, and one which he was sure would be as unwelcome as he would be. Either way, what was important was the envelope in his pocket. That was all that mattered. He took a left, leaving behind the chaos of the accident and emergency ward with its army of sick and needy patients wanting attention. He passed doors, labelled with black signs and white text: Radiology, X-Ray, Orthopedics. It was quiet now; quiet enough to hear himself think. His shoes clacked against polished floors, and he scratched at his cheek, half wishing he had made the effort to shave.

It became apparent to him that he had been one of the lucky ones, and had managed to come out of the ordeal at the hotel unscathed, unlike the person he was here to visit. As much as he knew how well off he was, he also knew that some scars were worn on the inside, like badges, reminders of a life changing event that could never be forgotten.

He had discovered that some, like him, were able to wear the scars well, and some days he could even forget he had them. Others, however, were less fortunate, picking and scratching at them until the wounds opened and they bled to death. Of course, the memories of what happened that night still lived within him, lingering in the back of his mind along with the guilt that festered alongside it, and occasionally lurching into his consciousness to remind him of their presence.

Mostly they were images, snapshots of that night forever burned into his memory. When those awful recollections decided to present themselves, they were mainly of the tree in the forest, the gnarled giant stretching toward the heavens. He recalled the way he hadn't quite understood what he was looking at until he saw the bodies, slick with rain and blood, writhing against the nails and barbed wire that held them in place.

He remembered the way his cameraman Sean had screamed, high-pitched and filled with a raw terror which was almost as terrible as the carnage displayed ahead of them. Sean's scars had run just as deep as his own, but sadly, he'd been a picker, and as a result, the wound had stayed open and become infected. He'd been discovered just a week earlier by his mother, hanging in the closet in the bedroom of his apartment, his bloated body freed from the horrors of that night.

Dane reached the elevator, just managing to squeeze in as the door closed. He stood, staring at his warped, hazy reflection in the polished steel doors, thinking it was a good approximation of how he'd felt inside since the incident at the hotel. The doors chimed and opened, his distorted mirror image disappearing to reveal a tranquil pale green corridor. Unlike the chaos of downstairs, this part of the hospital was infinitely calmer. He knew exactly where he was going. He'd been here several times before. Taking a left, he passed private rooms, some shrouded in darkness, others lit subtly by discreet lamps. The silence here pleased him, and other than the whir and hum of life-support machinery, it was total.

Room 411 was at the furthest end of the corridor. Like the others, it was designed to be as homely as possible, a feat almost achieved if not for the presence of an ugly grey hospital bed and a large bank of expensive equipment keeping its occupant's vital organs functioning . He didn't knock as the door was open when he got there. Instead he waited, looking at the broken slab of meat being kept alive in the loosest sense of the word by the network of tubes and wires snaking out of his body.

Not for the first time, it struck Dane that Bruce Jones would have been better off if he'd died at the hands of his maniac brother. Instead, the machines whirred, clunked and beeped, and Bruce Jones' heart kept beating, and his lungs kept inflating and deflating. No machine, however, could save his brain. It had been damaged beyond repair when Henry had attacked, and the doctors had said there was no hope of recovery. In spite of that, Bruce's wife, Audrey, sat as always by his bedside, holding his limp and unfeeling hand.

Dane thought it odd how his face was so worry free (apart from the misshapen skull, that was) as he slept through an ordeal from which he would never regain consciousness. Audrey bore the burden enough for them both, appearing nearer to fifty than her thirty seven years. She noticed Dane standing by the entrance, and turned away, stroking her husband's hand.

"You got your way, finally," she said without looking at him. "I bet you're glad it's over at last. I told him not to go to that place. I told him you and your brother were trouble, but he was too stubborn to listen."

"We've already been through this. None of what happened is my fault. I suffered too."

"Not enough," she said, glaring at him. "That brother of yours should have hung for what he did instead of getting to live out his days in a hospital."

Dane said nothing. Instead, he looked at Bruce, trying to understand why he felt no sympathy.

"My brother is sick—"

"Don't you dare make excuses for him or you can turn around and leave."

"Audrey, you asked me to come here today."

"Don't give me that shit. Those lawyers of yours have been hounding me since the accident. All I wanted was to be left alone to look after my husband."

"I wasn't hounding you. I was offering you help when I thought you might have needed it. God knows, you don't need a reminder like that hanging around your neck."

"Don't cheapen yourself by lying. You wanted something Bruce has and you haven't let it go since," she said, glaring darkly in his direction.

"Audrey, please…"

"You don't need to beg. I'll sign your papers. Chalk up another win for the Marshall boys."

He made no outward reaction, yet inside his adrenaline spiked.

"Why the change of heart?" he asked.

"Why the hell do you care? You don't know him. You don't know any of us."

Dane looked at his shoes, then remembering he still had the bunch of cheap flowers in his hand, set them down on the dresser. He didn't expect an answer, and was trying to think of something else to say when she responded.

"It's time to let him go. This isn't Bruce. He'd have hated this… being kept alive by machines. You know, I can't even remember his voice anymore."

"I'm sorry."

"We have a daughter, you know. She's seven. Every day she asks me when Daddy will be home. Do you have any idea how hard it is to keep lying to her? To keep giving her hope?"

"No, no I don't."

"That's why I decided it's time to say goodbye. It's time to move on."

"You're switching off life-support?" Dane asked, eyebrows raised.

"I can't do it anymore," she said softly, the anger fading out of her voice. "I don't have the strength. He's not coming back, I know that. I just… It feels like I'm giving up on him."

"He'd want you to move on."

"Don't you dare tell me what he'd want. You don't know anything about him."

"I'm sorry."

"Yeah, everyone is. It's just a word though. I'm the one who has to live with it."

Dane again decided silence was the best response. Realizing she wouldn't be able to goad him into an argument, she sighed and dabbed the corners of her eyes with a tissue. "Give me the damn papers. I want to spend some time with my husband before I let him go."

Dane handed her the envelope he'd been holding since his arrival. As was becoming routine, he held his tongue, this time not so much out of respect, but interest as he watched her open the envelope. Time seemed to slow as he watched her take a pair of reading glasses out of her bag and look through the documents. As he watched and waited, he became aware of everything going on around him, almost as if he were tuning into his surroundings at a more acute frequency than normal.

Everything seemed sharper, more intense: the steady hiss-wheeze of the machines keeping Bruce alive; the overpowering sickly sweet smell of his soon-to-be widow's perfume; even the distant sound of someone coughing somewhere down the corridor, all of which were secondary to the sight of Audrey as she scanned page after page of documentation. She caught him staring at her and screwed up her face.

"Jesus, you look like a vulture standing there."

"The paperwork is no different to the versions we've sent you before. Nothing has changed. I have no intention of ripping you off."

"You think I care about a patch of dead land in the middle of an even deader town? As far as I'm concerned, you can have it. I just want to be sure this will be the end of it."

"I understand. Your husband didn't care much for the land either, which is why he'd agreed to sell it."

"Yes, to your brother, right before he did this. It would have been much easier for you if they'd completed the sale before he decided to lose his mind, wouldn't it?"

He was shocked by the venom in her eyes.

"I'm not making any excuses for him," Dane said. "What he did was inexcusable. I just don't want to be associated with his actions. I was a victim too."

"You were no victim. You have your life; you have your health. What about me? What do I have?"

"I'm sorry," he replied, staring at the floor so he didn't have to look at her. "I don't know what you want me to say."

"I don't want you to say anything." Her voice was filled with emotion.

Before he could reply, she scrawled her signature on the bottom of the final page, slipped the documents and pen into the envelope and held them out to him.

"There. You win."

He took the envelope, unsure what to say or

do.

"Would you like me to stay? For the end, I mean," he asked, not because he wanted to, but because it seemed like the right thing to say.

"Are you serious?" she replied, face contorted into a grimace. "I couldn't imagine anything worse. Just go, get out of here and let me say goodbye to my husband in peace."

"Okay, I'm sorry. I just thought—"

"Get out!" she screamed.

Dane hesitated a few seconds more, torn between doing as she asked and trying to reason with her. In the end he chose the former, leaving Audrey to say her last goodbyes to her husband.

CHAPTER 4

Kimmel shifted into third, the black Jeep growling in response as it rolled across the blacktop. In the passenger seat, Fisher grunted and glanced across at the General, the gold buttons on his green suit jacket glittering in the mid-morning sun. Golden autumn leaves were displaced as the Jeep flashed past the sun-bleached sign welcoming them to the town of Oakwell. Fisher fidgeted, his polyester coat rustling against the seat.

"It's not what I expected after the way your people built it up," he said, glancing at Kimmel.

The General returned the glance, already disliking the skinny, sunken-eyed government official. "We're still at the town boundary. Give it a chance."

"You know, a lot of people in my office think this is a complete waste of time."

Kimmel snorted. "They always do until they see it for themselves. I've heard this a million times before."

"Are you trying to frighten me, General?"

"What do you mean?"

"Well, all this paranormal talk. Ghosts. Entities in the woods. It doesn't seem like something a military man like yourself would entertain."

Kimmel grunted as the Jeep passed under the trees, the road ahead masked with sun-spotted shadows. Fisher waited for a reply which didn't come.

"General?"

"What?" Kimmel snapped.

"You didn't answer my question."

"What question?"

"About scare tactics."

Kimmel gave Fisher a quick look and saw it all over his face. The half-smile, the raised eyebrows. He didn't believe any of it.

"Do you think the government would send you all the way out here if they didn't have legitimate concerns about this?"

"My understanding is it was you who requested someone be sent out here to assess the situation. I'm told you have some concerns for the safety of your men."

"Damn right I have."

"And the scientists; you refuse to let them conduct their work? I'm told you banned them from going about their duties."

"I did."

"Please, don't take it so personally, General. I'm here to understand why. I'm led to believe you have an extensive military presence here which should be more than capable of handling this situation."

"I came here with thirty men. Good ones too. Fine soldiers, the kind who keep this country safe so people like us can keep polishing seats with our asses."

Fisher didn't rise to Kimmel's goading. Instead, he turned more toward the General, eyes devious and sharp. "So I'll ask again. Why am I here?"

"Because five of those men have been lost under my command and I won't put the rest at risk any further."

"Some might say losing five men in a low threat mission such as this could be the fault of the man in charge."

"I hope you're not trying to pin this on me, Fisher. I'd be very, very careful if you are."

"I'm not blaming anyone. As I said, I'm here in a completely impartial capacity. My job isn't to take sides. The fact is, Washington has some doubts about the validity of your claims."

"You think I don't know that? Trust me, Fisher. Before I came here, I'd have been right there with you. Do you think I don't know how ridiculous it all sounds? Do you think I like reporting back to Washington and knowing how it must appear?"

"Then help me understand. How have you been so helpless here?"

"I don't follow."

"Don't you have weapons? Resources?"

"Of course," Kimmel snapped. "You have to understand, Fisher. This is something guns can't handle. My men are afraid."

Fisher watched the General, waiting for him to elaborate, perhaps for a punchline for a joke which wasn't coming. Instead, he stared at the road, brow furrowed, hands lightly touching the steering wheel.

"And what about you? Are you afraid?"

"You bet your ass I am," Kimmel grunted, his

candid response surprising Fisher.

The Jeep slowed as it pulled onto Main Street, the storefronts all telling a similar story: *Foreclosure*, *Closing down sale*. Some had already bitten the bullet and were sagging, dilapidated, boarded-over husks, whereas others were just managing to stay open, although it was obvious at a glance that the battle was a losing one.

"Jesus, this place is a dump," Fisher grumbled.

"It didn't used to be. Believe it or not, this was a thriving little town until not too long ago."

"So where is everybody?"

"Didn't you read the report we sent you?" Kimmel said, more than a little irritated.

"Skimmed it. I didn't want the content to influence my decision."

Asshole.

As tempting as it was, Kimmel didn't say it. Instead he stared at the road. Main Street and its scatter of dying businesses soon gave way to denser tree cover which overhung the road on both sides, shrouding the Jeep in an artificial gloom.

"You can't stay up there for long," Kimmel said, more to himself than to Fisher.

"At the hotel?"

"The hotel is bearable as long as you have people with you. I'm talking about the clearing out back in the woods. Anything more than twenty minutes and you start to feel it crawling around inside you. Nobody is allowed up there by themselves. Always groups, and then in short spells."

"Who made that rule?"

"I did," Kimmel snapped, "after one of my men castrated himself up there then pulled out his own eyes."

Fisher swallowed, his Adam's apple bobbing in his throat.

He's starting to understand, the General thought as they continued down the bumpy track.

Fisher remained silent, hands folded neatly in his lap.

"You might not know this, Fisher, since you 'skimmed' the report, but there have been over seventy eight recorded deaths in and around these lands over the years."

Fisher glanced across at the general, waiting for him to elaborate. When he didn't, Fisher pressed. "That sounds like a lot of people."

"Those are only the ones we know about. Since we started to actively monitor the site, we've found countless bone fragments. Just last week one of my men found a complete human skull out in the woods. So far we haven't identified it."

"Still, you can't attribute those deaths to the house or this… clearing you mentioned. People die all the time. Natural causes, old age, strokes, heart attacks."

"Fair point, and there have been documented cases of those here too. What we also have are the other deaths. The murders, the suicides. The mutilations."

"Mutilations? What the hell do you mean by that?" Fisher asked.

"If you'd read that damn report I sent you,

you'd already know all this."

"I'd rather hear it from you."

"What the hell do you think it means? People who stay up here for any length of time do things to themselves or to the people they're with. We've had hangings, stabbings, bludgeonings. We've had people drown themselves in the river, others have set fire to themselves. Perfectly sane and rational people have spent time in that place and transformed into brutal, violent psychopaths without warning or explanation."

Despite his unwillingness to believe, the hairs on Fisher's forearms bristled. "What about the fire that burned the place to the ground. Were your ghosts responsible for that too?"

Kimmel glared across the seat, making Fisher aware that he may have overstepped the boundaries with his comment. He cleared his throat and set about keeping on track.

"I remember a little bit about this part," Fisher said. "There was a couple who lived in the house. I remember reading about how the husband got burned up in the fire, the uh, Sandersons I think it was."

"*Samsons*. Steve and Melody. You're right about the burns to the husband. He got it pretty bad. He's dead now."

"He was killed during the massacre at the hotel, right?"

Kimmel glared at Fisher. "So you do know *something* about what happened out here."

"Just vague things I remember from the news at the time. It was a councilor wasn't it? Went and hacked up a bunch of people?"

"It's not how it happened."

"But that's the gist, right?" Fisher said, reverting to his 'I don't quite believe all this' smile.

"The stuff reported in the news was only half of it. For the record, Henry Marshall was an upstanding, law abiding citizen who had never had so much as a parking ticket before he decided to build that damn hotel."

"People don't just change. Maybe there was some kind of trigger, but people like that are inherently disturbed."

"I saw his psychological evaluations. It shows a complete turnaround in behavior directly in line with the building of the hotel and the mess that came with it. I see that as more than just a coincidence."

"So what do you think tipped him over the edge?" Fisher asked, interested enough again to drop his cocky smile.

"You know what I think. Don't try to railroad me into giving you a reason to doubt what I'm telling you."

"Come on, General. You got me all the way out here. I'm interested in your angle on this. That's part of why I'm here. The people back at Washington have a lot of respect for you. Do you think they'd have entertained this had it been anyone else who'd called it in?"

Kimmel flicked his eyes across to his passenger, expecting to see the cocky smile he was rapidly growing to hate. Instead he saw a sincere and level gaze, awaiting a response. Kimmel sighed and organized his thoughts.

"Did you ever hear of a guy called Donovan?"

"Of course. Violent psychopathic serial killer. All round nasty son of a bitch. I read up on him out of personal interest way before I ever got involved with this case."

"Well, what you won't have read is the link between him and Henry Marshall."

"What kind of link? Donovan was long dead before the massacre at the hotel."

"Oh, I know. As I said to you earlier, the stuff in the press and what happened are two different things."

The Jeep suddenly emerged from the overhanging branches into blazing sunshine. Ahead, beyond the overgrown gravel driveway stood the boarded-up shell of the Hope House hotel. Yellow weeds clung to the foundations, growing in sparse clumps and waving in the bitter breeze. The building itself was a slate-colored block against a backdrop of pale blue sky. Sheets of metal had been placed over the windows and doors, keeping access from curious souvenir hunters. Graffiti, ranging from the lewd to the inventive, adorned every square inch of the building, which, even in the bright light of summer, was both imposing and intimidating.

Green tents of various sizes stood in formation in what would have been the car park, and soldiers shuffled from one to another, carrying equipment and paperwork. Kimmel pulled the Jeep up in front of the hotel and shut off the engine, which began ticking monotonously as it cooled. He waited and watched as Fisher leaned forward in his seat, peering up at the building through the windshield, taking it all in. He went on with the story, wanting to finish before they got out of the vehicle.

"As I was saying, the stuff released to the press and the facts are completely different. Everyone knows Marshall went on a murder spree, leaving six people dead and another critically injured.

He hasn't spoken a word about it since despite numerous attempts to find out why he did it, or what changed his personality so quickly in such a short space of time. Since you didn't bother to read my report, what you won't know is that, for whatever reason, Henry Marshall became obsessed with Donovan."

"Bullshit," Fisher said, eyes bright with curiosity and, Kimmel thought, maybe just a little bit of apprehension now they had arrived at the hotel. Kimmel nodded at two of his men who had approached the Jeep to verify it as the General's. They returned to their duties at the tent nearest to the hotel entrance.

"I wouldn't bullshit about any of this, Fisher. The fact is, Henry Marshall murdered his wife some five days before his murder spree and left her to rot in the house. We found her sitting in the chair, head back, mouth open. Goddamn it, I never smelled anything so bad in my entire life. The maggots had eaten out her eyes. It was a mess."

"Jesus Christ," Fisher said, swallowing hard.

"That's not all."

"Go on."

"All over the house, in every room and on every surface, Marshall had written or carved the word Donovan. He'd even hacked it into his wife's stomach."

That left Fisher speechless, which earlier would have pleased Kimmel immensely. Now that they were at the hotel, however, all he could think of was the dull tingle in the pit of his stomach. "Alright, that's enough talk. Let's get this over with," the General said, climbing out of the vehicle.

Fisher followed suit, his breath fogging in the bitter autumn air.

"General Kimmel," he said, now all business. "Let me get one thing clear. I'm here to decide if there are valid grounds to close this town down due to your claims. As I'm sure you can understand, the reasons for your request are far from normal and have caused my superiors great concern, not to mention the headaches that would come with having to explain why we were sealing the place off. I like you, General, and I can see why people respect you. I just hope you're not wasting my time."

Kimmel stared back at him over the hood of the Jeep, his brilliantly sharp blue eyes watching Fisher. As much as he had done a good job of hiding it, the General could still see a hint of something lingering just beneath the surface: it wasn't quite fear, not yet anyway, but it was definitely uncertainty.

"I appreciate you have a job to do, Fisher," Kimmel snapped. "Much like I have one to do too. The difference is, you can do yours from the safety of an office. My men are in danger here."

"Forgive my ignorance, General, but this is hardly a warzone."

Kimmel showed a flicker of a smile, just enough to show the tips of his teeth, which unsettled Fisher. "You ask any single one of my men and they would gladly transfer out to Iraq or Syria or any other hellhole on this planet if it meant leaving here."

"I find that incredibly hard to believe."

"What's so difficult? In warfare, you know your enemy. It's just another man. This... This is something else."

"Then why don't you show me what has you so spooked and we can both get back to doing our jobs?"

"Okay, let's do it."

Fisher started toward the hotel, but Kimmel stopped him. "No, not there. Like I told you, down here is fine. If you want to experience what I'm talking about so you can report back to Washington, then you need to follow me."

Kimmel headed toward the rear of the hotel. Fisher followed, striding to keep up. They walked without speaking, the sounds of the forest accompanying them as they eased down the slight hill toward the river.

"I hope you didn't take any offence at my words," Fisher said as they made their way toward the bridge. Two of Kimmel's men were waiting there, both armed. They stood and saluted as he neared. Kimmel returned the gesture as he strode past them, spit-polished boots thudding with dull regularity against the wooden boards.

"No offence taken. I understand you're skeptical. It's normal when facing something that makes no rational sense."

"With all due respect, requesting a shutdown and quarantine of an entire town makes no rational sense either. If I don't find good reason to authorize this, then it won't happen. You better be sure your ghosts will be out to play this morning."

As they reached the opposite bank, Kimmel veered to the left, making for a well-worn trail through the trees.

"They're not ghosts," he said as the pair went under the cover of the canopy, the drop in temperature noticeable as they left the sun behind. "This is something else entirely."

"We'll see."

Kimmel stopped and turned to face the government official. His brow was furrowed, lips pursed. His cheeks were red from both cold and anger. "Look, I know you don't believe any of this. You've made that clear enough. For your own sake, I ask you to at least respect the situation."

"My job requires me to come into this with an open mind."

"It doesn't seem open. In fact, if anything, you seem determined *not* to believe this."

"What is it, General? Are you afraid I won't experience this evil juju you keep talking about with such conviction?"

"No." Kimmel started to walk again, putting his hands in his pockets. "I'm afraid that when you experience it, you won't know quite how to react."

They went deeper into the woods. For Kimmel, it was a journey filled with dread. For Fisher, it was one of curiosity. He was lost in thought, listening to the pleasant sound of birdsong, when he almost walked into the General who had stopped ahead of him.

"What's wrong?" Fisher said, trying to ignore another ripple of goose bumps on his forearms.

"Nothing. We're here," the General replied. His booming, authoritative voice was gone, replaced instead with meekness and uncertainty. His eyes darted toward the trees, lingering on the darkened tangle of roots and branches which hid secrets away from his gaze.

Fisher smiled, glad to see the General's discomfort. "Come on then, General Kimmel. Let's see what it is you want to show me." Before the general could respond, Fisher strode toward the clearing and back into brilliant sunshine.

He felt it immediately. The circular clearing bristled with an ominous energy. Fisher smiled, a nervous gesture which quickly faded. His throat was dry and he stared bug-eyed at the circular patch of dirt in which nothing grew. He realized then what it was that disturbed him so much.

It was the silence. The absolute, deathly silence. He could hear the ragged rattle of his own increasingly labored breathing as he soaked in the atmosphere. He realized he was clenching his fists, and forced himself to relax, if only so Kimmel wouldn't be able to see how afraid he was. And he *was* afraid. He felt incredibly exposed, and crossed his arms over his chest, rubbing his biceps as he stared into the surrounding trees, sure he could see people moving just outside his field of vision.

Kimmel.

He wouldn't be at all surprised if it was Kimmel's men out there, creeping around and trying to put the frighteners on him. He could imagine how they would laugh at him later, making fun of how the little man from the government had been so easily spooked.

"I know what you're thinking," he heard Kimmel say at his shoulder. "But it's not my men. That much I can guarantee you."

"Then what the hell can I see moving out there?"

"The dead. Those who are destined to stay here for eternity."

"Come on, Kimmel, don't screw around with me. I—"

Fisher turned, expecting to see Kimmel right beside him. However, the General wasn't there. He was hanging back on the edge of the circle, shifting his weight from one foot to the other as his agitation increased.

"How did you do that?" Fisher asked, his voice wavering. "You were right here next to me. I heard you."

Kimmel shook his head. There was at least ten feet between them, and Fisher knew it was impossible for Kimmel to have said the words which he'd heard so close he could feel hot breath on his neck.

Kimmel was looking at him now, a frown on his brow. Realization came to Fisher that everything the General had said was true. He turned to leave, and felt something stop him, an icy grip on his upper arm. He stared at it, his eyes seeing nothing but his suit jacket despite the feel of fingers digging into his skin. Without warning, the trees shuddered, a coordinated wave traveling from left to right, each flutter of every leaf and branch coming together in a crescendo of noise.

He heard Kimmel – the real Kimmel – his voice distant and distorted as if coming from miles away instead of the ten feet which separated them. Fisher bit down on his tongue hard enough to draw blood, which seemed to increase the oppressive darkness stifling him. He was vaguely aware of men dragging him away from the inner periphery of the circle, fatigue-clad soldiers who wore the haunted expressions of men to whom this was nothing new. The soldiers half led, half dragged Fisher out of the clearing, back into the relative safety of the woods. It was a feeling akin to breaking the surface of the water after a particularly deep dive, gasping in precious air – *clean* air without the toxicity of that which existed within the clearing. Kimmel appeared over him, face looming in half-focus, a look of concern and smug satisfaction etched on his face. Fisher didn't care though; he knew what had to be done. He swallowed, the taste of blood from his cut tongue thick and coppery in his mouth.

"Now do you understand?" Kimmel said, leaning close enough for Fisher to smell the minty scent of his chewing gum. "Now do you get it?"

Fisher nodded, unable to shake the vertigo.

"Then you know what we have to do? Damn it, Fisher, talk to me!"

"Close it down. Close the whole damn place down."

Kimmel nodded, the relief on his face clear. "It's about goddamn time."

Fisher barely heard him. He could still feel the cold on his skin where the phantom hand had grabbed him, and hear the devious, sinister voice which he mistook for Kimmel. Worse than all of that was the fact that he couldn't explain any of it. All he knew was Kimmel was right. Whatever existed there in the clearing was evil.

CHAPTER 5

Isaac Samson woke screaming again. This time it wasn't the dream of the man with the knife, but the other one where he was dead, cold and alone in the dirt. Strangers surrounded him, staring, their voices distant echoes as the black things with slimy, slick tentacles emerged from the ground and grabbed him, pulling him under, the soft earth falling onto his open eyes and filling his mouth as he was dragged to whatever lay below.

As he thrashed around in his sheets, his mother didn't run to him, nor did she soothe his cries like she had when the dreams had first started. Instead, she sat at the kitchen table, head resting on her folded arms. This, after all, had become a regular occurrence. Physically and mentally exhausted, she didn't know what she was supposed to do. She had been offered help by the authorities of course; invitations to counseling and therapy sessions for them both. She didn't want to put her son through that, however, and had decided to ignore the persistent letters. Even child services had made contact in regards to Isaac's wellbeing.

The carefully worded letter had infuriated her, and she suspected that her busybody neighbor had been responsible for having involved them. Like the others, she had ignored all attempts at communication. Her son's screams faded as he found a calmer place in his dreams. Melody was glad he hadn't woken up. She was starting to resent him for the almost nightly routine which was getting worse week on week. Her phone pulsed on the table, and she gave it a cursory glance. Another text message from her sister, the seventeenth, along with the twenty or so calls that she'd failed to return. Melody wondered if it was perhaps she who had contacted the authorities out of concern and not Mrs. Richter. God knew she could hardly blame her for it. Although it wasn't a deliberate decision, she had cut herself and Isaac off from everyone, partly because people wouldn't understand what they were going through, but mainly because of fear. She only had Isaac left now and was determined to protect him no matter what.

Isaac started to cry, low moans coming from his bedroom, calling for her as he always did. Still, she didn't move. Instead she stared at her hands, flat on the tabletop. Her phone pulsed again. Another message from her sister. Isaac continued to whine and beg for her to go to him.

Three weeks.

The number reverberated around her mind. Three weeks since she'd had a full night's sleep. Three weeks since she'd last been able to think, or to function.

Three weeks since Isaac had slept without crying, or wanting, or needing.

Three weeks.

Rage, alien and unexpected, exploded within

her. She swept the cup of cold coffee and the fruit bowl onto the floor, both of them shattering. She half turned on her chair, and before she could stop, she was screaming at him to shut up, to keep his whining mouth closed and go to sleep. Melody was crying herself now, an outpouring of emotion that she'd held onto for what felt like a lifetime. Isaacs's cries took on a different tone.

They were cries of confusion rather than fear. She barely heard them. Instead, the outpouring of anger continued as she raged at her son, then, as quickly as it came, it faded. She leaned her elbows on the table and put her head in her hands. Isaacs's cries echoed around the apartment, not stopping until the police arrived.

CHAPTER 6

James Fisher stood on Oakwell's Main Street, watching as Kimmel's men loaded the last stubborn residents onto busses ready to be transported out of the town. He remained impassive, eyes hidden behind reflective aviator glasses, as the proceedings unfolded. Some of the residents, those who had decided to try and sit out the slump or had only known life in Oakwell, had been difficult to move, and it had taken the presence of soldiers with weapons to persuade them the alternative accommodation that had been arranged was for the best. Fisher hadn't spoken of his experience at the clearing to anyone, and even though he was some distance away from it, he could still feel its clammy, sickening touch on his skin. He checked his clipboard, marking off another bus as it closed its doors and took its unwilling passengers away.

Kimmel strode over and stood beside him.

"Any trouble?" Fisher asked.

"Nothing we couldn't handle. We should have the town emptied within the week."

"Are they accepting the story?"

"Mostly. The old timers don't seem too convinced. They've lived here long enough to know there are no sinkholes under the town. I suppose it's going to have to suffice. What I want to know is what happens then?"

"What do you mean?" Fisher asked, turning

toward the General.

"Once you empty this place. What then?"

"Nothing. We seal it up and forbid access. A small team will be stationed here on the outskirts of town for a while to deter the curious. With luck, the forest will reclaim this godforsaken place and that will be the end of it."

"What about what we found under the house. Surely that changes things?"

"You don't sound much like a man who wants to be out of here, General Kimmel. Why all the questions?"

"Come on, Fisher, you know what I've had to deal with up here. You visited for half an hour. I've been here for a couple of weeks. I'm just having trouble leaving a mission half-done. It's not in my blood."

Fisher nodded, then took off his glasses, folded them over and slipped them into his jacket pocket. "I think under the circumstances, this one is best forgotten. You did your best, General. Nobody can ask any more of you."

"It's my men I'm worried about. The ones I've already lost."

"How so?"

"Do you know what it was like to tell their loved ones? Good men who didn't deserve to die that way. Men with lives… families. Telling a family member that their nearest and dearest died valiantly in battle is easy. How do I explain what they did to themselves up there?"

"We both knew how difficult this would be to keep a lid on, General. There will always be questions, there will always be curiosity. Sometimes the best thing to do is nothing at all. Let it fade from people's memories."

"That still doesn't answer my question about what's under the house. Those tunnels go deep. We need to explore them."

"And you can rest assured they will be. Just not yet."

"When?"

"Why do you want to know?"

"Because I'm curious. I want to know why I was sent up here to investigate then barred from entering the one location that might give us some answers. Pardon my French, Fisher, but this whole situation fucking stinks."

"Look, I won't insult your intelligence, General. I did that when I got here and regretted it instantly. You know how this works. There's a chain of command. We all have our orders. You follow yours, I follow mine and so on up the ladder. Your involvement is done here. You did a fantastic job but we can handle it now."

"I can't say I'll be sad to leave the place, no matter how curious I am," Kimmel sighed, staring out over the sorry-looking town.

"I'm glad we have an understanding. Go ahead and pack your belongings. You're free to go."

Kimmel looked down Main Street, beyond the crowds and the busses to the sloping green landscape of trees beyond. Like Fisher, he could feel the clearing up there, somehow watching him, somehow aware. He shuddered, and walked off down the street, anxious to leave the town of Oakwell behind for good.

CHAPTER 7

The office was cold, clinical almost. The man behind the desk stared at Melody with sharp eyes, his expression neutral. Aged somewhere in his fifties, he was dressed in a pristine charcoal suit, his graying hair swept into a side parting. She could smell his aftershave, strong and expensive, and was increasingly aware of how bad she must look. Her hair was frizzy and wild, eyes darkly rimmed from lack of sleep. She folded her hands on her lap and waited for the man to speak.

"Mrs. Samson, as you know, child services are concerned only with Isaac's welfare. We have no intention of causing undue disruption."

"When can I see my son? It's been two weeks since you took him."

"Please, try to understand, we want what's best. For both of you."

"I know that, Mr. Styles. But I'm fine now. It just all got on top of me. Since my husband died…"

She lowered her eyes and picked at her thumbnail.

"We appreciate the difficult circumstances. We also appreciate the strain you must be under. I understand you rejected all offers of help from the authorities?"

"I don't need their help. I'm just tired. Isaac… he's having these nightmares. I'm just… it all got a little bit too much for me."

Styles nodded and referred to the file on the table. "Yes, we read the report. Night terrors. Probably post traumatic due to the recent events in Oakwell. Our concern is making sure the correct support network is in place."

"It sounds like you're saying I'm a bad mother."

Styles smiled. Patient and calm. "Mrs. Samson, how much do you know about PTSD?"

She looked back at him blankly.

"Don't worry, I'll explain it all. PTSD stands for post-traumatic stress disorder. It manifests itself in people who have suffered a particularly violent or traumatizing experience. After reading your file, I think both you and your son may be suffering from this condition, which has caused the situation to escalate to this point."

"Are you saying I'm incapable of looking after my own child?" she snapped.

"Not at all, Mrs. Samson. I'm simply trying to give you an explanation of why this situation has developed."

She cleared her throat and folded her hands in her lap. "Go on."

"Sufferers of PTSD usually relive their traumatic experiences. Sometimes in the form of flashbacks or vivid and terrifying nightmares, more so when faced with daily reminders of the event in question."

"There are no reminders, Dr Styles. I moved away, started afresh. I don't know what else could be affecting him."

"There *is* one other common denominator, Mrs. Samson."

"What?"

"You," Styles said, giving her that smile again, the one which was mostly confidence mingled with just enough empathy not to be smug.

"What do you mean?"

"You were there, Mrs. Samson. When Isaac experienced the trauma of your husband's death, he saw you too. *You* are his connection."

"Are you saying I'm causing this?"

"No, or at least, not intentionally. However, I do believe that your continued presence in his life right now is having a detrimental effect on his wellbeing."

"I love him. I love him more than anything," she said, dabbing the corners of her eyes with a crumpled-up tissue.

"Your love for your son isn't in question here, Mrs. Samson. I'm sure you'll agree his wellbeing is our priority. The fact is that in the weeks since he was taken into care, he has shown a remarkable improvement. I think that warrants further discussions."

"Are you suggesting I just give him up? He needs me."

"Not at all. What I'm saying is that nobody expects you to have to do this by yourself. There is support available. Your sister has told us that she is there to help if you need her."

"You spoke to my sister? You have no right to do that."

"Please, calm down, Mrs. Samson. Try to work with us here."

"How dare you go to her? This has nothing to do with my sister. Nothing to do with you. I want my son now."

Styles leaned forward, his face a carefully engineered mask of sympathy and authority. "Mrs. Samson, I'm not sure you understand the seriousness of the situation. My job is to do whatever is best for the child."

"*I'm* what's best for the child. He's *my* son. He's all I have left."

"I appreciate how you feel, Mrs. Samson, and believe me, I understand. Try not to see us as the enemy here. We're trying to help you."

She slammed her hands on the desk, causing Styles to twitch. "Then give me my son!"

She shrank back, knowing how she must sound. Knowing how she must look. Styles adjusted his tie and steepled his hands across the file.

"Frankly, Mrs. Samson, we have concerns, not just for Isaac, but for you too. Both of you have been through a very trying experience. I'm sure you'll be the first to admit that you're feeling the strain of the situation and you should have sought help. What we need to do is determine what's best for you as well as Isaac. That's the key here."

"Look," she said, voice trembling. "I know I should have accepted help. I see that now. If you want me to talk to your counselors, or your therapists, then I will. Just give me back my boy. He's all I have."

Styles said nothing, just continued observing her, then turned his attention to her file. "I think one-on-one counseling sessions would be in your best interests, Mrs. Samson. I would also like to refer you to a doctor with regards to prescribing you some medication to help you during such a difficult time. It seems clear to me that, despite your best efforts, you are still struggling to cope with the tragic loss of your husband. I think both you and your son are suffering from severe PTSD, and despite it seeming otherwise, you are both negatively affecting the wellbeing of the other and hindering both of your recoveries. It's for this reason that I have decided to place Isaac into short-term care until you're in a better position to provide the care and stability he needs."

"No, you can't do that!" Melody said, gripping the edge of the table. "He needs me. We need each other. You can't take him away from me."

"What your son needs is stability, Mrs. Samson. He needs to be able to flourish in these important years. He needs a stable environment where he can receive treatment and get well. Surely you want that for him as much as we do?"

"Please, I'll do whatever it takes. Just don't take him away from me."

"I'm sorry, Mrs. Samson," Styles said, closing the file. "This is for the best."

"What about second chances? Don't you people see that I need him? I need to protect him?"

"Like I said, if you accept the help we are offering and show improvements within a reasonable timescale, this should only be a short to midterm solution."

"I need him with me. What if those things come back for him?" she shrieked, immediately regretting saying anything. Styles sat there and took it. She imagined he was used to it by now. Bearing bad news, taking the backlash from aggrieved parents who were about to lose a child to the system. She cleared her throat and looked him in the eye, hoping to appeal to his humanity. "Please don't take my son. He's all I have."

"I'm sorry," he replied, holding her gaze. "There's nothing else I can do. The decision has been taken."

"What do I do now? What am I supposed to do now on my own?" She was sobbing again, her voice a shrill, hysterical shriek.

"Accept the help we're offering you. We will review your case again in due course."

"I can't do that. I need my boy!"

"I'm sorry, Mrs. Samson. I truly am."

"Can I at least see him, explain to him. Say goodbye?"

Styles shook his head. "I'm afraid not. It wouldn't be fair to confuse him when he has already made such good progress. I think the best thing we can do is let him settle into a pattern of normality."

"Please, I just want to hold him. I need to explain."

"I'm sorry," Styles said firmly. "This is for the best. As I said, we will review the case again in due course. In the meantime, attend the counseling. Take the help we're offering."

"Why are you doing this? Why are you taking him away from me?"

"It's not our intention to cause upset. We want what's best for the child's welfare."

Melody nodded, and stared down at her hands. They were trembling. The entire situation had taken on a surreal quality. It was almost as if it were happening to someone else and she was only vaguely aware of it. Still in a daze, she left the office, distantly aware that she was alone in the world.

CHAPTER 8

Petrov strode toward the building, its glass and steel façade glittering in the sunlight. Eyes hidden behind his sunglasses, he mapped out the locations of the security guards and hoped none would recognize him. He walked with confidence past the two men by the door, neither of which gave him a second glance as he entered the spacious marble-floored reception area. The American flags hanging from the walls fluttered as Petrov strode to the main desk, the sharp tap of his shoes echoing around the cavernous space. He stopped at the counter and took off his glasses.

"Can I help you?" the receptionist asked, glancing at him from her computer.

"I'm Detective Alex Petrov. I need to see James Fisher."

"Do you have an appointment?" the woman shot back.

"No. I'm a police officer. I need to speak to him now please."

"One moment please," she said, turning back to her computer, her fingers clicking at the keyboard in a blur of movement.

Petrov remained impassive, knowing what was to come.

"I'm sorry," the receptionist said. "We don't have a James Fisher in the building."

"I know he works here. I've been trying to

track him down for weeks now."

"I'm sorry," she flashed him a thin smile, "I can't help you any further."

"You do realize I'm a police officer?" Petrov said, watching as two more security guards appeared from one of the rooms behind the counter.

"Do you have an arrest warrant or any other official paperwork?"

Petrov smiled. She was good. Very good, and sharp to boot. "No, I don't. I just need to speak to Mr. Fisher about a case I've been working on. I understand he now has control of the location and I need access to it."

"As I said, there's nobody of that name here."

"Come on, lady, we both know that's not true. I traced him here. I know this is where he works."

"If you don't leave, I'll have to have security escort you from the premises."

"Look, this is important. If you can just get him down here—"

"I'm sorry. I can't help you."

Petrov considered arguing, maybe even putting on a little pressure. He decided against it, however, because he was sure it wouldn't work. Government run buildings like this one didn't seem to take too kindly to any form of interference from regular law enforcement.

"Fine," he said as the security guards approached from behind the counter. "I'm going."

The receptionist gave him a cold smile as he turned and headed back the way he came. He paused and returned to the counter.

"Do me a favor. If he happens to show up here by chance, give him my card and ask him to call me."

He placed his card on the counter.

"Like I said, he doesn't work here. I've checked the system."

"If you happen to check again and find him, just make sure my card gets to him. Tell him it's about what's under the house. He'll know what I'm talking about."

He waited to see if she would pick up the card, or at least acknowledge him. Neither happened, she just greeted him with the same cold look of indifference. Petrov turned and left the building, determined more than ever to meet up with the mysterious James Fisher and find out what he had to do with what was happening at Hope House.

CHAPTER 9

Dubbed by its operators as 'The Rat', The GT16 was the culmination of more than three years of top level military research. Resembling a small radio-controlled car, the prototype unit was equipped with an array of cutting-edge equipment. Everything from temperature sensors to high resolution night vision cameras with real-time video recording made the unit a useful tool in the field. It sat at the foot of the subcellar as its operator made final checks to the unit's controls. Soldiers flitted around the area, unsure what to do or why they were even there.

"Hey, Linus, is that toy car of yours ready or what?" one of them said, nudging his friend.

"This 'toy' costs more than your house, Hopkins," Linus fired back over his shoulder as he remotely adjusted the focus of the unit's camera.

"I don't know why the hell they're putting that thing down there. Surely it would be easier for a few of us to go and check it out."

"It could be unstable. That tunnel looks to go right under the river. You don't want to be stuck down there if the roof collapses."

"I don't want to be down here at all. This place is weird," Hopkins said, glancing around the foyer.

"Shut up man, we're not supposed to talk about it. They already canned General Kimmel."

"There's nobody here but us right now. Besides, Kimmel will be fine. He'll be back behind his desk in no time."

"This is a pretty fucked-up situation, I'll give you that," Linus said as he activated and deactivated the night vision camera of the GT16, watching as the image on screen went from black to grey then back again. Satisfied, he switched on the powerful lights on the front of the unit, illuminating the dirt tunnel ahead.

"You don't say. Have you heard that shit in the trees at night?"

Linus turned slightly, staring at Hopkins, expecting to see him grinning. Instead, he saw a tense and frightened man, pale face and blue eyes darting into the shadows and back. "What about the trees?"

"There's something out there. You can hear it. Crying. Screaming. I don't know what it is, man, but I don't like it."

Linus considered it for a moment, then turned back to the controls. "Probably just your imagination. I wouldn't worry about it."

"That's easy for you to say. You haven't been stuck out here."

"Well, I'm here now. The quicker you shut up and let me get on with this, the quicker we can all get out of here."

"Don't let me stop you."

"I have to wait," Linus said.

"For who?"

"For me," Fisher said as he walked into the hotel. He stood at Linus's shoulder, watching the screens. "Is it ready?"

"Yes. It's good to go."

"Alright, let's see what we have. Whenever you're ready, pilot."

Linus licked his lips and pulled his seat closer to the desk. "Video feed is live and recording in real time. Temperature sensors are online. Ambient temp is at a steady four degrees. Proceeding into the tunnel."

Linus picked up the unit's control, which looked like a more elaborate version of a child's toy remote. With twin thumb operated joysticks taking care of direction and speed respectively, the controller also had an LED display showing temperature and other telemetry. Linus teased the joysticks, the image on screen shuddering as the vehicle moved down the tunnel.

"Go steady, pilot. I want to get a good look at everything beyond the chamber room."

"Got it," Linus mumbled as the unit rolled slowly toward the doorway, its lights banishing the shadows. The GT16 entered the chamber where Petrov had discovered the altar with the human-animal hybrid. This had been removed soon after discovery by Fisher's men, yet no further investigation had taken place. Linus piloted the unit across the room, then brought it to a stop. He leaned over to his computer console and input a command.

The image on screen moved as the camera turret on top of the vehicle extended and swiveled, giving a panorama of the room.

"Which door do you want me to go through?"

Linus asked.

"The one straight ahead," Fisher said. "The others are closed rooms."

"What's in them?"

"None of your business. Just do as I say."

"Yes, sir."

The turret descended back into position, and Linus continued on, into the dark.

"Pretty steep downward gradient here," he said over his shoulder.

"Is it going to be an issue?" Fisher said.

"No, I'm just keeping you informed. We're having a few issues with the exterior lights though. See how they're flickering?"

"Can we go on?"

"Absolutely. Worst case, we can switch over to the night vision. It's not a problem."

"Good. Just go easy. We don't know what's down there, but if it does go under the river like we suspect, there could be water, not to mention general instability."

"Depending on the water level, it could be a problem. This unit can only go so deep."

"Alright, let's just take it as it comes, we don't know anything yet."

They carried on, the tension palpable. The images on screen rolled by steadily. Beyond the door, the change in elevation was immediately apparent. The walls were rough, and had been cut with less care than the rooms. The unit went deeper, the flickering of the spotlights increasing.

"Temperature is down half a degree," Linus reported.

"Can't you do anything about those lights?" Fisher snapped.

"I can switch over to night vision. Should be more stable."

"Do it."

Linus flicked the switch, transforming the on-screen image into greenish-grey hues. The GT16 ambled on, delving deeper into the tunnel. Water dripped from the ceiling, and at intermittent sections of the tunnel, wooden supports had been erected.

"Temp down to three degrees," Linus said, then paused.

"What is it?" Fisher asked.

Linus didn't answer. He picked up a pair of headphones and put them on, simultaneously accessing the computer's audio recording log.

"What is it, dammit?"

"I thought I heard something."

"Like what?"

"I… uh, I'm not sure," Linus muttered, his frown deepening as he replayed a particular section of the recording. "I suppose it's nothing."

Fisher glanced around the foyer, wishing there were less shadows outside of the cone of light they stood in. "Can that audio feed be broadcast into the room for us all to hear?"

Linus didn't answer. He was still staring at the audio waveform on screen as he replayed the same section over and over.

"I said—"

"Yes, it can," Linus cut in, taking off the headphones. He blinked, looked over his shoulder at Fisher, then back at the controls. He appeared different. Disorientated somehow. For a moment, he just sat there, staring at the screen.

"Well, go on then, let's hear it."

Fisher's command appeared to do the trick, snapping Linus out of his stupor. "Sorry," he muttered, and manipulated the controls. The hotel foyer filled with the hiss of static. Linus adjusted the audio levels, then picked up the controls for the GT16 and continued on into the tunnel, rough dirt walls and slick roots giving way to a man-made wooden frame built around the perimeter of the passageway. Water dripped in clockwork rhythm as Linus brought the rover to a halt.

"We're about to pass under the river," Linus said, checking the GPS positioning. Fisher leaned over his shoulder and looked at the map.

"Of course, this all makes sense now. There's a raised sandbank just under the surface of the water. It was used to cross it before the bridge was erected. This tunnel must be the cause of it."

"What do you think is down there?" Linus asked, looking at Fisher.

"That's what we're here to find out. Proceed when ready."

Linus complied, making the transition from dirt to wood easily. The image on screen flickered and distorted, causing Linus to double-check the telemetry.

"Problem?" Fisher asked.

"No, I don't think so. Could just be water landing on the sensors. Temp has dropped two full degrees. It's just above freezing down there."

The unit moved on, leaving the wooden frame behind. The path started to curve as the ground fell away in an even steeper gradient.

"How far under the surface are we?" Fisher asked.

"We're under the forest now, so readings are difficult to take accurately. We were only a few feet below the surface when we passed the river sandbank. Now, it could be twenty-five, maybe thirty feet."

"Hey, did you see that?"

Fisher and Linus turned to Hopkins, who was staring at the screen.

"What?" Fisher snapped.

"Something moved down there."

Everyone stared at the screen, the shades of grey showing no movement.

"Shall I move on?" Linus asked.

"Proceed," Fisher replied, forcing himself to relax and stay focused on the task at hand.

The unit rumbled on, and this time they all saw it, a flicker of something, a shadow almost as dark as the tunnel, moving just on the edge of the cameras range.

"There's definitely something down there," Linus said, his throat dry, the words almost scratching as they came out.

"Impossible. Nobody's down there. It's been sealed up for years and guarded around the clock ever since it was discovered."

"Are you telling me you didn't see what I did? Something moved."

"I saw it too," Hopkins said.

"Nobody asked you for your opinion, Private."

"What do you want me to do?" Linus asked.

"Proceed as planned. Move on."

Linus complied, the night vision cameras melting away the dark as the unit rolled deeper. This time, a form, opaque yet not quite as dark as its surroundings, flitted across the screen. There was no doubt that it was humanoid as the thing turned and retreated out of the visible range of the cameras. As if to emphasize its existence, the sound of footsteps accompanied it.

Fisher wanted a drink, and even though he had been more than three years sober, he would have given anything for a good shot of whisky to help clear his head. "Move on," he said, wiping the sweat from his brow despite the chill.

The GT16 went even deeper, following the tunnel. Other sounds began to filter through as the unit relayed them to the control room. Subtle sounds which were hard to pick out from the static and the hum of the vehicle's forward motion. The low pained moan of a woman. Unintelligible whispers, some pleading, many offering more sinister sound bites, appeared seemingly at will; some from the hidden depths of the tunnel, others close enough to the microphones to distort as they exploded into the hotel foyer.

All three men, Fisher, Linus and Hopkins, were transfixed in morbid fascination. Fisher gritted his teeth, eyes wide. He was struggling to find that balance between fight or flight. Linus was faring little better. The steady hands with which he had operated the unit were shaking. His entire body felt numb as he watched events unfold. Least surprised of all was Hopkins. He had seen it before. He'd experienced this and worse since he'd been stationed at the hotel with General Kimmel, and watched with a resigned sense of foreboding. Terror for him had given way to a strong desire to leave the Hope House site and its secrets behind for good.

The unit traveled deeper. As it did, the shape of the tunnel changed.

Gone was the carved, deliberately cut shape which had come previously.

Now the way ahead was filled with giant roots from the denizens of the forest above. Still the GT16 went on, and still those shadows on the edge of their vision appeared and disappeared. The screen shuddered and filled with distortion before returning to normal.

"What's happening to the picture?"

"I uh, I don't know. It shouldn't be doing that. Something's wrong. The sensors are all over the place."

Fisher stared at the telemetry screen. The temperature indicator was fluctuating wildly, showing anywhere from minus ten degrees to fifty plus. As he watched, something rolled out of the darkness – an object, or more accurately objects, on the ground ahead. Fisher stared, not sure what to do. Linus brought the GT16 to a halt and turned to Fisher.

"Do you want me to try the spotlights again?

Just in case that's not what it looks like?"

Fisher knew of course that there was no doubting what they were looking at, but nodded anyway, something in him needing to see just how far it went, just how bad it was. Linus activated the light-switch, the picture on screen going dark as the transition was made to the spotlight. As the cavern illuminated, Linus shrieked and threw his chair back.

This time, whatever had been flirting at the edge of the shadows came at them. It was both something and nothing, humanoid but also strangely formless. The GT16 shuddered and tipped onto its side as the thing that attacked it melted away into nothing. Accompanying the assault was a noise that none of them would ever be able to forget. It was almost the sound a lion would make when threatening a rival. A deep growl, filled with malice, charged with so much aggression and anger at the intrusion that Fisher already knew any investigation planned for the catacombs was over.

Some things, he decided, were best left alone. The GT16 lay on its side, the image on screen distorted and shaking, but still showing the scene beyond. A split second later, its feed was cut as all power to the unit was lost. They had already seen it though.

Fisher recounted grainy photographs from the Second World War, particularly the atrocities undertaken in gas chambers and concentration camps. It was a similar feeling, a similar scale of unimaginable genocide, made more frightening by the attack on the GT16.

"Pack everything up. I want this place sealed off. All doors. All windows," Fisher ordered, still fighting against the image they'd seen. "I want everyone out of here within the hour."

Hopkins nodded and left the hotel, the relief on his face clear.

Although the screen now displayed static, Fisher could still see well enough in his mind's eye what existed in the tunnel.

Bones.

The ground was littered with human bones.

CHAPTER 10

Known as the Romanian Bermuda Triangle, Hoia Baciu Forest covered an area of more than two hundred and fifty hectares. Its bizarre history of paranormal activity, UFO sightings and other unexplained phenomena had made the forest one of the most intriguing and feared locations in Europe.

Emma Barrett trudged through the woodland, hands thrust in pockets and head down against the steady drizzle which had been falling for three solid days. Her boots were splattered with mud, and her breath fogged in the chilly air. Although it was mid-morning, the day was dull from the heavy gray cloud cover, which, as miserable as it was, still wasn't enough to deter her from her journey.

Behind her, cheeks flushed from the cold, was Alex Brett. Like her, he was a survivor of the Oakwell massacre, and from it a relationship of mutual need had grown. They leaned on each other when times were tough, helping each other find a way to cope with the events of that awful night. Emma couldn't help but think of those who had survived, and considered, not for the first time, perhaps the dead were the lucky ones. In the aftermath of the massacre, she had become obsessed with paranormal phenomena.

Against the advice of her family, she dived

into the subject, doing anything she could to distract herself from the event where she'd lost almost all of her friends in a single night. The more people around her told her that it was a one-off incident, and that she just happened to be in the wrong place at the wrong time, the more determined she was to prove otherwise. It had become an obsession which led her to Japan and now Romania in the search for other areas sharing similar traits to the clearing in Oakwell. Using the savings that she'd one day hoped to purchase her first home with, she'd spent more money than she knew she should in order to fund her investigations.

Emma lost her footing, slipping in the wet mud, which pulled her thoughts back to the task at hand. The ground angled downhill now, and she knew they were nearing their destination.

"You see the trees here?" Alex said from behind her.

"Yeah, let's stop and take some photos."

She took a moment to catch her breath, ignoring the drizzle as it pattered on her raincoat. The trees ahead of them were abnormal, the trunks growing in mysterious S-shapes, twisting back on themselves before continuing their reach for the sun.

"You see how they're all like this, exactly the same shape and direction?" she said over her shoulder as she snapped photos from various angles.

"Yeah, it's especially odd because the same species elsewhere in the woods are fine. You see the charring there?"

"Where?" she asked, lowering the camera.

"There, on the lower branches. Just like the locals said it would be."

"Oh, yeah, I see it now," Emma said, leaning closer.

"You think someone did this on purpose?"

"I doubt it," she mumbled, inspecting the damage. "The locals here are scared of this place. In all fairness, I can see why."

"Tell me about it, it's creepy here, it's just like… like the other place."

Emma glanced at him. "You okay?"

"Yeah, I'm fine, it's just… this is all a bit too familiar, you know?"

"I get where you're coming from. I appreciate you agreeing to come out here with me. Especially so soon after Oakwell."

"It was good to get away. Although I'd have preferred sunshine and a beach rather than Romanian rain," Alex replied, almost forcing a smile. "This place has a weird vibe, don't you think? It's heavy… oppressive. It's a lot like the forest back home."

"It is. Which is why we're here. Come on, let's go on. It should be just a little further ahead."

The pair moved on, past the misshapen trees and deeper into the forest. Alex was right. There was an atmosphere here that she hadn't felt since her time back in Oakwell forest. There was the same kind of dark oppression, the heaviness, and a feeling of anxiety that came back all too clearly. The only other place she'd visited that gave off such a skin-crawling sensation was Aokigahara forest in Japan. It was better known as the Suicide Forest, a place where, year on year, people would go to end their lives.

Such is the density of the vegetation there, sitting as it does at the base of Mount Fuji, that many of the bodies are never found, while others leave behind photographs of family or loved ones, or tents which had been the location of their last night's sleep before the owners headed into the trees to find a place to take their leave of the world.

Unlike Alex, who had been swamped by the events in Oakwell, Emma had tried to use it in a positive way. She was desperate to understand what they had experienced in Oakwell, and perhaps by understanding, learn to live with it.

Convincing her parents to let her go on this and the trip to Japan had been easy, although she hadn't told them the reason for her wanting to come.

She simply explained she needed to get away from the town, away from the memories, and they in turn were happy to oblige. Any guilt she felt for deceiving them was pushed aside by the thought of finding out what had happened and why. She had experienced things that couldn't be explained by any way she knew, and was determined to discover the truth, no matter how far she had to go.

The land ahead leveled out, and traveling became easier. The darkness between the branches grew lighter, and she spied the break in the trees ahead. Her heart, already working hard from traversing the landscape, started to beat a little bit faster.

"This is it," she said. "We're here."

Alex followed her as she walked into the clearing, her stomach tightening at the similarities between it and the one in Oakwell. It was formed into a rough circle, one which, based on the geography of the place, shouldn't be there. Nothing grew in the middle apart from a thin, sick-looking covering of yellowish grass. The silence was almost total, and both Emma and Alex were grateful for the steady song of the rain.

"Holy shit, it's got the same feel…" Alex whispered.

Emma nodded. She scanned the clearing, opening up her senses to take in everything. It was remarkable. She lifted her water bottle, her shaking hands having difficulty unscrewing the cap.

"Let's get started. We have a lot to do," she said, forcing herself to venture further into the clearing.

"Do you want me to get some soil samples?"

"Yeah, I'll take some photos and video, then we can do some EVP work."

"You really believe in that stuff?" Alex asked.

"EVP?"

"Yeah."

"Actually, I do. I've heard quite a lot of convincing recordings."

"I'm not sure I buy into it all. Recording the voices of the dead… It all sounds a little bit farfetched to me. Besides, it's easy to mishear things. Background noise or static can sound like voices if you want it to."

"Still, I'd rather have the recordings than not."

"Hey, you're the boss. I'll set it up," Alex said, grateful for the distraction. Emma took another moment to look around, then set to work. She had no intention of staying in the clearing any longer than she needed to.

"You know, when you head back there, I won't be able to come with you. To Oakwell, I mean," Alex said.

"I know. I understand. You experienced more than most. I'd never ask you to go back."

"It's just too much for me. I hoped that working with you might act like a form of therapy and let me find the strength to do it. Truth is, I'm no less scared now than I was then."

She paused, looking over her shoulder at him. He had never opened up, never spoken to her or anyone else about what had happened.

"Are you alright?" she asked.

"Yeah, it's just... I can still feel it, you know? That thing crawling around in my head. I'd like to think it was all a dream, that maybe I imagined some or all of it. Then I remember how it was, how little control I had. I couldn't put myself through that again."

"I know how hard it is for you. I wouldn't ask you to go back there. Have you ever thought about seeing someone about it? A doctor or something?"

"Come on, you know better than that. What would a doctor say? They'd either tell me there was nothing wrong, or they'd put me in a nuthouse and throw away the key."

"It's not healthy to keep things like this to yourself. You need an outlet. Someone to talk to. Therapy maybe?"

"I don't *want* to talk about it. That's the problem."

"You know you can talk to me if you need to. I understand. Hell, I'm probably one of the few who does."

"I appreciate that, although I probably won't take you up on the offer. To tell you the truth, I was worried you might be angry."

"Angry? Why would I be?"

"I don't know," he said, forcing a grin. "I know how much figuring this out means to you. I thought you'd be disappointed."

"Not at all. I respect your decision. How about we talk about this later and focus on getting these samples, then we can get out of this rain?"

"That's one thing I can agree with you on. It's cold here."

"Tell me about it."

They went about their tasks, Emma taking photographs, Alex collecting soil samples.

"Hey, Emma?" he said, looking at her from where he crouched.

"Yeah?"

"Why are you so determined to do this? To go back there after everything that happened?"

"I've asked myself that same question. I think

it's something I feel obliged to do. I don't know if it'll prove to be a good or a bad thing, but I feel like I don't have a choice. If I don't at least try, I'll regret it."

"Maybe," he said, staring off into the distance.

"Anyway, let's get on with this. I don't want to be here after dark."

"I don't know why we're even here at all if I'm honest. This link you keep talking about with Oakwell. It's... flimsy."

"Look, I just find it interesting. This place is said to be the way it is after fifty local peasants were killed in the forest and their enraged spirits trapped there. I think it's well worth looking into."

"But for what?" Alex said. "What can we do?"

"I don't know," Emma replied, wishing she had a better answer. "Maybe I can find some common link – something that ties them together."

"The problem is, we're not looking for something physical. Shit, Emma, I don't have to tell you. After all, you were there too. What do you expect to find?"

"Who knows? Either way, it's getting late. We can talk it over later when we're back at base camp."

"What I wouldn't give for a hot bath and a soft bed," Alex said with a sigh, casting a frown to the grey, rain-filled skies.

"Quicker we get on, quicker we can get back."

"Yeah, I suppose so."

"Besides," Emma said, trying to lighten the mood. "Next time, you can pick where we go."

Alex didn't answer, a frown crossing his face,

and he wondered if he should tell her that this would be his last trip with her. He decided against it, only because it didn't seem right. He set about collecting his soil samples as the rain continued to fall.

II

Just a few days after returning home from Romania, Alex Brett waited for his stepmother to pass out. It usually happened a little after ten pm, however tonight, she had won at bingo and had started drinking early.

As always, he had stayed in his room, waiting for her to fall silent and stop shouting at whatever she happened to be watching on the television. Just after nine, he went downstairs, moving quietly, heart beating fast.

It was like Groundhog Day, every single day that passed a repeat of the day before. She lay on the sofa, snoring lightly, greasy hair fanned over the pillow, filthy dressing gown pulled up to reveal her ugly, scabby legs. He stared at the television, which was showing a gameshow to the empty room. Quietly, he grabbed the remote and switched it off, bringing silence to the house.

The first moment of doubt entered his mind, and in immediate response, he heard them, those creeping whispering things which had never left his head. He had, of course, tried to deny them, to ignore them in the hope that distance would free him from their grasp.

He knew, however, from the things they said and the images they showed him, that not only were they still there, but they were growing stronger. He wasn't sure if it was him or them that had planted the idea in his head for what he was about to do, and he supposed it didn't matter now. All that mattered was the decision had been taken.

He moved past his snoring stepmother, giving her a disgusted sneer as he went into the kitchen, then through the side door leading into the garage.

This was his father's space, and unlike the rest of the house, was clean and pristine. Cold and clinical, even. Spotless concrete floor, a rack of gleaming spanners on one wall, a workbench neatly organized against the other. The car was, of course, gone, and would be until his father finished work at the bar, busting heads at the door if anyone got rowdy. Alex absently wondered if he would still store his pickup truck in the garage afterwards. Quickly following that thought was another which said it didn't matter.

He crossed the room to the workbench, moving aside the blue plastic drawers separated into compartments that contained all manner of nails and screws. What he wanted was at the back, hidden from sight.

The cigar box looked alien somehow, its yellow illustrations ill-fitting with the clean efficiency of the rest of the garage. Alex knew what it contained was as cold and clinical as the rest of his father's possessions. He flicked open the lid, revealing the handgun inside.

Underneath it were photographs of his mother. He slid the first picture out. The colors were faded, but the image was still clear. It appeared that Alex's father had taken it. In the photo, his mother sat on a beach, feet buried in the sand, sun hat perched on her head. She was smiling for the camera. Alex was astounded by how happy she looked. He couldn't remember much about her, apart from the times at the end when his parents were barely on speaking terms.

It made him sad, and as if it were waiting for the right moment of weakness, the thing in his head spoke, reminding him that he was doing the right thing. That it would be better all round if he were dead. For reasons he couldn't explain, he folded the photograph and slipped it into his pocket, then turned his attention to the gun.

It was a .38 that his father had purchased some ten years earlier and had never used. Alex wondered if he even remembered he owned it. He took it out of the box, surprised at the weight in his hand. It felt awkward, uncomfortable even, but incredibly real. The thing in his head guided him through, instructing him on how to load the weapon, how to ensure the safety was off. He followed its lead, doing as he was advised without thinking what the result would be, what it would mean when everything was ready. He disengaged the safety, and stood in the silence, weapon at his side, listening to the house. Apart from the hum of the striplight, there was absolute silence.

Kill the cunt.

It was a command, an instruction delivered to him that left no course for argument or negotiation. On legs that were out of his control, he walked silently back through the kitchen, and stopped at the head of the sofa where the dirty, snoring form of his stepmother slept. With absolute calm, he held out the weapon, touching cool steel to her temple, his finger poised over the trigger. It would be so easy, such a simple thing to do. Certainly, it would be better for his father.

Just pull the trigger. Go out in a blaze of glory.

Alex drew breath and pulled away. It wasn't *his* idea at all, but the idea of the thing in his head; the tumorous mass which had festered and grown there since he'd first been exposed to it at the clearing in Oakwell forest.

Yes.

It was definitely time to do what he had to in order to ensure he remained in control. With an extraordinary effort, he retreated toward the garage, longing for the cool, clean order of it all, desperate to be away from this woman who had been trouble since day one. Back in the sterile space, he closed his eyes and counted back from twenty, each number banishing something from his mind.

When he got to one, he felt better, more in control. He opened his eyes, horrified to find that he had wedged the gun into his mouth without realizing he was doing it. It was behind his front teeth, digging into his palate, angled toward his brain. The thing in his head was delighted, filling his mind with visions of brain matter splashing all over the walls, of bone fragments hitting the floor, ruining the pristine garage.

He started to think about his father, how he would respond when he saw what awaited him, and immediately decided it didn't matter.

There was no way he was going to change his mind now. It was settled. He wanted to be free from those awful manipulative things in his head. Squeezing his eyes closed, his last thought was of Emma, and how he hoped she would understand what he had done and why. The alien thing tried to speak, but before it could, Alex pulled the trigger, extinguishing his existence before he was forced to hear the vile things it had to say.

CHAPTER 11

Melody Samson couldn't have imagined the cruelty life would throw at her after the fateful tidal wave of events at Hope House. Its horrors, and those which came after, had not only damaged her mentally, but had taken a physical toll. She had lost weight, and the laughter lines of her youth had deepened into their worry-driven cousins.

Crow's feet reached out from the corners of her eyes, which were dull, only showing the faintest glimmer of their former exuberance. Her hair, once thick and black, had thinned and started to gray. Worse than the physical and mental toll was the absolute loneliness she felt. When she lost Steve, she had clung to her son, thinking he would be enough to save her. Yet, like her, Isaac suffered with demons of his own. Plagued by nightmares of his ordeal at the hands of Henry Marshall and the sheer horror at seeing his father die in front of him, she supposed it was almost inevitable the nightmares would eventually morph into something worse.

Although she had been diagnosed with Post Traumatic Stress Disorder just like Isaac, she wasn't entirely convinced they were listening to the whole story. She'd had enough of the countless and mostly frustrating therapy sessions with the psychologists and doctors trying their best to tell her she didn't know what she was talking about, especially when it came to the horrors she had endured at Hope House. She had tried to be patient, and explain as thoroughly and slowly as she could exactly what had happened; however, the therapists seemed less interested in what she had to say, and more in trying to tell her that she needed to start facing up to the reality of the situation and not hide behind the supernatural.

They had prescribed her medication, and although she assured them she was taking it, the bottle remained unopened in the kitchen drawer. She knew that everything she'd experienced was real, and no matter who tried to tell her otherwise, she believed it completely. The weeks since she'd been ordered to seek help had been an endless void of misery.

Her nights were sleepless, her days spent walking around her empty and silent apartment like some forgotten ghoul with nobody to haunt. It was only during her therapy sessions that she put on a mask of relative normality. She smiled and tried to be as casual and ordinary as possible, all with the goal of getting her son back in her care.

Melody sat once again in Styles' office, knowing that his decision would have an overwhelming impact on the rest of her life. She tried to read him, to second-guess what was going to happen, but it seemed Styles was more than used to dealing with such cases, and his poker face held true.

"Would you like a glass of water, Mrs.

Samson?"

She looked at him. Blinked. The reply stuck in the back of her throat. "No, I'm fine, thank you."

Styles nodded curtly, and addressed the file in front of him. "I see you've been attending the sessions. I'm glad to see it. How are you finding them?"

"They're fine. Very helpful."

He watched her, dark eyes probing. She imagined him sniffing the air, sensing her lie. "That's good," he said, turning back to the file. "Very good," he added.

"Mr. Styles, please, can I see my son? I don't even know how he's been doing."

"Isaac is doing fine, Mrs. Samson. He continues to show excellent progress. His night terrors are being controlled by his medication and he seems to be responding well to his new environment."

"Does that mean I can take him home?"

"Mrs. Samson, the reports from your sessions show you to still be dealing with intense grief after the loss of your husband, which is quite understandable given the recent nature of such a traumatic experience," Styles said, ignoring her question. "It seems you continue to persist with these very rich and vivid stories about supernatural beings somehow attaching themselves to your family. Indeed, these reports say you were quite vocal about this."

She stared at her hands, spinning her wedding ring around her finger, which was almost too thin to hold it anymore. "I've been unwell. I was confused. Overtired."

Styles held up a hand. "Please, let me finish."

She shifted in her seat, sensing that things were taking a turn in a direction she didn't want them to go.

"As I was saying, the subject matter discussed during your therapy sessions has, frankly, caused some concern. Although Isaac is showing good progress, you, unfortunately have proven to be less responsive. Now I know that trauma such as this can take a long time to recover from, even without the added stresses of life as a single parent. My job, and that of the state, is to provide the best and safest environment for all parties involved in any particular case. That's why the therapy sessions we organized for you are so important, as they give us the opportunity to assess your progress ahead of any decision we make."

"Please, I'm really trying to get over this."

"I understand that, Mrs. Samson, and I don't want you to feel like we are in any way rushing you. In fact, it's quite the opposite. In cases like this, children naturally seem more receptive to recovery than adults. This is just one of those cases where Isaac is making faster progress than you are. It's perfectly normal, in fact, it was to be expected."

"What does that mean?" she asked.

"It means that we have a very delicate situation here which has been the subject of much discussion and thought with myself, your doctors and Isaacs's carers. As I said during our first meeting, our job is to provide the best care we can in assisting both you and your son in your recovery. With that said, I think it's wise if, for the time being, you and your son remain separated, especially after Isaac has shown such good progress."

"You can't do this. Six weeks you said. Six weeks as long as I did the therapy."

"No, I said we would review the case, which we have in great detail. Believe me Mrs. Samson, this isn't a part of the job I enjoy. The board have decided that it would be in everyone's best interests if we extended the current arrangement until you are more capable to offer Isaac the stability he needs."

"You can't take him away from me. You have no right. He's my son."

"And we have a duty of care," Styles snapped. "Mrs. Samson, I take no pleasure in making decisions like this. I'm just a small cog in a very big wheel. Sometimes we agree, sometimes we don't. In this case, the decision to keep Isaac in a settled home where he can be monitored and treated for his condition whilst also giving you the time to recover further is the best option for everyone. I'm sure you can understand that we aren't your enemies here. We are doing this to help you. Both of you."

"None of this helps me," Melody shrieked. "You're stealing my son. I won't have it. I'll go to the press, I'll take legal action."

If Styles was concerned, he didn't show it. He closed the file and folded his hands on the desk.

"Mrs. Samson, I think it's important you look at the bigger picture here. The very last thing we want to do is break up families, especially when they've experienced the kind of terrible trauma you and your son have been forced to endure.

At the same time, you must see the reasons for our concerns. There is a very real and valid concern that if you were to be given back custody of your son, he would regress to a similar state to when we first became involved. Not to mention the added pressure and stress of caring for him would hinder your own recovery and make your condition worse. I hope you can understand that that this is for the best. The long term goal is to help both you and your son recover from the ordeal you have endured."

"You can't just take him, not without my say so. I have rights. I need to give permission."

Melody knew how she must sound. She could hear the shrill tone herself and could imagine how everything she said made the situation worse. Even so, she wasn't about to go down without a fight.

"I'm afraid we can, Mrs. Samson. We have the power to do whatever is in the best interests of the child," Styles said, straightening the folder on the table top.

"His best interests are to stay with me!"

"No disrespect, but we need to protect your son from the real world rather than these paranormal delusions."

"I knew it," she said, glaring at Styles. "You don't believe any of it, do you? The things I told you, the things I told your therapists."

"I don't want to get drawn into this now, Mrs. Samson. The decision has been taken. I'm sorry it wasn't what you wanted. I hope that once you've calmed down, you can find a way to work with us. Our end goal is the same. Would you like a drink? Some time to compose yourself perhaps?"

"No," she mumbled, shaking her head. "I don't see there's much point, is there? I'm not going to get him back. You said so yourself."

"Short term, Mrs. Samson. Keep attending the therapy sessions. Before you know it, things will be back to normal."

She stood, feeling alien, distant from herself. She walked to the door, placed a pale hand on the handle, and then turned back toward Styles. "It won't work like that though, will it, Mr. Styles?"

"Why's that?" he replied, eyebrows raised.

"Because you just told me that the things I *know* to be absolutely true were lies. And I know they're not. How can we ever find a way to fix this if you don't believe what I'm telling you? How can I get my son back if you don't believe me?"

"Mrs. Samson—"

"Forget it. I'll show you. I'll prove it to you if that's what it takes."

Although she wanted to unleash her rage, she knew it would do her no good. Instead, she opened the door and left the office. Only when she was safely in her car did she let it out. As she sobbed, holding nothing back, she realized that there was a good chance she would never see her son again.

PART TWO:

REAWAKENING

CHAPTER 12

THREE YEARS LATER

It was his sixth adoptive family. Now ten years old, Isaac Samson had become convinced that nobody wanted or loved him. Some of the families he'd been sent to had been fine with him at first, doing everything they could to make him feel as welcome as possible. However, the persistent night terrors proved to be a universal problem that many of them weren't prepared to cope with.

The other, more serious issue was that of his mother, who tracked him down at every new home demanding to see him. He had been with Grant and Tanya Gaunt for two months, and so far they seemed nice enough, and were even handling his nightmares better than most. Grant was a headmaster at a local school. Slim and blond, he was quiet and serious, with a firm belief in traditional entertainment.

Reading, art and music were actively encouraged in the house, and as the days went by, Isaac had started to see a happy, funny man behind the serious exterior.

Tanya was the polar opposite of her husband. Happy and outgoing, she loved children, and took

Isaac in with unconditional love from the start. Some days, he could almost forget all that had happened. The upset, the trauma. Other days, a deep, all-consuming darkness overcame him. Today was one such day, and as he always did, he sat in his bedroom, unable to muster any enthusiasm or excitement for anything. His sole joy was reading, and it was something he had taken to vigorously, devouring a novel per week, sometimes two. Mostly he read young adult and fantasy, and was currently blasting through the third Harry Potter book. To him, those worlds between the pages seemed like magical locations which swept him away from the mundaneness of his own existence.

Downstairs, Grant and Tanya were putting away the groceries together. Married for eleven years, they had tried to have children of their own without success. Adoption had seemed like the most obvious choice, and one which was still on the cards. For now, however, with their own careers to manage, it proved to be a better option to volunteer for the temporary care program. Designed with short term care in mind, it gave the children a stable environment in which to live and develop.

Grant was putting the milk in the refrigerator when the knock at the door came. He walked through the kitchen and opened the door, and instantly recognized the woman standing there. The agency had warned them that she might arrive.

Melody Samson had aged badly. She had lost

weight to the point of looking ill. Deep worry lines made her look older than she was, and her hair was greasy and graying. She tried to smile the way she used to but couldn't quite manage it. It seemed she had forgotten how such a simple gesture was performed.

"Hello, I hope you don't mind me arriving unannounced, my name is—"

"I know who you are," Grant said, keeping one arm across the doorframe. "You're not supposed to be here."

"Please, I don't mean any harm. I need to see my son. Is he here?"

"You can't do this. You've been warned. We were told to call the police if you showed up."

"Please, don't do that," she said, trying to look beyond Grant into the house. "Is he here? Can I just see him to make sure he's alright?"

"He's not here."

"Please, I just want to see him."

"Look, I appreciate your situation, but you can't do this. You need to let him go," Grant said, feeling more pity than anger toward the frail woman in front of him.

"I know it's easy to say, but try to put yourself in my position. He's all I have. I need to talk to him."

"He's fine. He has everything he needs."

"Is he... sleeping?"

"He's sleeping fine," he said, then as an afterthought, "How long have you known he's been with us?"

"A week. I've been trying to build up the

courage to knock on the door. Please, you don't need to call the police. I won't cause any trouble."

"You realize how difficult a position you've put me in? I'm supposed to call Mr. Styles if you show up here."

"Please, I won't cause any trouble. You seem like nice people. That's sometimes the worst part, you know? Not knowing what kind of family he's with," Melody said. She was wringing her hands, moving her wedding ring around her finger. She saw Grant watching her and put her hands behind her back.

"I still can't bring myself to take it off," she said, just about managing a tired smile. "It's all I have left."

"Look, I appreciate you've been through a lot, and God knows it can't be easy, but you have to go. I won't call Styles if you go right now, but you can't come back here. If you do, then you'll leave me no choice but to make that call. Do you understand what I'm saying to you?"

Melody looked at him. Strong features, blond hair. Handsome apart from his slightly crooked nose. She got the feeling that these were good people, and avoiding another brush with the police was also something she was keen to do.

"No, I understand. I'm sorry for coming. I just…" She couldn't finish, choking on the words.

"It's okay," Grant said. Calm, comforting, understanding. "Please, just go, okay? Before he hears you."

She nodded, fighting not to cry.

"Good luck with getting on your feet. I really

hope you do it," he said, then closed the door.

Melody stood there for a few seconds, unsure of what to do or where to go, then with the threat of the police looming and a few of the neighbors taking an interest, she retreated back down the path and got into her car. She drove away, letting the tears come, and feeling as low as she ever had in her life.

CHAPTER 13

Petrov slammed his fist on the counter as the security guards approached. "I know Fisher is here. The more he refuses to see me the harder I'm going to fight."

"We've told you before," the guard by the receptionist said. "You're not supposed to come here."

"I know, so my captain keeps telling me. Doesn't mean I'm going to stop though. Tell him I'm here," Petrov said as security closed in on him.

This was a regular occurrence. Petrov would arrive and kick up a fuss, security would throw him out. For reasons he couldn't quite explain, the Oakwell case was lingering in his mind, despite having been closed for almost three years. Part of it was because it represented the one blot on his record, the one unsolved case, although the reason it was unsolved was because he had been pulled from it almost immediately after finding the tunnels under Hope House.

The only name he had was that of Fisher, who proved to be frustratingly elusive. Undeterred, he had begun a campaign designed to track the man down so that he could at least speak to him about what he'd found.

Despite his best efforts, and employing some of his very best contacts in the police force, Fisher had remained invisible. An enigma. A ghost.

Nobody seemed to know him, or if they did, had no idea how to reach him. Petrov had searched every database to which he had access, all without a single hit. Petrov was sure whoever this Fisher character was, he was high up the chain within the government.

"Look, Detective," the security guard said, leaning on the counter in an effort to intimidate. "You are barred from entering this building. Make no mistake, we will be informing your superiors about this and suggesting they take the appropriate disciplinary action."

"It wouldn't be the first time," Petrov fired back. "You people seem to forget we're all on the same side here. I need some information in regards to a case. It's obstruction of justice."

"Only it isn't, is it. You already filed that motion without success," The guard fired back, the arrogant smile suiting him.

"Just five minutes. That's all I need and then I'll stop coming here and bothering you."

The guard shook his head. "Get him out of here."

The security guards moved in, taking him by both arms and frog-marching him toward the exit. Another stayed at his back to ensure there were no problems. Petrov wondered if they would actually throw him to the ground like they did in the movies, but in the end, they opened the doors and let him out, giving him a gentle shove.

"Don't come back here again. You're already in a lot of trouble, pal." Petrov wished he could have thought of a witty retort, something to make him look good, but nothing came, and he slinked away from the building, ignoring the stares of the passers-by who had witnessed him being ejected.

There was a bench in the plaza opposite the building. Petrov sat down and lit a cigarette, staring at the reflective glass façade and wondering if Fisher was in there somewhere watching him. On the off chance he was, Petrov gave the middle finger to the building then took a deep lungful of smoke.

"He'll never see you, you know."

Petrov watched the man approach. He had seen him earlier while he was on his way into the place he referred to as Fisher's building. Part curiosity, part police training, Petrov took stock of the man as he sat beside him on the bench. He was tall and broad-shouldered, maybe late fifties or very early sixties, with white hair, meticulously parted, and keen blue eyes, framed by a well-tanned face. Petrov could tell he was a man who looked after himself, perhaps one of those people who had a winter holiday home in Florida or southern France. There was an air of authority about him, and even though he was dressed in a gray suit with a white shirt open at the neck, the man screamed military. He sat on the opposite side of the bench, staring straight ahead at the building.

"Do I know you?" Petrov said.

"No, but I know you, Detective Petrov."

"Are you Fisher?"

The man laughed, while Petrov continued his assessment: Good teeth, possibly veneered.

Expensive aftershave. Nothing shelf bought.

"No, I'm not Fisher, although, unlike you, I know him. My name's Kimmel."

"General Kimmel?" Petrov said, turning toward the stranger.

"Formerly. I'm out of the forces now. Put out to pasture, as it were, after that whole Oakwell mess."

"You were there, right?" Petrov asked, sliding effortlessly into detective mode.

"I was, for longer than I would have liked. If you're about to ask me about it, there's nothing I can tell you. Classified information, you understand."

Petrov nodded, and took a pull on his cigarette. Noticing Kimmel watching him, he offered the pack. "Smoke?"

"No, not anymore. Haven't touched one in years."

Petrov raised his eyebrows, staring at the scuffed gold lighter that Kimmel was flicking open and closed in his hand. The retired General followed his eyeline and laughed, slipping the lighter back into his jacket pocket. "Good luck charm. Had it with me since my first tour in 'Nam. A lot of the guys then had crazy things they did to bring themselves luck. Mine was this lighter. Old habit I guess."

"Did it work?"

"I'm here aren't I?"

Petrov grinned and turned back toward the building across the plaza. "Can you tell me anything about Fisher?"

"There's not much to tell. He's nothing out of the ordinary."

"I mean about his involvement in—" Petrov hesitated, wondering if he should go on, or how much Kimmel knew. He was even entertaining the idea that Kimmel was there at Fisher's request to find out what Petrov knew.

"Don't worry, I'm not here as a stooge," Kimmel said with a wry smile, sensing the detective's concerns. "That son of a bitch did everything he could to discredit what I was telling him about that place, and as soon as he found out I was telling the truth, he cut me loose and shut me out."

"That makes two of us."

"Oh? What happened to you?" Kimmel asked.

"Three years ago I was the first officer on scene after the massacre. Standard bread and butter job, right? We have our lead suspect in custody, enough evidence and eye witnesses to guarantee a conviction.

It's all looking good, open and shut case, right? So we take Marshall in, he's a slam-dunk conviction, but we still have all this evidence to look through. There was a murder scene out in the woods, another in the hotel, along with a violent assault. Lots of loose ends still to tie up. So we start our investigation, taking our time as we always do, when we start to get the hurry up. Chief wants us done and out of there so the army can move in."

Kimmel waited, letting Petrov speak.

"Straight away, I get that feeling. Call it instinct, or whatever you want, but it's right there. There's no way the army should have any interest in this case, and then to top it off, I start to see the F.B.I. poking around, not to look at the case as such, but I get the impression they're there to keep an eye on us and what we're doing. The more stuff that happens, the more curious I get. I start to look deeper into things. Do some digging, do some research on the place. I find out it has this godawful history, things that would make even the most skeptical man raise his eyebrows, you know?"

"The murders and suicides," Kimmel said. "I know all about those."

"Yeah, well it was news to me. The more I dug, the more I was sure they were hiding something. Anyways, two weeks after, I get a call from my partner. He says he found something new and that I really should go check it out. I race up there, I mean, really race. This was my chance, you know? No F.B.I., no army, just me. I get there, and it's dark and it's raining. I have this feeling, this awful feeling of dread. I guess it was because of what I'd read about the place, but that didn't make it any less real. So my partner takes me to what he found. There was something in the house that had gone unnoticed before, something new that might have given me the answers I wanted."

"The subcellar," Kimmel said, glancing at Petrov.

"You know about it?" Petrov said, more surprised than he intended to show.

"Of course. Based on what you've said so far, the army team that you were under pressure from to get out of the way of was mine. Me and my men."

"So you know what's down there?"

"No," Kimmel said. "The hotel was off-limits to my team. We were there for a… different reason."

"Yeah, well that's where I might be able to give you some info that might shock you. I went down there."

"You entered the subcellar?"

"Briefly," Petrov said, ushering away the memories of what he had seen before they could flash into his mind. "There was something down there. Some kind of… altar. I'll be honest, it freaked me out, and I ran. Next thing I know, I'm frozen out of the case. I get hauled in front of my captain and told I was being put on something else. No explanation, no reason."

"And that made you even more curious I presume?"

"Damn right," Petrov said, glaring at the building across the plaza. "I tried to go back up there anyway, but the site was closed off. Army blockade, probably your men, General, based on what you just said. I showed them my badge, and then I tried to bully my way through, but they were having none of it. I demanded to know who was in charge, but they wouldn't tell me that either. Thing is, General, I have contacts, friends in both the police and the army. I made some enquiries, had some files pulled. Most of it was classified of course, but this one name kept coming up."

"Fisher," Kimmel said. Petrov nodded.

"Yeah, Fisher. I kept scratching and calling in favors and eventually linked him back to this place," he said, nodding to the building.

"I'm not sure I understand," Kimmel said, thumbing the tatty gold lighter as he spoke. "You said yourself that you had your perpetrator for the crime. The case was, for all intents and purposes, solved. Why pursue it? Why not move on to other things?"

"Oh I did. In my line of work there's always another case waiting around the corner, but that didn't mean I didn't keep trying. It's become a hobby of mine."

"Some might call it an obsession."

"They might be right," Petrov replied with a wry smile. "Whatever it is, I can't seem to shake it. I've tried to make contact with this mysterious Fisher character at least a dozen times, each without success. Everyone keeps giving the same story. It's like the son of a bitch doesn't exist. I'll find him though. I'll find him and then I'll find out what the hell they wanted up there."

"I'd advise you to drop this, Detective," Kimmel said, locking eyes with Petrov.

"What do you know about it?"

"Enough. More than I can tell you or anyone else at any rate. Just trust me when I tell you it would be better if you just forgot about the town of Oakwell and that damn hotel."

"I don't think I can do that."

"Let it go, Detective. Nothing good can come of it. They closed the town for a reason. If you ask me, sealing that place off was the best thing Fisher ever did. With luck, the forest will take it back and people will forget it ever existed."

"Don't you ever wonder about it? Don't you ever want answers?"

Kimmel considered it for a moment, elbows on knees, hands clasped together, head low. He almost looked like a man in prayer. Petrov waited, giving Kimmel time to formulate his answer. Eventually, the former General spoke, his tone soft and reflective.

"The problem with answers, Detective, is that you sometimes feel worse after getting them. I can't speak for you, but I and my men experienced something up there that, to this day, I can't explain. As clichéd as it sounds, there's evil up there. And it's something you'd do well to leave alone."

"What if I choose not to?"

Kimmel shrugged. "I can't do anything about that. Fisher was the same. Some people just have to find out for themselves. I've looked into you, Petrov. You have a superb record, cracked some big cases. You seem like a smart guy, which is why I made sure I was here today to speak to you. Can I suggest that maybe this is one of those occasions when you ignore that police instinct of yours and let it go?"

"Point taken. I'll consider it," Petrov replied.

Kimmel glanced over at him, and for the first time, Petrov saw the strain in his face. Sure enough, it was hidden behind the tan and the years of living well, but it was there nonetheless.

"No you won't," Kimmel said. "People like you never do."

"People like me?"

"Dogs, Detective Petrov."

"Excuse me?"

"People like you are like dogs with a bone. You cling on and chew until you break it. Sometimes, even the big dogs bite off too much. Sometimes those dogs choke. Forget this, Detective Petrov. For your own good."

Kimmel's jacket buzzed, and he took out a mobile phone, which was at least fifteen years out of date. He briefly checked the number then slipped the phone back into his inside pocket. Petrov was amused at the General's use of old school technology, and was about to comment on it when Kimmel stood, pulled out a pair of reflective sunglasses from another pocket and put them on. Petrov was glad those inquisitive eyes were hidden.

"I have to go. I'd say goodbye, Detective, but I have a suspicion you and I will meet again before this is all over."

"Maybe we will. I don't intend to give up on this."

Kimmel nodded, his brow creased with a troubled frown. "You remind me of one of the men who worked under me. He was determined, headstrong. Fantastic leader, brilliant soldier. Everything changed when we went up to that place. We found him in his tent, wrists slit, or more accurately, gouged. He had hacked out the veins on his left hand and it looked like he had been trying to work on the right before he bled out. Not one of those cry-for-help suicides. This was the real deal. The thing I remember most is the note he left. It was hauntingly simple and struck a chord with all of us."

"What did it say?" Petrov asked.

"It said 'I can't handle this anymore.' We'd only been up there for three days. If you insist on pursuing this, just make sure you're ready for the consequences."

Kimmel walked away, hands in pockets. Petrov watched him go, unsure what to make of the surreal conversation that had just unfolded. He remembered his cigarette, and glanced down at it. Unsmoked, it had burned down to a column of ash.

He flicked it onto the flagstones, and lit another while he searched for Kimmel in the crowd of lunchtime office workers milling around the plaza, hoping to convince himself that the encounter really did happen. The General, however, was long gone, lost in the crowd. Petrov sat there for a while anyway, smoking and trying to get his thoughts in order. Despite Kimmel's attempt to frighten him off, his warnings had instead made Petrov more determined than ever to find out what was going on.

CHAPTER 14

The diner was busy, a symphony of chatter and cutlery as people ate lunch.

Situated by a turnpike just outside Michigan, it was the perfect space for weary traveler and trucker alike to take a break and grab a bite to eat. The smell of coffee and bacon assaulted Emma's senses as she pushed through the door, taking a second to scan the crowd for the person she'd come to find.

She crossed the room, all fifties retro in style: white and red décor, reproduction posters on the walls from a time when Brylcreemed hair and leather jackets were the epitome of fashion. The counter was at the back of the room, beyond which was a partially open plan kitchen that was a hive of activity. Here, the smell of cooking food was even stronger, and Emma's stomach growled in an effort to gain her attention. She squeezed in between people eating plates of eggs and waffles, and waited to be attended to, all the time keeping a close eye on the kitchen through the pass.

"What can I get you?"

Emma's mind went blank, and she looked at the waitress, who waited with pen poised, smiling despite the fake, glassy-eyed look of someone jaded with her chosen profession.

"I'm looking for someone."

"Who ya trying to find?" she said, struggling

to make herself heard over the din.

"Uh, a Truman Lemoyne. I was told he works here."

"He does, he's a kitchen hand."

"Can I see him?"

"He's busy right now. Rush hour."

"Oh," Emma said, wondering what to do next.

"Why don't you take a seat and have a bite to eat? Things should be calming down in here soon. How do you know Truman?"

"I don't, I just… I need to speak to him."

"If it's urgent, I can bring him out for now."

"No," Emma said, finding a smile as false as the waitress's. "It's fine. No rush. I haven't eaten yet anyway. What would you recommend?"

"Depends what you like. Bacon and eggs?"

"Are they good?" Emma asked, glad of the chance to compose her thoughts before she met the man she had traveled so far to see.

"Award winning. You want coffee too?"

"Why not."

"Alright, you go ahead and take a seat. I'll bring them over."

"Thanks," Emma said, taking a seat at the counter, enjoying the ambience. She looked into the kitchen, searching the army of white-clad kitchen staff as they fulfilled orders. She wasn't even sure why she was staring. She had no idea which one was Truman Lemoyne.

The bacon was good. She finished it, not having realized how hungry she was. She was on her third cup of coffee, and now the diner was almost two-thirds empty, the early morning clientele having moved on to work or wherever else they were heading.

She was staring into her cup, her mind a million miles away, when the man approached the table. He waited, watching her as she swirled the last dregs around in lazy circles.

"Tina said you were looking for me?"

She looked up at him with a start, almost spilling her drink. He was slim, his skin dark and in stark contrast to his white kitchen porter uniform. He had short hair and a strong jawline, and although they were mistrustful at the moment, she could easily imagine his eyes being kind.

"Are you Truman?"

"You're her, aren't you?" he said, sitting opposite her without being asked. She noticed now that it wasn't mistrust she'd seen, but fear.

"Sorry? I don't think I understand."

"I knew you'd be coming to find me."

"Wait, you're saying you know who I am?"

"Not you specifically, but I knew someone would show up at some point."

"Look, I don't think I'm who you think I am," she said, wondering how she was going to explain her reasons for being there, when Truman's next words threw her off guard.

"You're here about my great, great granddaddy, ain't ya?"

It wasn't often she was speechless, yet this was one of those occasions. She stared at Truman, who broke off into a booming, hearty laugh that triggered a few glances from the patrons still inside the diner. "Shit, you should see your face!"

"Hang on a second, let's just go back…"

"Sorry," Truman said, folding his hands on the table. "It's just… I'm relieved you're here. I was startin' to think I was crazy."

"Why is it you think I'm here?" she asked.

Truman smiled. "Do we have to do this?"

"I'd just like to make sure we're on the same page."

Truman looked at her for a second, his eyes searching hers, the faintest hint of a smile on his lips. "Alright. Then let me take a guess. You're here because of my great, great granddaddy Isaac. And about that house in the woods where all the bad shit lives."

"How…" It was all Emma could manage to stammer before Truman broke into another booming laugh.

"I'll tell you all about it. First up though, let's get some more coffee. It looks like you might need it."

III

The coffee helped, although she was still

pretty shaken. She had built up to the idea of presenting her case to Truman on the expectation that he wouldn't believe it. The fact that not only did he believe her, but knew what she was there for, was a little too much to handle.

"So you dreamed about me?"

"It sounds creepy when you put it like that, but I suppose I did. I started to see that place whenever I went to sleep. A dream but not a dream. Like I was seeing something in the real world but at the same time not. It's hard to explain, but I know that place," Truman said, sipping his drink.

"Depends if we're talking about the same place. Can you describe it?"

"It's quiet there. In the woods. The house is set in a little cove, like a cut out in the forest. It's a good size, and there's a circular wall on the east corner running the full height of the house. Around back, there's a river and a bridge, and above the road in the forest leadin' to the house, there's a sign hanging on a wooden frame. The sign has the word 'hope' on it."

"How do you know this?"

Truman shrugged. "All I'm tellin' you is what I see in my dreams. I see other stuff too. Stuff I don't understand."

"What kind of things?" Emma said, leaning forward in her seat.

"Just images mostly. Things. I see him sometimes. He's the one told me someone would be comin', that I should listen to what they tell me. There are other things too."

"Like what?"

"I don't know… snapshots. Clips of things that have happen' at that place over the years. He tells me his body was freed 'cus it was taken far away from the bad place by the river waters. It's those unlucky sons of bitches who died there that are stuck. Trapped. I see what happen' to some o' them. I see all the people that died there, and I feel what happened to them. I know it's just dreams, but to me, it's real."

"What if I told you I knew what your dreams were about?"

"I'd be curious, but not too surprised. As I said, I guessed a way back these were more than dreams. It's just not the kind of thing you can go talk to someone about without lookin' like some kinda nut, ya know? I figured I'd just wait and see if someone turned up looking for me about it all. I guess this means I'm either crazy or involved in some freaky shit."

"Do you know anything about the place from your dreams? The real place?" Emma asked.

"I looked it up. Did some research online. A lot of what I read kind of tied in to my dreams. What I wanna know is, where the hell *you* come into this."

"When you were researching, did you read anything about the hotel?"

"Course I did. It was pretty much all there was about the place until I decided to dig a little deeper. Sounds like some nasty shit went down there over the years. Some real nasty shit."

"I was there. I survived it."

Truman gave her the look. The one she always got from people who knew she was one of those who'd lived to tell the tale. "Holy shit. Then I guess maybe you *do* know what the hell I'm talking about. Sounds like you were lucky," Truman said.

"If you can call it that. I..." she took a drink of her coffee. It was almost cold, but she barely noticed. "I lost some friends. Some good friends. They were killed that night."

"Yeah, well, losing people is never easy. If it makes a difference, I'm sorry for your loss."

"My family has a history there. It's... well, it's something I don't want to get into right now. When we know each other a little better, maybe. For now though, it's not important."

"Alright, no problem," Truman said, still gazing at her intently. "But I do need you to tell me what you want with me, and how you think I can help. As you can see, I'm just a guy who washes dishes for a livin'."

"How much do you know about your ancestor?"

"Not much. I tried to look into his past, but I couldn't find much. I know he came over as a slave in the early nineteenth century. I know he was married and had a wife and kid, other than that I couldn't find anything. If you came here to ask me what he has to do with that house, then I'm sorry but I ain't got a clue."

"I do. That house, the one from your dreams. He helped build it. He was working for a man called Michael Jones."

Truman nodded. "I read about *that* motherfucker. His company went under a few months after the house was built. He just upped and left one day. All of his debts were left to his brother and business partner. Good riddance if you ask me. Damn slave trader."

"That's the official story. What you don't know is your ancestor was the first man to die on those grounds when the house was being built."

"How do you know that?" Truman said, the mistrustful look appearing in his eyes again.

"The documented history of that place is only part of the story. My grandmother was from Oakwell, she lived there all her life. The townspeople buried a lot of things from the public. A lot of it was never officially recorded."

"So what happened to him?" Truman asked.

"There were a series of letters, correspondence between Michael Jones and Governor Hughes, which showed Michael's degeneration into madness. Later, after Michael had stopped responding to the letters, Michael's brother Francis contacted the Governor to announce the death of his brother, and made reference to a suicide – a hanging of one of the slave workers on the site.

That worker was your ancestor. Like his brother before him, Francis's letters took on a very dark and disturbing tone, and soon he too stopped responding. Concerned by the mention of the deaths on site and lack of communication from either of the Jones brothers, Governor Hughes sent some men to find out what was going on. They didn't find anything at the house, however they did locate the bodies of both Michael and Isaac. They had drifted downriver, and were found almost twenty miles away.

My best guess is that Michael was trying to get rid of the body so it wouldn't hold up construction. The assumption is that he slipped whilst trying to dump the body in the river, and got washed away along with your grandfather. He wasn't a good swimmer, although anyone who knows the history of that place knows it was no accident. It rarely ever is in that place."

"What happened to the other brother, uhh Francis?"

"Nobody knows. His body was never found, and he was never seen or heard from again. My guess is his bones are out there somewhere, undiscovered in the trees."

"This is some crazy shit, lady," Truman said, smiling nervously. "What does it have to do with me?"

She reached into her bag on the seat beside her, took out a folder and slid it across the table. "This is all the information I have on your ancestor and the house. It's everything I've found out about how I think we can stop this thing. My number is on the back. I can only stay for a few days before I have to move on as there are others who I need to help me with this. It's important for you to know I need everyone if I'm to make this work. Just think about it, okay?"

Truman pulled the folder toward him and leafed through the pages.

"I need some time with this. I need to get my head straight, it's buzzin' right now."

"I understand. The address where you can find me is in the front there."

"Let me think it over," Truman said, sliding out of the booth. "I'll give you a call if I think I can help you."

Emma nodded, watching as he went back into the kitchen. She sat for a few more minutes then decided whatever happened next was out of her hands. She glanced toward the kitchen, but couldn't see Truman. Finishing her coffee, she left in the hope that he would decide to join her.

CHAPTER 15

"You must be the new guy," the orderly said, striding across the room and thrusting out a shovel-like hand. "Name's Barry. People in here call me Bear."

It was an apt name, as Bear stood a good half foot taller than Barlow, who was almost six feet tall himself. Barlow shook the offered hand, watching as his own skinny appendage was swallowed by an ocean of cocoa.

"Pleased to meet you," Barlow said, filled with the nervous unease felt by those starting a new job. "I'm Ron."

Bear grinned. He had kind eyes and a dazzling smile which was infectious and set the new arrival at ease. "Well, Ron, you stick with me and you'll be just fine. I've been asked to show you around. You got your swipe card yet?"

"Yeah," Barlow replied.

"Door passcodes?"

"Uh, not yet."

"We'll sort those out later. For now, let me give you the grand tour of chez Crease."

Bear led Barlow through the main reception area and punched in his key code, granting access to the inner sanctum of the hospital. Eggshell colored walls were the prevailing theme as the décor tried its best to make up for the grilles on the windows and the locks on the doors.

"So, how long have you worked here?" Barlow asked.

"Twelve years now."

"Impressive. I take it you like the job?"

"Not all the time," Bear said, flashing that infectious grin again. "But for the most part, it's rewarding as hell, that is if you can handle it. This job isn't for everyone."

Barlow nodded, happy to stay on the fence rather than offer an opinion until he knew Bear a little better. "So," he said instead, "anyone in particular here I should be wary of?"

"You need to be wary of all of the patients here, for your own safety as well as theirs. If you're talking about anyone you might have heard of in the news, then the answer is yes."

"Who?" Barlow asked.

They came to a security door. Bear swiped the card that he wore on a lanyard around his neck. The magnetic lock clicked, and Bear held the door open, gesturing for Barlow to go through. They were at the top of a staircase, and Bear led the way as they descended three floors, the lighting now much duller compared to the bright, airy feel upstairs.

"I take it you're asking about the Oakwell massacre?" Bear said, pausing in the corridor.

Barlow said nothing, and Bear gave another grin. "It's alright. Everyone wants to know about that. Believe me, soon enough the hype will wear off and you'll be as sick as the rest of us of hearing about it. Come on, I'll show you what you want to see."

At the foot of the steps was a caged security station, manned by a small, wrinkled old woman who gave them both a bland look. Bear gave her a cursory nod and again punched in his code, granting them access to a long corridor with doors spaced regularly down both sides. As they walked, their shoes echoed on the polished floors.

"You know what happened I take it? During the massacre?" Bear said.

Barlow nodded, noting even Bear had lost some of his exuberance as they entered the secure wing of the hospital.

"A lot of people now don't seem as interested. You know what it's like, new things happen, people forget. Shit, there's always some new horror in the news to grab people's attention. For us though, we don't get to forget. We have to live with this every damn day."

"Are you from there? Oakwell, I mean…"

"No, not me. My brother lived there for a while though. His business went under and he moved away a few months before the massacre."

"I remember reading about it. Awful stuff."

Bear smiled, his eyes glimmering with something Barlow couldn't quite place. "You think reading about it is creepy, wait until you have to go face it every day."

"That doesn't help with the first day nerves," Barlow said, forcing a smile. Bear, however, didn't return it. His face had become tight, brow furrowed. He was all business now. It was as if he had left his easy going demeanor with the sour-faced hag at the security station.

"Hell, I'm not trying to freak you out or put you off, my man. All I want to do is make sure you're aware. We take precautions, and the staff here are damn good at their jobs, but you still need to stay sharp. Keep on your toes."

"I will."

"Alright, this is it," Bear said, coming to a halt at a windowless steel door. In the center, at head height, was a second door with a lockable hatch.

Barlow felt a surge of adrenaline mingling with his fear, making it all the more potent. He couldn't help but offer up a nervous smile, which again went unreciprocated by Bear. "He's really in here? Henry Marshall?" Barlow asked.

"He is. You sure you wanna see him?"

Barlow nodded, his mouth too dry to speak. Bear opened the hatch and stood aside, allowing Barlow to see inside.

The cell was small. Cold concrete. Iron bedstead. Stainless steel toilet and sink. The person inside was sitting on the bottom of the bed, facing away from them, staring at the corner of the wall. Barlow couldn't make out his face, just a sliver of flesh revealed through the greasy, graying shoulder-length hair.

"He always sits there like that," Bear said as Barlow looked on. "Just staring at that wall. He's docile enough, it's just creepy how quiet he is all the time."

"Maybe he's a little…" Barlow tapped the side of his temple with his forefinger.

"No, I don't think he is," Bear countered. "Sometimes, you'll catch his eye, and you can see all the lights are still switched on in there. It's like he's waiting for something. I don't know, my man, but whatever it is, it freaks me out."

Bear closed the hatch, locking it into place.

"Alright," he said, forcing a smile. "Let's go see about those key codes, and then we can grab a coffee. I don't like to be down here any longer than I have to."

Barlow didn't argue. The further away from Marshall's cell he got, the better.

CHAPTER 16

Truman followed Emma through the house, still unsure if he'd made the right decision in contacting her. She had brought him to the converted ranch house, both of them awkward and silent as they successfully avoided the elephant in the room about how they'd come to meet. The house was old, and Truman thought it almost certainly belonged to an older family. Dark wood floors with an overabundance of furniture and ornaments was the prevailing theme. Every surface Truman could see was covered with mementos or photographs. He suspected that at some point in the past, this would have been a vibrant family home, yet all that remained now were echoes of that time left to haunt the place like ghosts. Sunlight, gold and warm, filtered through the study windows, catching lazy swirls of dust in its beams. Truman only noticed this for a second before his attention was drawn to the wall. It was reminiscent of those police dramas, where the plucky detective would pin all of their leads to the noticeboard. Photographs, articles, notes, all linked together with color-coded string.

"This is the entire history of Hope House as I've been able to put it together," Emma said, standing aside to let him see.

Truman looked. Faces he didn't recognize. Photographs of places that he did from his dreams. It was almost too much to take in, and all he could do was try to assimilate it all, letting his brain filter the cluster of information in front of him. Something caught his eye and he stepped forward to a section of the wall, crouching to stare at the drawing. It was a reproduction of course. Any original would be in a private collection or perhaps even a museum. Even so, its impact was still the same. Truman looked at the image, and beside it, the slavery manifest.

"Holy shit, that's him," Truman said, pointing at the portrait of the man. "Isn't it?"

Emma nodded. "That was the only reference to him anywhere I could find. The drawing was from before he was brought over here to work. The slavery manifest is the only official mention of your ancestor."

Truman held out his hand, taking the picture by the bottom edge. "Do you mind if I take a closer look?"

"Go ahead."

He unpinned the photograph and sat in one of the high-backed leather chairs by the fireplace. He studied the photograph, committing it to memory.

"The nose is wrong."

"What?" Emma said, wondering if she had missed something.

"The nose on this drawin'. It's wrong. The real one isn't as wide at the bottom. And the forehead is too long. I can tell it's the same man, though, but he looks different in my dream." He looked at her, and she saw in him the same confusion that used to plague her until she started to understand. "What the hell's goin' on here?"

"It's easier to show you," she said, going to the window. She grabbed a jar from the ledge and handed it to Truman.

"What the hell is this?"

"Just take it. It'll all make sense in a minute," she said, taking a seat opposite him. "First, let me tell you what we need to do to stop this."

CHAPTER 17

Barlow had been working at Creasefield hospital for three weeks, and had just about found his feet. He had got to know the staff, made a few friends, and had a few close calls with some of the more volatile inmates.

"Hey, man, how's it goin'?" Bear said as he sauntered into the staffroom and made himself a coffee.

"I'm good. You?"

"All good in the hood, brotha'. You busy today?"

"I'm babysitting the rec room this afternoon."

"Screw that, my man, ask Todd to do it."

"And what will I do when Todd is doing my job?"

Bear grinned and leaned close, even though the staff room was empty. "You know when you first started here, and you had a little look at Henry Marshall?"

"Yeah."

"Well, I'm down to turn his room this afternoon. Nothin' too taxing. Just changing the sheets, making sure he hasn't got anything stashed in there. I need someone to help me out if you feel like it."

"You sure you want to tempt fate? It's Friday the thirteenth you know," Barlow said, smiling.

"Come on, man, surely you don't believe in

that shit. How about it, want to help me?"

"Absolutely, count me in," Barlow replied, just about managing to hide his nervousness.

"Alright, that's a deal. Meet me downstairs at eleven and you can give me a hand."

"Eleven tonight?" Barlow asked.

"Hell no, not eleven tonight. This ain't some horror movie. After morning break, dumbass."

Barlow grinned, the tension lifted. "I was just checking. I don't think I'd wanna be in there with that guy at night."

"I hear that. See you at eleven."

Barlow waited until Bear left the room before he let the false smile melt from his lips. As much as he had liked the idea of getting up close and personal with someone as notorious as Henry Marshall, now that it was a reality, he wasn't quite so sure. No matter which way you looked at it, the man was a killer, and as insane as they came. He knew how it would be. Even in mid-morning light, the shadows would still seem a little deeper, the atmosphere just a little more intense. There was no denying that, light or dark, they would still be in the presence of a mass murderer. Taking a last look around the empty staffroom, Barlow finished his drink and went back to his duties.

II

Fire.
Blood.
Pain.

A vague awareness that this experience was more than just a dream. These were memories. Experiences from strangers somehow shared across some kind of mental wavelength.

Signs proclaiming no access to a place forbidden for a reason.

Friends bickering.

Friends laughing.

Friends dying.

Always friends dying.

A beautiful rosebush in a circle of death. Pink petals, green stems with sharp thorns.

A rain of blood. Flooding the earth.

Pink flowers blooming.

Life fed by death.

Friends screaming.

Friends dying.

Secret voices all around.

In the trees.

In the ground.

In the brain.

That sound, that scraping sound that makes the teeth hurt. The sound of dead things dragging themselves through the earth.

Only, this sound isn't part of the dream.

This is somewhere else.

That screech, that scrape.

The confusion replaced by recognition.

Suddenly, it fades.

The bloody rain, the screaming, the dying friends.

All gone.
Reality, a blanket with a stuffy, mildew taste.
No more roses.
No more circle of death.
No more screaming.
No more dying friends.
Only that sound.
That scraping sound.
Reality.
My world.
My prison.
Not for long.
Not for long.
Not for long.

Henry Marshall's eyes flickered as the door to his cell scraped open on unoiled hinges. He was in his usual position, sitting at the foot of his bed and staring at the wall, his visitors at his back. He rarely moved from that position. He liked to stare at the walls where the corners met. To focus on the line where the bricks converged, where the walls of his prison were at their strongest.

The years since his incarceration hadn't been kind to Henry. The bloated belly grown from too many public luncheons as he schmoozed with his fellow councilors was long gone. He had lost at least eighty pounds, his face now gaunt and heavily lined, his once perfectly styled hair now dirty and touching his shoulders. Gone were the clean-shaven cheeks and winning smile.

This version of Henry Marshall wore a beard as dirty as his hair, and those perfectly maintained veneers had yellowed. Usually, such intrusion into his space would have been ignored. Not today though. Today was different. Today the voices were answering his call.

"Hey there, Mr. Marshall, it's me, Bear. I'm just here to check over your room, okay?"

Henry didn't move. Bear looked at him, the familiar sight of the back of his head, the only real sight he had seen since Henry was first institutionalized. He turned to Barlow, who was standing by the door, eyes wide.

"It's okay, you can come in."

Barlow did as he was told, still staring at the man hunched over the bottom of the bed. Starstruck wasn't quite the right word. Awestruck maybe, and although he didn't want to acknowledge it, fear crawled around inside him with malicious intent.

"What do you want me to do?" he said, his words feeling like they were falling out of his mouth instead of projecting into the room.

"We need to change his sheets. Help me to get him to stand up."

"Is that safe?"

Bear strode across the room and leaned close to Barlow, the scent of his spearmint chewing gum potent as he spoke.

"Look, my man. You can't show fear here. You need to be strong. This guy is a pussycat. He's harmless. I've turned this room hundreds of times.

Trust me, you don't need to worry, okay?"

"Sorry, I'm just... It's fine."

"Alright, then help me move him."

Bear grinned and moved back toward Henry Marshall, standing at his shoulder.

"Okay, Mr. Marshall, you know the drill. Stand up please and move against the wall."

Normally at this point, Henry would comply, allowing himself to be led like a child to wherever Bear wanted him to go. Today, however, he remained where he was, still staring at the corner of the wall, brow furrowed in concentration.

"Mr. Marshall, come on. Please."

Still Henry didn't move.

Although disturbed by the change in behavior, Bear didn't want to spook Barlow, so he laughed it off.

"Come on now, Mr. Marshall. Just like always. We'll be in and out of here in just a few minutes."

Bear put a gentle hand on Henry's elbow and guided him up. Docile and compliant, Henry Marshall obeyed, allowing himself to be led toward the corner.

"That's it, Mr. Marshall, just like always. You just wait there until my friend and I are done here, then we'll leave you be. Okay?"

Henry gave no response or acknowledgement, and Bear turned toward Barlow, a relieved smile on his face.

"You see, my man? This job is all about respect, both giving and receiving. If—"

Bear saw Barlow's eyes grow wide just a split

second before the pain exploded through him.

Henry Marshall, the man who had remained a docile mute for the last three years, had struck. Driven on by the voices in his head, he showed no mercy, biting down hard on Bear's throat and tearing away a mouthful of flesh, rupturing veins, severing arteries. Bright red sprayed across the white painted walls in an arcing jet as Bear fell to the ground, hands clutching at his open throat as he choked and gargled. He spasmed and twitched, performing a slow half circle on his back, leaving a bloody trail in his wake.

Barlow looked on, too afraid to move, unable to do anything but stare. Henry was on him in two steps, deftly avoiding the gurgling, flopping Bear who was still desperately trying to cling on to life.

Barlow tried to step back, but there was nowhere to go. Henry's hands were on him, gripping his face. Squeezing. Squeezing.

Barlow saw no compassion in Henry's eyes, just a distant emptiness behind that blood-drenched beard. That image would be the last he would ever see as Henry jammed his thumbs into his eyes. He managed not to scream until the first eyeball popped, spilling over his cheek in a gelatinous mass. His legs buckled, but with a firm grip on the inside of Barlow's eye socket, Henry pulled him upright, just seconds before the right eye popped. Like its twin, it exploded in a liquid jelly mass. Barlow thrashed and twitched, an anguished roar of pain and fear escaping from his lips.

Henry tossed him to the floor, absently

wiping his wet thumbs on his white t-shirt. He took a deep breath, listening to the sounds of feet racing toward him. None of that mattered to him now. All that mattered was getting out.

He reached down and snatched Bear's keys from his belt and the pass from around his neck, not even glancing at the dead man's stare.

He paused to reach under his mattress, pulling out a toothbrush, the handle split and sharpened into a makeshift blade. Henry took a deep breath, feeling more alive than he had in years, then, driven on by the symphony of voices in his head, set out to meet those who were coming to stop him.

III

The first of them arrived before he'd reached the end of the hall. The voices drove him on, controlling him, Henry trusting their instructions without question. The orderly stopped, his eyes widening as he saw the blood. He reached down to grab his personal alarm from his belt but it was too late. In a single fluid motion, Henry attacked, thrusting the sharpened toothbrush toward the man's face. Either by instinct or reaction, the orderly threw up an arm, the toothbrush piercing the flesh of his bicep.

Blood spattered onto the floor as the man screamed. Henry was already behind him, forearm around his throat, the bloody, makeshift dagger held toward his face. The orderly calmed, sensing the gravity of the situation as Henry marched him to the security gate.

"Open it," he whispered, foul breath hot in his prisoner's ear.

"No, I won't do it," the orderly panted.

The voices in Henry's head told him what to do. He pressed the point of the toothbrush to the side of the orderly's eye, the point wavering just inches from the eyeball.

"Open it," Henry repeated.

The orderly swiped his card and punched in his number; the door clicked open, allowing them access to the main part of the hospital.

The woman in the caged security station glanced up, then stood and pushed her chair away from the desk. Henry saw her eyes go to the alarm, but the black things in his mind had already reacted. He slammed his prisoner's face against the cage, pushing the sharpened toothbrush into the soft flesh around the eyeball.

"Don't," he grunted. "Out of the cage."

She stood frozen, hands clasped in front of her, torn between what she had been trained to do and what instinct was telling her.

Henry pushed his weight against his captive and pulled Bear's blood spotted lanyard out of the waistband of his pants. "You either come out of there now or I'll kill him and come in after you," he growled.

That appeared to do the trick, and the skinny woman moved to the door, opened it and came out into the hall, sliding across the wall as if she were trying to push her way through it to keep her distance from Henry.

"Just calm down. Don't do anything stupid," she said, voice trembling.

"Open the door," he whispered, pulling his prisoner away from the cage and pressing the makeshift knife into the soft flesh of his throat.

"I can't do that," the woman said. Although shaken, she didn't seem as terrified as Henry's current prisoner was. She held his gaze as he peered over the shoulder of his terrified captive.

The voices came to him, whispering their instructions. Without thought, he reacted.

The sharpened toothbrush easily pierced the flesh on the orderly's neck, sending a great spray of arterial blood across the eggshell walls. Henry tossed him aside, leaving him clutching his throat as he squirmed on the floor, blood pumping out with frightening speed. The woman gasped, for the first time starting to understand the gravity of the situation. Henry was already on her, hand clasped around her throat, leaving a bloody smear, his nose inches from hers. He touched the toothbrush to her cheek, leaving a bloody impression on her skin.

"Door," he said, his dead eyes never leaving hers.

This time she complied, deciding that her life was worth more than the job. He grabbed a handful of her hair, keeping his weapon close to her neck while she swiped her card and punched in her code.

As the door clicked open, she glanced back to

look at the orderly on the floor. He lay motionless, eyes staring at the ceiling, one arm still clutched to his neck, which was now trickling blood rather than pumping it out. She realized that although she recognized the man, she didn't even know his name. Henry shoved her through the door. Ahead of them, a staircase loomed.

"How do I get out?" he hissed in her ear.

"You can't. It's a secure unit. Please, just let me go."

"Take me outside."

"Please, don't kill me," she said, finally breaking down. She blinked back tears, and Henry could feel her trembling against him. He liked it. The almost palpable taste of fear in the air emanating from the woman pleased him. More importantly, it pleased the dark thing in his head. He marched her up the steps, still holding her by the hair. They encountered nobody on the staircase and ascended the three flights to the top of the secure area.

"Which way out?" he said.

"Please, just let me go. I have a family," she said between gasping sobs.

"Which way?" he snapped, leaning closer to her.

"Through the door," she stammered. "Then turn right and go to the end of the hall. There's a door to the right; it will take you to the parking garage. You can get out to the street from there."

The voices in Henry's head asked a question, which he in turn relayed to the terrified woman.

"What about staff? How many will be up

there?"

"Not many," she sobbed. "It's shift change. It'll be quiet. Please, don't hurt me. I've done everything you asked."

"Open the door," he grunted.

This time there was no hesitation. She punched in her code, Henry watching over her shoulder as she pushed the magnetic keypad. It was all he needed.

Mustering all of his strength, he slammed the woman's head into the wall, the sound making a horrific wet crunch as her skull impacted against the concrete. That would have been enough, but the rage was strong, the voices encouraging. He did it again and again, the woman's face destroyed, leaving a bloody, smeared impression on the wall. She was already dead by the time he tossed her down the steps, her body tumbling to the first floor landing, the pulpy mess that used to be her face unrecognizable. She twitched once. Twice. Then was still.

Completely calm, Henry turned back to the keypad, swiped the card, and punched in the woman's access code which he had already committed to memory.

The upper floors had a different feel to the ones below. He followed the dead woman's instructions and walked down the hall. A staff member exited one of the doors and the two locked eyes for the briefest of seconds before Henry plunged his homemade knife into the staff member's throat. He didn't even look back as the gurgling man slid to the floor, legs kicking as he bled out.

The woman hadn't lied. The parking garage was cool, a light breeze ruffling Henry's beard and feeling somehow alien to him. He saw his opportunity immediately.

A doctor, one he recognized from his rounds in the secure wing, had just arrived and was taking his briefcase out of the back of his car. Henry was already moving. He closed the distance, coming up behind the doctor, who was unaware of what was about to happen. He never saw it coming. Like the others, Henry plunged the blade into his throat, tossing the doctor to the concrete. This time, the frenzy was uncontrollable. He straddled the doctor's chest, bringing the blade down again and again into his face and neck until it snapped, a shaft of bloody white plastic embedded in the doctor's cheek.

Breathing heavily, he stood, pausing to pick up the doctor's keys and close the trunk of the car. He waited, listening to the things in his mind. He re-opened the trunk and grabbed the doctor under the arms, straining to lift him into the small space, folding him in, making him fit. The voices telling him how he could be used later, how he might be needed. When it was done, he re-closed the trunk and wiped a forearm across his sweaty brow. He stood, savoring the absolute silence around him, calmness and serenity filling him as he eased himself into the driver's seat, encasing himself in the pine-scented confines of the vehicle. He sat there for a moment, trying to catch his breath. The alarms in the hospital began to sound – a monotonous wail that spurred him into action. He started the engine and slipped the vehicle into gear. Then, with a squeal of tires, Henry Marshall was on his way, free within the world.

CHAPTER 18

It was a sobering thought for Melody Samson, one which she wasn't sure how to deal with. She'd been existing for the last few months with some form of hope that her symptoms were anything other than cancer. She had watched herself change, shriveling and withering as the days went by.

The first tumor had been found in her stomach six months after she'd lost Isaac. Chemotherapy treatment had started immediately, which resulted in the cancer regressing. She considered herself one of the fortunate ones to have survived such a ruthless killer. However, the story for her wasn't done yet, and rather than being defeated, the disease had just been resting, recuperating before coming back to finish the job. This time its attack had been remorseless. It had gone into her bowel.

Although she was convinced death was coming, she was determined not to give up hope until the visit from the doctor to give the results of her latest series of tests. He came to the house, face somber with just the right amount of sympathy. She, of course, didn't think anything of it. Doctors, as a rule, were often somber. It wasn't until he started to talk, to explain the situation that she truly understood and started to acknowledge the stark reality. She nodded in all the right places, only hearing snatches of his words.

Nothing more can be done.

Even though her mortality had been at risk for a while, to hear the finality of it made her entire being ache with the desire to live on. She asked him how long she had, staring through him and trying not to break down, doing all she could not to think about Isaac until he had gone. She prayed for enough time, something she had come to realize was so precious and fragile. His answer floored her.

Two years, maybe less.

Maybe less.

That was the one that hit home. The doctor forced a smile and suggested she spend as much time as she could building memories with her friends and family, which was easy for him to say. He wasn't the one limited to just a couple of years (maybe less) or who had a son he wasn't allowed to see. His life would go on. He would be present for whatever the future held. All she had was a precious twenty-four months (maybe less) to right wrongs, rectify mistakes, and most importantly, clear her conscience and get her son back before she was erased from existence. The world, of course, would keep turning without Melody Samson. Nobody would know. Nobody would care. For a while, *she* didn't think she cared, however, now that it was real, now that she knew it was going to happen, she wanted to go on living more than ever.

What a joke.

The relationship with her sister that had once been so strong had been irreparably broken by the events that took place in the aftermath of the hotel attack; so much so that she'd moved away, leaving no forwarding address. At the time, Melody was convinced she didn't care. However now, with this latest news, she wanted nothing more than to confide in her sibling or hug her and take comfort from her, things she knew were impossible.

Now, some four hours after the doctor had delivered the devastating news, she sat at the kitchen table, her coffee cold and untouched, absolutely paralyzed with dread and unsure what she was supposed to do. There was a knock at the door, a sharp rat-a-tat-tat. She wondered if it was that bitch from next door looking to get the scoop on why the doctor had made a house call, but the tone of the knock wasn't like that of Mrs. Richter. This was an authoritative call. On weak legs, she crossed the room and opened the door.

"Melody Samson?"

There was a flicker of recognition when she saw the man standing in the hall. Her mind sifted through its fractured contents, trying to put a name to the face, to recall where she knew him from. He was tall and broad, with chiseled features, sandy hair and matching stubble. His eyes were a piercing blue and he was dressed in a sharp black suit, the purple shirt underneath open at the neck.

"Yes," she replied, still in a daze.

He thrust a hand toward her. "Detective Alex Petrov. I wonder if I could speak with you for a moment."

The name triggered a memory. "You were there at the hotel. You investigated it," she mumbled.

"I did. I believe I interviewed you shortly after the death of your husband."

"Yes, I remember. It's all a bit of a blur to be honest. Why are you here now?"

"It would be better if we could talk inside," Petrov said.

She stepped back and opened the door further. "Come on in."

The detective entered the apartment, remaining stony-faced at the mess. Dishes were piled high in the sink, and empty takeout containers filled the countertops. A dozen empty wine bottles told him how she'd spent most of her nights, and a prickle of embarrassment made her blush.

"Sorry, I haven't had a chance to tidy the place yet."

"It's alright," Petrov said, declining to tell her he had seen much worse places over the years.

"What's this about?" she asked, wringing her hands as she stood by the table.

Petrov looked at her, shocked at how her appearance had changed in the relatively short space of time since he'd last seen her. She had the look of someone struggling with ill-health. She was pale and exhausted, like she was tired of the world kicking her in the teeth on a daily basis. It didn't make the reason for his visit any easier. He cleared his throat and followed procedure.

"Mrs. Samson, what I'm about to tell you may come as a shock. What I want to do is remind you not to panic. Everything is under control."

"What's happened?" she asked, keeping eye contact with him.

"Henry Marshall escaped from Creasefield hospital yesterday, injuring several staff members in the process. For obvious reasons, we wanted to get out here and check on you."

Melody felt her legs tremble and, for a moment, she thought she was going to collapse.

"Are you okay?" Petrov asked, putting a hand on her elbow and leading her to the kitchen table. She sat and put her head in her hands, the influx of information proving difficult to deal with.

"How did he escape?" she finally asked, still staring at the table top.

"We don't know the details yet apart from that he waited until the morning shift change to do it."

"Was anyone hurt?"

"I'm afraid so. Several staff members were hurt trying to restrain him."

"Is anyone dead?"

Petrov hesitated, trying to decide how much to say. It was obvious that Melody wasn't coping at all well, and he was determined not to push her any further.

"We don't have information on that at this time. I came straight here to ensure you were safe."

"So where is he?"

"We don't know. We have our best people on it."

"Oh god, do you think he's coming after me?"

"We don't think so. I just came here as a precaution and to advise you to stay on your guard. I'm going to have officers keep a regular watch on the place until we get him back. We've set up roadblocks and have an extensive search team on the case so he won't be out there for long. Just keep a close eye on your surroundings. Watch people. Make a point of noticing those things you might normally ignore. If you sense anything – and I do mean anything – is wrong, you give me a call straight away, no matter what time it is." He handed her a card with his number embossed on the front.

"I will," she said, feeling detached and distant as she slipped the card into her pocket. "Please, do your best to find him. The idea of him out on the streets…"

"Don't you worry about that, Mrs. Samson. I'll do whatever it takes to find him. That I can promise you."

It was easy to believe him. The intensity in his eyes was utterly convincing, and it was enough to take the edge off her fear until something dawned on her that made her feel nauseous.

"What about my son? What if Henry Marshall goes after him?"

"No, we've already considered that. Marshall has no way of knowing where he is, and no means of finding out. Chances are, the only thing on his mind right now is escape and lying low. Even so, I'm having an officer go out to your son's foster home to advise them of the situation."

"Okay, thank you," Melody said, making sure

she was very careful in her response so as not to alert the detective.

She had learned from her therapy sessions that nobody in an official capacity would believe her account of the supernatural forces at work on her and her family. She was also convinced that Henry Marshall's escape was no coincidence. She suspected that, far from wanting to run away and lie low, he would want to make a very different use of his freedom.

She also knew that, despite Detective Petrov's assurances, Henry Marshall wouldn't need to access police records or other confidential documentation in order to find out where Isaac was. He had access to the things that had attached themselves to his psyche to guide him. Somehow she remained calm, despite the urgency to get to her son and make sure he was safe. The last complication she needed was to be arrested or arouse suspicion. She glanced at her watch, calculating the time it would take to get to her son before Henry Marshall. Now at least, with her own death a certainty, she had nothing to lose.

CHAPTER 19

Petrov stood at the entrance to the park, his eyes scanning the thin scattering of people who were enjoying its amenities. A couple of joggers made another lap, iPod buds wedged in ears. A man played catch with his dog, the muscular Alsatian retrieving the tennis ball with eager energy. Kimmel was waiting exactly where he said he would be. He was sitting on a bench, his eyes hidden behind dark sunglasses, briefcase on his lap. He looked impeccably smart: charcoal suit, leather shoes.

You can take the man out of the army, but you can't take the army out of the man, Petrov thought as he approached the former general. Kimmel saw him and stood, setting the briefcase on the bench.

"Thank you for agreeing to meet me, Detective," Kimmel said, holding out a hand. Petrov shook it, the old man's grip still firm.

"Not a problem, General. I have to admit, your phone call made me curious. I didn't expect to hear from you again."

"You wouldn't have if not for… uh… recent events. Please, take a seat."

Petrov sat beside the General, a wall of silence between them. He was about to break it when Kimmel began to speak.

"I asked you to come here when I learned of Henry Marshall's escape yesterday."

Petrov said nothing, even though his curiosity was already piqued. He glanced at Kimmel, but the General was staring straight ahead as he spoke.

"I don't think I need to tell you where he will be heading, do I?"

"Oakwell. We think he'll try to make his way there," Petrov said, waiting for confirmation from Kimmel. There was no response. "We have roadblocks set up; we'll catch him before he gets there. Even if we don't, we'll ambush him in the town. He won't escape us."

"I wouldn't underestimate him."

"Don't worry, we don't. He's already killed six people."

"Even more if your men try to restrain him."

Petrov turned to face Kimmel, unsure of why he was so angered by his comments. "He's just a man. I appreciate you come from a military background, General, but this is my world. Don't hype him up to be more than he is."

"What if he is more? More than you think anyway."

"Come on, General, if you have something to say to me, just say it. What's your point?"

"How much do you know about that place? Oakwell I mean."

"I know I don't like it. I know it interests me. I know it has a history."

"Do you remember when we last spoke in the Plaza? You were telling me about how you were removed from the case without warning and have been trying to figure out what happened ever since. I think you will agree it has become some kind of an obsession for you?"

"I was fine with it until your people threw me out," Petrov replied.

"Not me. Fisher. He threw me out too, remember?"

"What's your point, General?"

"My point is, that place is unlike anywhere else in the world. It changes people. Twists them and corrupts them until even they don't know who they are anymore."

"I'm aware of the stories. And for the record, I don't believe them."

"That's why I asked you to come," Kimmel said, turning toward Petrov and taking off his sunglasses. His eyes were tired. "The fact that you don't believe them worries me."

"I appreciate your concern, but it's unwarranted."

"Please, just hear me out," Kimmel said. He was holding the sunglasses, absently folding and unfolding one of the arms. Noticing what he was doing, he slipped them into his pocket. "I was like you once. Saw everything in black and white. That place changed me though. It changed all of us."

"I'm sorry, General, but I really don't have the time to sit here and listen to this. I'm up to my neck in a manhunt as you well know. From the message you left, I was under the impression that you had a specific reason to meet me here."

"Yes, yes I do," Kimmel muttered, reaching into his briefcase. He handed Petrov a brown folder. The detective took it and opened it. Inside was a diary, the front red and water-damaged.

"What's this?" Petrov asked.

"I want you to read it."

"I don't understand."

"As you know, I'm not allowed to divulge anything to you about what happened up there when we took over. Privileged information and all. The fact that I'm retired now makes this easier, especially as what you're about to read doesn't officially exist. To be honest, when we found it, I had no idea what the hell to do with it. I hesitated before calling you at all, Detective Petrov, but I think in light of these most recent events, it would pay for you to read it."

"What is it?"

"A diary made by one of my men during our brief stay on the hotel grounds. I won't say anymore yet as I don't want to influence you. We found it buried under his tent when we were clearing it away. I didn't know what the hell to do with it so I just took it with me and kept it quiet. Truth be told, I wish I'd never laid eyes on it."

Petrov took the diary out of the folder and turned it over in his hands.

"You want me to read it now?" Petrov asked.

"I'm sorry for being so vague, but I don't want to influence you in any way. Please, just read it."

Petrov stared at the General, who seemed to have a little of the fire back in his eyes as he held his gaze. He glanced around the park, finding it even more bizarre that life went on around them as normal. The dog and its owner still played catch. The joggers still lapped in tandem, and Kimmel still stared and waited, now opening and closing the dull gold lighter instead of messing with his sunglasses. Petrov turned to the book, reading the name penned on the front.

Lance corporal Frederick Landro
D.O.B 10/9/83

Holding the diary brought with it an intense feeling of foreboding. He could feel the waxy, slick texture of the cover, and the book smelled faintly of damp. The first dozen or so pages had been torn out, leaving jagged edges in the gutter of the book. The text written inside was small and neat, the handwriting slanting toward the top right of the page.

June 9th 2014

This should have been an easy assignment after the last two years of hell spent in the desert wondering if each day would be my last.

What a surprise, then, that I would gladly take that life back if it got me away from this godawful place. We've been told by General Kimmel that this is a sensitive situation, and one we're not allowed to discuss, even amongst ourselves. The whispers still get around though.

You hear about things that have happened and hope to God the stories have been exaggerated. Worse still is the feel of this place. It has a dirty, sinister vibe which is making the rest of the men stationed here cranky. Some of them bullshit that it doesn't bother them, but their eyes tell a different story.

It doesn't help that we're not allowed into the hotel. What bullshit! That place is kitted out with all the mod-cons and here we are slumming it in tents in the car park. Typical. The waiting is the worst part. We're set to patrol the area in groups. I'm scheduled in for my first taste of it tomorrow.

A couple of the guys who came back in this morning said it's not too bad until you get to the clearing across the river. That, they said, was unlike anything they had ever experienced.

Kimmel shut them up before they could go into detail, which prompted me to start this diary and log what happens. I'm curious, and although I won't admit it to the others, a little afraid. Some soldier I am! Let's hope tomorrow goes smoothly and without incident. So far, despite the ominous threat of some unseen presence, all is quiet.

June 10th

It's done. My first visit to the clearing across the river is behind me, and it was every bit as bad as I'd been told it was. I'm just glad I wasn't alone. Even so, the three of us who went there could all feel it, although explaining what it felt like is difficult. Mills and Layfield didn't even try.

All I can tell you is that it's like something crawling around inside your head. You feel dirty, if that makes sense. Mills went up there all full of piss and vinegar, which to be fair to him is all he's ever been since I've known him. Since we came back to camp he's been quiet.

Layfield has gone the other way. He's trying too hard to show he isn't afraid, although I don't think he's fooling anyone. It's almost like we're dead men walking. Each of us waiting our turn to have to go back up there. If it were up to me, we would burn this place to the ground.

Unfortunately, we have a job to do. Kimmel says their scientists need us to accompany them up there so they can do their tests. I don't think whatever is up there is anything science can fix, but as I said earlier, I'm a soldier and I'll do as I'm told. I'm tired now, and think sleep (if I can get some) will do me the world of good.

June 11th

I dreamed last night, a garbled mess of scenes. I saw a blond-haired man on fire at the base of a huge dead tree. As he stood there, arms agape, it started to rain blood. Then, as if that wasn't bad enough, dead children started to fall, their bodies impacting on the ground with the most explosive sound. I woke up drenched in sweat and twisted around my blankets. How I didn't scream, I don't know.

I was thinking of asking Mills or Layfield if they had experienced anything similar, but Mills wouldn't make eye contact with me, and I didn't see Layfield during breakfast this morning.

One interesting snippet I did pick up was about what the scientists we're babysitting are up to in the clearing. One of the boys overheard Kimmel talking about it. According to Cameron, the scientists are interested in the dirt. That tells me there's something up there they either want to weaponize or keep out of the reach of others. Either way, I hope they find whatever the hell it is they're looking for soon so we can leave this place behind.

I never imagined I'd be wishing for an uncomplicated warzone to take my mind off a patch of damn dirt in the middle of nowhere. Anyway, I'm depressing myself by writing this and I need to give my report to Kimmel soon. Everyone who goes to the clearing has to report in. Research apparently. Best to get it over with I suppose. God, I hate this place.

June 12th

There was something in the woods last night. We all heard it. It sounded like children crying, or maybe that's not the right word. It was more like wailing. Mills locked eyes with me across the fire we were sitting around, and we didn't need to say a word.

I looked for Layfield to see if he was also looking in my direction but, like the others, he was staring into the trees, trying to think of anything to explain away the sounds he could hear. For the first time today, I realized just how much I miss my wife. I just want out of here. It's obvious by now we don't belong in this place. Worse, we're not wanted here, and I worry about what might happen if we overstay our welcome.

June 13th

Everyone is tense today. We heard more noises from the trees last night. Like the night before, it sounded like children, although there were other sounds too. Mills told me he thought he heard them call his name. I know that can't be true because I heard them say mine. What the hell is out there?

June 14th

Layfield is dead. One of the guys found him hanging from a tree just a few feet from the edge of the camp.

I thought for sure that would see the end to this stupid assignment, but as is the way with the government, a dead soldier wasn't about to get in the way of what needed to be done. If anything, activity has increased. People are in and out of the hotel like ants, bringing in lights and equipment. God knows what they're doing, but whatever it is, we have been frozen out. Even Kimmel seems a little put out by it. He thinks this is his show, but this thing about the hotel being off-limits showed everyone that he has someone up the chain pulling his strings.

Poor Layfield was shoved into a body bag and left in the car park ready for transportation back to the city. For him at least, this ordeal is over. It's not the most dignified way to go out, but nobody expected people to die up here at all, so this is the best we could do under the circumstances. One of the guys said he'd left some kind of fucked up suicide note in his pocket, although, as it always is with speculation, nobody seems to know what it said.

As I write this, I can see Layfield's body bag by the edge of the path, and it dawns on me that although we're trained to handle death, it's still a shock to see it up close. Speaking of close, it's getting dark and the tension is starting to ramp up a little. People are wondering if we will get a repeat performance from the forest tonight or not.

I'm almost certain that we will. It's funny, because the more you ty to ignore them, the more sense they start to make. My turn to go on patrol tomorrow. To say I'm not looking forward to it is an understatement. I just hope I can do what I need to.

June 15th

Last night was the worst yet. The noises, as I predicted, were out there again.

I'm sure I'm not the only one who thought they were louder, as if each night brings them closer to the camp. What the hell is this place?

June 16th

Really tense in the camp today. Everyone knows what's going on here but they're either too proud or too afraid to say anything. I suppose I can't complain too much, as I'm guilty of the same thing.

Last night, someone took Layfield's body from where it was waiting for pickup. We were sent out into the woods to look for it, but interestingly enough, we weren't asked to check the clearing. The official word from Kimmel is that animals must have dragged the body into the woods, although nobody believes it.

Even the General is starting to look tense and, dare I say it, a little afraid. I keep hearing my name whispered by the trees. Can't say anything about it though. It's tense enough already.

My turn to patrol the clearing tomorrow. We're taking a couple of the scientists up there to get more samples. The vibe in the camp is bad. Nobody wants to be here and I suspect a revolt isn't a million miles away. It's been dark for a couple of hours now and the voices in the woods have just started. I considered putting my iPod on so that I could get a little sleep, although if I'm honest, not being able to hear them is worse.

June 17th

Early morning entry today as I'm heading out to the clearing in an hour and I have new information to share.

Last night was the worst since we arrived. I don't think these things like us being here. The noise was awful, and even hunkered down in my bunk, I could hear some of the guys losing it. Some screamed. Others cried. I even heard someone praying.

It's obvious by now whatever exists here is evil. There is no use in denying that anymore. This, I suppose, is what being a soldier all is about. The TV ads and the posters asking you to sign up don't mention we're expendable, or that we might have to face things like this. Kimmel has set up armed command posts around the perimeter of the hotel, which is laughable, a token gesture at best.

Everyone knows this thing can't be brought down with bullets. Can't blame Kimmel too much though, I think as a lifelong military man, guns have always been his go-to response. It's time for my patrol and I can feel the nausea lingering in the back of my throat. With luck I'll be back in one piece so I can pen another update. Writing this diary has helped me to handle this situation. I wonder how many of the others are doing something similar. Anyhow, enough of that shit. I'm just delaying the inevitable. It's patrol time.

Second entry today. Needed to write. Clearing atmosphere worst yet. I threw up twice. One of the scientists bludgeoned his colleague to death with a fancy bit of equipment they were using to take measurements. We tried to stop him but the voices were just too loud. I know I shouldn't, but I've started to listen to them. What the hell is happening?

June 18th

All patrols to the clearing are on hold due to what happened with the scientists. I'm glad as it gives me more time to listen to the voices in the trees. Some of the things they are saying make sense. I overheard Kimmel on the radio (phones don't seem to work here) to one of his higher-ups asking to abort the project. He said the best thing to do would be to shut down and quarantine the entire town. Can't argue really.

The fact he's so concerned has got me thinking about what to do with this journal. One thing is for sure, I can't let anyone see it. This stuff is top secret no doubt, and the last thing I want is to be explaining myself in a military prison. I hope I can sleep tonight without the nightmares plaguing me.

June 19th

Shadows on the walls of my tent shaped like tiny hands. I can't handle this anymore. Listening to the voices helps. They make a lot of sense when you give them a chance.

June 20th

Gogoku Gogoku Gogoku Gogoku Gogoku Gogoku Gogoku Gogoku Gogoku Gogoku Gogoku Gogoku Gogoku Gogoku Gogoku Gogoku. I fucking hate that word. It's all I hear. All I think about. I sometimes want to scream. Worse are the times when I want to laugh, because I know it will sound as broken and splintered as my mind feels.

June 21st

Kimmel thinks he's so clever. Thinks we don't know what he's up to. He deserves to suffer for bringing this upon us. The voices told me. It's all his fault. Him and his scientists, digging in the ground to get to whatever is underneath. He thinks his secrets are safe, but they hear it all and they tell me.

It's almost dark now, but I don't fear those sounds, those disembodied wails and phantom hands. Not anymore. Now I see why they are so mad. It's Kimmel. All because of Kimmel and his stupid idea for bringing us up here. Tomorrow will be the day it all changes. Tomorrow is the day I put things right.

June 22nd

My turn to guard the perimeter tonight, but I have something else in mind. The clearing is off limits, yet the voices tell me I need to go up there to learn the secret of why they are here.

Screw Kimmel and his rules. I'll do things my way from here on in. There is one small issue, and that is this journal. I don't want anyone to find it, and at the same time I refuse to destroy it as it might prove useful for others if something should ever happen to me. I could hide it in the forest, god knows it's dense enough, but I wonder if it would last the test of time or rot into dust. I don't think I'd like that. It doesn't seem right. Either way, I'm late for the briefing. I wouldn't have bothered going but I need to make sure everything appears as normal as possible. I'll give some thought to the dilemma about this journal and update later as to my decision.

Just about to head out, but have decided what to do with this journal. The night is close, and already those voices hide in the wind. Strange that just a few days ago they filled me with such fear, but now they sing me the sweetest of songs.

I will admit to being a little nervous about heading up to the clearing tonight. If I'm caught I'll be court-martialed for sure, and yet I can't quite seem to resist the lure of what the voices tell me I might find up there. I have decided, in light of my pending possible arrest, to seal this journal in plastic and bury it. If all goes well tonight, I will of course return and this will be just another entry to add to the others.

If, on the other hand, this happens to be the final entry, and whoever is reading this found the journal buried in shallow earth and wrapped in plastic, you should assume that I either got caught disobeying orders, or something worse happened to me up there in the clearing. Either way, I will do my best to get back and update later as to what the voices said. Until then, it's time to put this journal in the dirt until I return.

Petrov looked through the remaining pages, hoping to see a continuation of the journal, but was greeted with blank pages.

"That's all there is" Kimmel said. He had put away the lighter and reverted to hiding his eyes behind his sunglasses, leaving him as unreadable as when Petrov first arrived.

"Where did you find this?" Petrov asked, his throat dry and itchy. He badly wanted some water, something to help rinse away the irritation.

"At the temporary camp up there at the hotel. That's as good an illustration as any of what that place does."

"What happened to him, the man who wrote this?"

Kimmel shrugged. "We don't know. He just… disappeared. Left all of his belongings in his tent. We found the diary by chance when we were packing his stuff away. It was barely buried under the topsoil."

"What do you mean he disappeared? Where the hell did he go?"

"People disappear all the time, you of all people know that," Kimmel said, his face impossible to read.

"So why show me this? What were you hoping to achieve?"

"I hoped it might make you cautious, even though I know it won't deter you from chasing him up there."

"I think we'll be fine. We have good men on this."

"I'm sure you do. Just do me a favor."

"What's that, General?"

"Don't have your men waiting up there for him. That place… it's not good for people."

"Even the town? I was under the impression it was just the clearing and hotel that were bad news."

"That whole place is bad," Kimmel replied, almost sighing the words. "Whatever's up there is spreading. We closed it off for a reason."

"You're suggesting we just let him go?"

"Not at all. I'm suggesting that you let him enter the town then go in after him."

"Impossible. There are too many places he

can escape to. We couldn't possibly cover all that woodland."

Kimmel removed his glasses again, and this time Petrov was sure he was looking at the Kimmel of old, the intensity in his face once more changing the detective's impression of him. "If you send men up there to wait for him, they'll die."

"Why are you trying to frighten me off?"

"I'm trying to help you. Fisher was the same. Didn't believe it until it was right in front of him. Please, just listen to what I have to say."

Petrov held the diary toward Kimmel. "Here, I have to go."

"Keep it. Read it again."

"I don't think—"

"I'm confident you're a smart enough man to do the right thing, Detective Petrov. Keep the diary. The damn thing brings nothing but bad memories for me anyway. Read it again and ask yourself if you really want to risk the lives of your men by sending them up there."

"What if you're wrong?"

"What if I'm right?" Kimmel countered. "Are you really prepared to live with the consequences if I am?" He stood, fastened his jacket and picked up his briefcase. "Good luck, detective. I really hope you make the right decision."

Petrov watched the General leave, walking briskly down the path as the jogging couple came in the opposite direction. He sat there for a while, half watching the tireless Alsatian chase its ball until both owner and dog were tired of the game and made their leave. He stared at the diary, hating that Kimmel had got under his skin enough to almost convince him that there could be something to his story. "Screw this," he muttered, then stood and walked back to his car, hoping the drive back to the station would at least allow him to clear his head and decide what he should do about the whole Henry Marshall situation.

CHAPTER 20

The search for the fugitive Henry Marshall was in full swing. Scores of police were scouring local woodland with dogs in search of the escapee. In addition, local and national news had been alerted, warning the public to remain vigilant and to report any sightings. As Petrov had promised Melody, roadblocks had been set up in an effort to capture Marshall before he could get too far. Embarrassed that the escape had been perpetrated so easily, the authorities had thrown a lot of resources at it in an attempt at damage-limitation.

Thirty six year old Karl Sloane had been manning one such roadblock for the last five hours. It had been drizzling steadily, and even with his rain poncho, the officer was soaked to the bone. Traffic had been light, for which he was grateful, however, he knew that when rush hour came, it would be absolute chaos.

They knew Marshall had stolen a vehicle, but hadn't reported it to the press. The last thing they wanted was for him to know they were aware. The hope was that he would be stupid enough to try and pass the roadblock. Karl put a hand on the butt of his gun. They were authorized if need be to use lethal force to stop Marshall if they encountered him, which was a proposition Karl wasn't looking forward to.

His hope was that the threat would be

enough. Two cars approached the roadblock. He waved the first one through to his position, his colleagues keeping an eye on the van behind with the tinted windows.

The first vehicle was a grubby red Ford. Karl waved it closer and held up a hand. The vehicle stopped as instructed and Karl motioned for the driver to wind down the window. She was a lone female in her thirties. Business suit, hair pulled back and tied at the rear. She glanced at Karl, then his weapon.

"Traveling alone, miss?" Karl said, following the script. Going through the motions.

"Just heading home from work. What's this all about?"

"Have you seen the news, ma'am?" Karl said, keeping a close eye on the van behind.

Something about it didn't sit right with him, and it made him nervous.

"I heard about that man escaping. Is this related to that?"

"Just precautionary. Have you seen anyone or anything suspicious during your travels today?"

"No, not a thing," she said.

"You haven't been flagged down or noticed anything out of the ordinary?"

"No, nothing. I came straight from work."

Karl glanced at the van, hating that the windows were blacked out. It would be an ideal vehicle if someone wanted to make an escape.

"Alright," he said, standing up straight. "Go straight home and keep your doors locked. If you see or hear anything unusual, report it straightaway to the police. There's also a dedicated number being aired on both radio and television."

"I will. Thank you, officer."

He waved her through, turning his full attention to the van. He put his hand on his gun, and locked eyes with his colleagues, the silent message received. *Be careful.*

II

Henry lay in the pitch black, knife to his prisoner's throat, the thrum of the engine vibrating as the car rolled forward. He recalled his former life, before the blood, before the death. Back when he was just a councilor, a man like any other, filled with pointless ambitions. He recalled a statistic from the time he tried to enforce a new traffic calming bill. It stated that approximately forty-seven percent of people would stop to offer assistance to a vehicle stranded by the roadside. Henry had needed just one. He had staged the scene perfectly. The doctor's body had come in useful, and once Henry had sat it in the car by the side of the road, hood open, he waited in the trees, watching, waiting for someone to take the bait.

He recalled fishing trips with his father when he was a boy, hot sticky summer days spent by the water's edge, waiting for a bite, waiting for something to break the monotony. This was much the same. The sporadic traffic had, for the most part, passed without stopping. He was patient, careful not to be seen. Eventually, the bait was taken and someone was fool enough to stop. As always, he let them guide him, acting completely in accordance with their commands. In the end, it was easy. He waited now, his hostage weeping and terrified, Henry anticipating passing the roadblocks so he could do as his new masters commanded. He pressed the knife harder into the flesh of his prisoner's neck as he waited to be set free.

III

Sloane waved the van toward him, his two colleagues approaching the passenger side, surrounding the vehicle. A fourth officer waited by a patrol car beyond the roadblock on the off-chance that someone tried to crash through it, his dog leashed and tense. Karl approached the driver's side window, motioning the driver to wind it down. The driver was somewhere in his early twenties and had a narrow face and large nose, which Karl thought gave him the appearance of a rat.

His eyes shifted and darted at the police who surrounding the van, causing Karl to raise his alert level even further. He had seen nervous behavior before, and this was a classic example. Across from the driver, in the passenger seat, sat another man. They shared the same strangely proportioned facial features and shifty demeanor.

"Where are you boys heading?" Karl asked, the smell of marijuana drifting out of the van.

"Just on our way home," the driver said, eyes still darting. "What's this all about?"

"Just the two of you?"

"Yes, just us."

"What's your name?"

"John Smith."

Karl nodded. John Smith was a false name if ever he'd heard one, and certainly wasn't given in any sort of convincing manner. For now, he let it slide. "Have you picked anyone up on the road today?"

"No, like I said, it's just us."

"What's in the back of the van?" Karl asked, adjusting the grip on his gun.

"Nothing."

"Step out of the vehicle please."

Karl could see in the driver's eyes that the man wanted to run, and probably would have if he'd had the guts. He was afraid of something; that much was obvious. Reluctantly, he complied, climbing out of the vehicle. He was much shorter than Karl had expected, only standing shoulder high to the officer. Without being asked, he turned and put his hands on the hood.

"Alright, I see you know the drill," Karl said as he patted him down. The driver half turned toward Karl, speaking quietly, the words changing the game as far as Karl Sloane was concerned.

"He's in the back," the driver whispered.

Karl saw then that it wasn't agitation, but fear causing the driver to act so strangely. Acting on instinct, Karl cuffed the driver and sat him on the ground. He motioned to his fellow officers across the front of the vehicle, beckoning them over, sharing the information.

Now caution was out of the window. With both driver and passenger cuffed and on the ground being watched by the dog-handler, the other three officers drew their weapons and converged on the rear doors of the van. Karl swapped his gun hand, wiping sweat from his palms on his trouser leg before reverting to a more familiar weapon stance. The officers took up firing positions as their colleague placed a hand on the door.

The three men looked at each other, knowing the gravity of the situation, knowing the danger they faced.

The one holding the door mouthed the countdown from three to one then yanked it open, Karl and his fellow officer pointing their weapons at the man crouched in the back, bellowing instructions. However, it wasn't the snarling blood-covered Henry Marshall they saw, but a skinny runt of a teen who shared the same genetic pool as his siblings. He lay on the floor of the van, hands behind head, terrified at the aggression in the officer's voices, wondering why an outstanding arrest warrant for the robbery he had committed a month earlier would require roadblocks. He, like his brothers, had no idea that the officers were looking for a much bigger and more dangerous fish, one which was sadly almost a mile up the road and away from their net.

IV

Three miles away, Leanne Patterson pulled her dented and dirty red Ford off the road and put her head on the steering wheel. The temptation to tell the police at the roadblock what had happened to them had been great, but the knowledge of what would happen if she did was greater.

The instant she'd been waved through, the tears had come, and now her face was streaked with make-up. Trembling, she did all she could to compose herself, as the ordeal wasn't over yet by a long shot. The road was quiet, a tree-lined stretch of highway with little to no traffic. She got out of the car, eying the trees, wanting to run but knowing it was impossible. She was a restraintless prisoner. She approached the rear of the car and opened the trunk, stepping back as terror once again overwhelmed her. Henry Marshall held the knife to the eight year old boy's throat. He glared at the woman as he struggled to his knees, one bloody hand still gripping the boy's shoulder. Like his mother, he too was red-eyed from crying. The two locked eyes, and Leanne heard herself telling the boy it would be all right, that, just like the man had promised, they would be set free just as soon as they had helped him.

She had only stopped because she saw the car

by the side of the road, hood open, hazard lights flashing, driver slumped across the wheel. Her intention was to check on him, to see if she could help. The area where the car had been was isolated, overgrown with a low hanging scrub of trees by the hard shoulder, and she didn't like to think of whoever it was stranded out here having no access to a phone.

In hindsight, she should have driven away, and yet, she couldn't do it. She'd got out of the car, curious but in no way afraid, at least not until she'd approached the driver's side door and saw the blood. Saw the mess of his mangled flesh. She never saw Henry come out of the woods; he'd waited until her back was turned before dragging her into the trees, away from anyone who might help her.

She didn't care for herself. All she could think about was her son who was sleeping in the back of her car.

He had pinned her to a tree, hand around her throat, eyes blazing. She had told him she would give him money, even give him the car if that was what he wanted, just as long as he left her alone. The man stared at her, and she saw nothing in his eyes. No pity, no compassion. No emotion. She could just as easily be looking into the eyes of a shark.

He held a penknife to her throat and told her what he wanted. He needed her to get him safely through the roadblocks and away from the police checks.

She responded by telling him again that he

could take the car as long as he let her and her son go. Something changed in his eyes at the mention of her son, a light of recognition that told her she had made a huge mistake.

His next instruction had been simple. Get him past the police blockades and he would let them both go. If she told anyone or was stopped and the car searched, her son would be killed. She'd watched as he climbed into the trunk, taking her terrified son with him and telling her to remember his instructions. Now she'd complied, she could only hope that he would do as he promised.

Henry struggled out of the car, filthy, bloody and wild, a chorus of demonic voices in his head, guiding him.

"In there," he grunted, motioning toward the scrub of trees at the roadside.

Leanne shook her head. She didn't want to go in there with him. She didn't want to be far away from any potential help which may come along, which she suspected was the exact reason he wanted the privacy. She'd heard on the radio who he was and what he had done. With no choice but to comply, she closed the trunk of the vehicle and walked toward the tree line, Henry and her son following.

"Please, I did everything you asked, just let us go," she begged as they left the road.

Henry said nothing. He pushed the knife closer to her son's throat and gave her a thin smile that said more than words ever could.

Leanne did as he instructed, and he followed her into the woods. The voices chattered in his head, instructing him, guiding him away from the shreds of doubt in the little humanity that remained within him. Any semblance of the man he used to be before he became a slave to them was almost completely gone. There was no compassion left. No morals. Just an overwhelming desire to serve his new masters. The three walked deeper into the woods, two in hope of freedom, one lost to the voices of the dead.

Two hours later, as day turned to dusk, Henry Marshall returned alone. New blood covered old on his clothes, and fresh dirt coated his hands. He had tasted them, the woman's flesh bitter with fear, the boy's sweet with innocence. He felt better, stronger, and knew it would be something he would experience again. He scrambled down the small bank, checked the road was clear and climbed into the Ford. He adjusted the seat for his frame and shifted the mirrors so he could see, his dead eyes showing no remorse for the atrocities he'd just committed. The car started smoothly, the engine idling. Henry could hear them within its sweet notes, the voices of his guides, telling him where he must go, telling him what he had to do. He selected a gear. Parking brake off. Accelerator depressed, clutch lifted. The car pulled away. Henry Marshall had been given a mission, one which he would complete at all costs.

CHAPTER 21

Isaac sat at the table, arms folded, head down. He was refusing to play ball, making a point to his foster parents by using the childish logic that if he didn't eat, then he would get his own way. The disagreement had started, as most of these things do, over nothing. Isaac had been instructed to take out the garbage before sitting down to eat, one of the jobs he'd been given when he first moved to the house.

Today, however, he wasn't in the mood to comply. He had suffered a particularly harrowing dream the night before, one which, as always, was compellingly real enough to make him wet the bed. It was something that he was embarrassed by, and although Grant and Tanya never chastised him for it, he had gone on the defensive anyway, stubbornly doing all he could to defy them. Tanya had reacted with patience and understanding, trying to put a positive spin on things. Grant saw it as a slap in the face of his authority.

"Come on, honey, eat up. You said you like spaghetti," Tanya said, fixed grin in place as she glanced at her husband sitting opposite. Stubborn to the last, Grant wasn't about to let it drop. He set his fork down and sipped his drink.

"Look, Isaac, if you want to stay here, you have to contribute to the family. I don't think a few household chores are unreasonable, do you?"

"Grant, Honey, let it go," Tanya said, keeping a close eye on Isaac who was doing all he could to convey his anger. Arms folded, head down.

"No, I think we need to address this," Grant fired back. "There are certain rules that need to be adhered to. That's how society works. With this and the bed wetting, I don't know," he sighed and picked up his fork, twisting spaghetti onto it. "I just think we need to address it as a family."

Isaac muttered something under his breath.

"What was that?" Grant asked.

"Leave it, honey, let's just have a nice meal together, okay?" Tanya said, hoping her smile would win her husband over.

"No, I'm sorry, but I want to hear whatever was said. My father always taught me the value of discipline and respect."

Isaac slammed his hands on the table. "You're not my father!" he screamed. "And this isn't my house. Just leave me alone," he ran upstairs, leaving Grant and Tanya shocked at the table. They waited until his bedroom door slammed closed, then sat silent for a moment. Grant tossed his fork back on his plate and rubbed his temples.

"Jesus, I didn't mean to go off on him like that. It's been a rough day. I guess I just brought it home with me."

"Don't worry, I'm sure it will be alright," Tanya replied, the smile now replaced by a furrowed brow as she set her own fork down. Like her husband, she no longer had an appetite.

"Should I go talk to him?" Grant said with a sigh.

"Maybe let him calm down first."

"Good idea"

"Come on, you can help me with the dishes," Tanya said, trying to lighten the mood.

She stood and kissed him on the head.

"Hell, why not, I don't feel like eating now anyway," he replied, stacking his plate on top of hers and following her to the kitchen. "What should I do with Isaac's?"

"Leave it for now. He might want to eat it later."

"Got it."

He went to scrape the plates into the bin and remembered it was full to bursting. He locked eyes with his wife and the two shared a smile.

"Don't say a word, okay?" he said, setting the two plates on the side. "I'll just take it out myself and have a word with Isaac about it later."

She smiled, a real one this time. She turned toward the sink and started to fill it with water, arranging the pans and dirty cutlery on the side. Grant pulled the sack out of the bin and set it between his feet, scraping the food into it. He handed the plates to Tanya and tied the sack.

"How about a little drink tonight?" he said, picking up the garbage and walking to the back door.

"Maybe, as long as you give me a foot rub."

"Deal."

He opened the door and stepped outside, almost walking into the filthy, bloody man who was waiting there. A flicker of recognition flashed in Grant's eyes seconds before Henry Marshall slashed his throat. Dropping the sack on the ground, he staggered back into the house, blood spewing from his neck, spraying the door, spattering onto the hardwood floor. Henry stepped forward for every backwards step Grant took, crossing the threshold of the property. He shoved Grant with one hand, sending him sprawling to the floor where he gargled and bled. With the other, he slammed the door closed behind him. Tanya started to scream.

Henry closed the distance to her without breaking stride, his every movement delivered with purpose. Tanya's natural reaction was to scramble away, but there was nowhere to go. She bumped against the work surface, pans and glasses clattering to the floor. Without any hesitation, Henry grabbed her by the hair and plunged her face-first into the sink. She thrashed her arms and kicked her legs as the scolding water burned her skin, dimly realizing what was happening.

As hot as it was, the water didn't bother Henry. He stared at his black ghostly reflection in the window above the sink; eyes dead, calm despite the pain he felt distantly up to his forearm. He pushed her face deeper, mashing her nose into the stainless steel bottom. Water spewed out onto the floor as Tanya scratched and clawed for anything she could lay her hands on, but her oxygen-starved brain was already starting to fade, and her desperate clawing only resulted in more dirty dishes being sent tumbling to the floor. Henry waited and listened to his masters as they soothed him through the process, telling him she was close to the end.

She stopped flailing.

One twitch.

A reflexive jerk of the foot.

Silence.

Still he held her there, waiting until they told him it was fine to stop. His own pain from the scolding water was irrelevant. He lived to serve them now. The boiler groaned, and in the sound he heard the approval he sought. He let go of her hair and removed his pink, blistering arm. They allowed him to feel the pain now, the voices in his head telling him he should savor it, should let it consume him. He gritted his teeth, looking at the swollen skin, the dull throb of his ravaged flesh lighting his pain receptors and sending the agony around his body.

Released from Henry's grip, Tanya's body slid to the floor, eyes open, mouth agape. Like his arm, her face was red and blistered. He stared at her body as water continued to spill out over the rim of the sink. Without thinking, Henry reached over and shut off the tap, plunging the house into silence. Now all that remained was what he had come here for. There was a knife on the floor, knocked from the work surface by Tanya's flailing arms, and he picked it up, wincing at the pain of flexing his scalded hand around it. He switched, moving the knife to his undamaged left hand. Satisfied, he set off through the dining room to begin his search for Isaac Samson.

II

Isaac lay under his bed, feet pressed against the wall, eyes wide. His field of vision was narrow, but enough. He could see the bottom of his dresser, the bottom portion of his bedroom door which he had closed. He'd seen the man coming toward the house from his bedroom window and knew it was the man from his nightmares. Grant and Tanya had always told him it was just a dream, and that it couldn't hurt him. Now he saw the man was real, and knew he had come for him. He heard the footsteps, slow and deliberate, as they ascended the steps. With no means of escape, Isaac pushed himself further into the corner and prayed he wouldn't be found.

III

The night had cast the house into a shadow-heavy tomb. Amid the silence, Henry Marshall moved with deliberate leisure, knowing the boy was upstairs without any route by which he could escape. As a child himself, Henry had always feared the dark, but now he saw it as his ally. Those who dwelled deep in his consciousness waited for him to complete the task they had set him. He knew how vital it was, how important the boy was to them, and by proxy, to him. The message had been clear. The child had to die.

Henry reached the top of the stairs, pausing to assess the layout. Four doors; one open, three closed. He could imagine the boy cowering, hiding somewhere, probably in a closet or under a bed. It would be easy. He would butcher the child in such a way that he would be unidentifiable. Only then would his task be done and he could join his masters in death.

He opened the first door immediately to his left. A bathroom: Small, pristine, white tiled. Nowhere a boy could hide. Henry walked further down the hall, making no effort to keep quiet, knowing that every creaking floorboard, every sound of opening doors would increase the boy's terror, and as he had come to discover, scared flesh was the sweetest tasting.

He opened the second door, this one an office or study of some kind. A desk filled with clutter around the computer, bookshelves filled with books on science and history, geography and politics. Henry stepped inside, looking for anywhere a young boy could be hiding. He looked behind the door, under the desk, between the two filing cabinets. The room was empty.

Striding back out, he paused again. The other two doors were a little further down the hall. The idea of building up the fear in the child was too much. Henry started to whistle, a happy jingle. He started to walk, deliberately, slowly. He dragged the tip of the knife blade across the wall, hoping the sound would filter through to wherever the boy was hiding. He came to the final two doors, each on opposite sides of the corridor.

One was plain white, the other adorned with a poster of a sports car. It was plain to see which one was Isaacs's room. Henry turned toward it, slowly depressed the handle and opened the door. Like the rest of the house, night had almost taken it. Shadows were long and black. Outside, just a sliver of golden orange daylight remained. Henry stepped into the room, taking it in. It was a child's room; that much was obvious, however there was no personality to it. The room was little more than a blank canvas to which Isaac had just started to add his own touch.

"I know you're in here," Henry said, watching for any sign of movement. "Just come out. I won't hurt you."

Henry looked around the room. There were only two places the boy could be: the closet, or under the bed. Henry reached out and flicked on the light, dismissing both shadows and hiding places alike. He turned toward the closet then stopped, looking toward the bed. He moved toward it and sat down, elbows resting on knees.

"I know you're under there," he said. "They can sense you. You can never hide from them."

He waited for a reply, enjoying the game, trying to imagine the fear the boy must be feeling.

"You know you have to die, don't you? You were meant to die before. If you come out, I'll make it quick. I'll make sure it doesn't hurt."

Again he waited, listening, giving the words a chance to sink in.

"If you make me come under there to get you, then you'll suffer. You'll beg for death by the end."

Henry grinned as the voices in his head told him what to say, whispering ideas to him.

"If you're hoping the light that saved you before will do the same, then you'll be disappointed. That power is long gone. He can't save you now. I won't ask you again. Come out now."

Henry waited, listening to the house, listening to the voices in his head.

"Alright," he said to the room. "We can do it your way."

He stood, grabbed the bottom edge of the bed and lifted it up. Lying there on the floor, looking up at the man he never imagined could be real, Isaac cowered. He had never been more afraid. He could taste it in the back of his throat, could feel it in the way his heartbeat raced. Some inner instinct told him he had to act, and he did so without thinking.

He scrambled to his feet, surprising Henry as he ran past him. Henry let go of the bed, swinging the knife at Isaac. The blade sliced the air inches from his face. Isaac was in the hall, but there was no respite. Henry Marshall was just a few steps behind him, face contorted in rage. Isaac ran, feet thudding on the wooden floor, driven on by something beyond terror.

He charged down the steps, two at a time, too afraid to look but able to hear his pursuer close behind him. He snatched at the front door, twisting the handle, fumbling with the lock. He could sense Henry behind him, and darted to his left, again trusting his instinct.

Henry slammed into the door, screaming as his burned arm was sandwiched between the wood and his own body. Isaac charged through the living room, conscious of how vital time was, how every second was crucial, and also knowing that his only chance to escape was through the back of the house.

Barely missing a beat, Henry was back on him, a vision of rage as he ran through the room. Isaac pushed through the door to the kitchen, intending to go to the back door. Instead he stopped, gasping as he saw the bodies of Grant and Tanya.

Blood.

Blood everywhere.

Grant had bled out spectacularly, and yet somehow still wasn't quite finished. He lay twitching, eyes wide, hands clutched to his own throat to stem the flow. Tanya lay where she had fallen, still staring at the ceiling, blistered and burnt, and obviously dead. Again, Isaacs's instinct saved him, and he ducked to one side. The knife sliced the air where Isaac had stood seconds earlier. He ran for the other side of the room, determined not to look at Grant as he passed him.

The door loomed in front of him, his way out, his exit. A glimmer of hope that he might escape. He reached out for the handle then slipped on the bloody floor, going down on his side and slamming into the kitchen cupboard. He scrambled around, pushing himself into the corner.

Henry Marshall stood triumphant, breathing heavily, knife hanging limp at his side. Both of them knew there was nowhere else to run, no way of escape. Marshall stepped toward him, adjusting his grip on the knife.

He stepped over Grant, his grin wide and yellow. Isaac pushed against the wall, kicking his feet against the bloody tiles. Henry reared back, face twisted into a grimace. But, before he could swing, Grant grabbed at his legs, using the last of his strength to pull Henry off balance. Henry stumbled, and although Isaac couldn't decipher the words, Grant's weak gargles were clear enough.

He scrambled to his feet and opened the back door, leaping off the porch and running into the night. Enraged, Henry plunged the knife up to the hilt into Grant's skull, the blade passing all the way through and embedding in the floor. Henry pulled it free, the scraping, wet sound incredibly loud in the otherwise total silence. Without giving the body a second glance, he hurried out into the night after Isaac.

IV

He ran, arms and legs pumping, skirting around the house with no idea where he was going. His fear had become a living thing, growing inside him, spreading into his bones.

Even at such a young age, he was aware of what had happened, and knew that the man from his nightmares, who had impossibly appeared in the real world, wanted him dead.

He thought about Grant and Tanya, and a fresh surge of grief hit him. In the back of his mind, he knew he was once again alone in the world. More than that, he wondered what he had done wrong to constantly have the families he was sent to live with taken away from him. He ran into the street, feet thumping on concrete, shadow thrown into four ghosts running along with him by the streetlights.

He couldn't go to a neighbor, as he knew what the man would do to them – he would do the same as he had to Grant and Tanya. Instead, he had to get away, find somewhere to hide. He reasoned that the man who was after him was old, and couldn't keep up on foot. At the same time, anyone who could come out of his dream world and into the real one might not operate by the same rules as everyone else.

He put his head down and pumped his arms and legs, pushing himself to the limit. Ahead, the street gave out onto a main road that dropped downhill toward the shops and cafés, supermarkets and bars. Places where there would be people, places where he would be safe if he could get there. He exploded out of the street, almost losing his balance as he veered right, heading downhill.

The lights of homes he passed looked so

inviting, but he kept going traffic honking at him as he ran into the road, then back onto the path. Isaac was getting tired now, and his breathing was coming in short, sharp gasps. He looked over his shoulder, pleased to see there was no sign of the man, and risked slowing to a jog, keeping a close eye on the exit to his street. As he regained his breath, a car skidded to halt beside him. He stared at it, frozen in place, unsure what he should do. The door was thrown open by the driver, who leaned over the seat.

"Come on kid, get in," the female driver said, staring at him.

He hesitated. She looked familiar, although why, he didn't know. He looked in the back of the car. There was a man there, dark skinned. He glanced out of the back window then back at Isaac, clearly agitated.

"Come on, we don't have much time," she snapped.

A squeal of tires distracted them as the battered old Ford driven by Henry Marshall rocketed out of Isaac's street, almost clipping a motorcyclist going in the opposite direction. It was all the encouragement Isaac needed. Whoever these people were, they were better than the man who was trying to kill him. He clambered into the passenger seat and shut the door as Emma floored the accelerator, the car snaking away, leaving thick black lines of rubber on the road.

"Put your seatbelt on," she said as Isaac leaned over the seat to look out of the back window. The twin headlights were getting closer, following them as they navigated the streets.

Now that the initial panic was over, Isaac started to cry, blinking away tears. "That man…" was all he could manage between sobs.

"It's alright, we'll get you somewhere safe," Emma said, glancing in the mirrors.

"He's still back there," Truman said from the back seat. The chase went on, Emma cutting down side streets, trying everything to get away, but no matter what they did, Henry stayed with them, never more than a dozen yards behind. Now, with suburbia at their back, she pulled onto the freeway, changing gear and letting the car stretch its legs. Isaac watched the speed increase as the needle climbed to fifty, then sixty.

"It's workin', we're losin' him," Truman said, grinning as the headlights began to shrink into the distance behind them.

"Who are you, what's going on?" Isaac said, not crying anymore but clearly shaken. "That man killed Grant and Tanya…"

"It's okay, just relax, you need to calm down," Emma said.

"It's not okay. They died and it's all my fault. If I hadn't come to live with them…"

"Stop that. This isn't your fault."

"Oh shit," Truman said. Isaac turned to look; Emma saw it clearly enough in her mirrors. The headlights of Henry Marshall's car were coming closer, growing larger as he closed in.

"Floor it, do somethin!" Truman said.

"I'm going as fast as I can."

The red Ford pulled out into the opposite

lane, causing oncoming traffic to weave off the road to avoid a collision. Henry accelerated alongside their car, glaring across at them. Isaac screamed as the Ford broadsided their car, slamming into it hard and sending it off the road. Emma tried to correct, to catch the slide, but the speed was too great, her skill level too low.

The car skewed right, then left as she tried to correct the spin. One wheel went off the edge of the tarmac and into the dirt, making any hope of regaining control impossible. The car left the road and slid down the grass embankment before the tires found purchase in the soft earth, flipping the car over into a high speed roll.

Glass shattered, metal crunched and deformed as the car shed body parts. Its passengers were tossed violently, screams lost in the shriek of broken metal. To those inside, it seemed to go on forever before the car came to rest some twenty feet down the embankment on its roof, smoke rising from a broken radiator, ferns and branches pushing into the spaces where the rear window once was.

Silence.

Isaac came to, blood in his eyes and mouth, head ringing and neck sore from the impact. He was hanging upside down, still held in place by his seat belt. He breathed in, separating scents. Copper. Oil. Pine. Next to him, Emma was also conscious, and like Isaac, was allowing her shaken brain to reset itself. Her face was bloody, but she looked otherwise okay. In the back, Truman had come free of his seatbelt and was lying face down on the car roof, hair covered in tiny fragments of glass, blood pouring from a nasty gash on his arm.

Swimming in and out of consciousness, Isaac heard the distinct crunch of feet on grass as someone approached the upturned car. He hoped it was help, someone coming to aid them after seeing the accident, but he knew without doubt that it was the man from his nightmare.

He wanted to scream, but could only let out a pained moan as consciousness threatened to leave him again. A sound punctuated the night. Sirens growing closer, a symphony of them. Isaac closed his eyes, trying to clear the headache which raged without reprieve. His awareness of what happened next was vague, filled with gaps as he drifted away then back to consciousness again.

The car started to rock as hands yanked at the door handle, trying to pull it open. Isaac cowered away from the feet he could see from his inverted position. He recognized them of course; they were the same ones he'd seen from under the bed. Their owner dropped to his knees, and Isaac screamed. He was face to face with the man from his nightmares, the thin, cracked glass of the rear window the only thing separating boy from pursuer. Henry grabbed the door again, teeth gritted in fury as he tried to yank it open. Isaac stared at the buckled door, aware that the bent steel was all that was preventing the man from gaining access. Emma mumbled, and was now also watching as Henry tried to gain access to the car. He head-butted the glass, eyes wild and filled with a fury neither she nor Isaac could comprehend. He slammed his fist against the car, paying no heed to Emma. He stared only at Isaac, the boy cowering in response.

More people were coming now, other drivers who had seen the accident and were racing down the banking to help. Henry stared at Isaac, face contorted into a mask of rage, and then he was gone, fleeing from the scene like a phantom into the night.

The other people who had abandoned their vehicles to help now surrounded the car, trying to figure out the best way to get them out. Someone brought a tire iron and smashed the front window, and two of their potential rescuers crawled in to assist them. Isaac and Emma barely heard their questions, both were too busy looking out into the night for Henry Marshall.

Hands on Isaac now, dragging him out into the light, his scrambled brain unable to comprehend what was happening as he fought to stay conscious. A silhouette above him, a face, the features unclear. He was moving now, those hands, which had pulled him from the car under his armpits, pulling him away from the wreck. He could see the vehicle now. Upside down, smoldering. Broken.

He stared at the sky, the pale moon like a beacon of light to protect him from the black thing that seemed hell-bent on hurting him. He concentrated on trying to bring it into focus, trying to force himself to stay awake and fight, but it was all too late, too much to ask. The light of the moon, which represented his freedom, was slammed closed as his body gave in and he lost consciousness. As darkness filled his world, he imagined the monster that was chasing him parting his blood red lips and giving a smug, humorless grin.

CHAPTER 22

The road had been sealed off. Police had arrived *en masse*, and were questioning witnesses as to what had happened. Truman, Emma and Isaac waited in the back of an ambulance, their wounds dressed, Isaac still drifting in and out of consciousness. The paramedics had already assessed him and had assured them he would be fine, but would need to go to hospital for observation.

"We can't let these assholes get us to the hospital. They'll find out we fed them a load of bull," Truman said, dabbing the small head wound with the pad he'd been given.

"I know. I'm just waiting for an opportunity to slip away. Besides, I want to be sure Marshall isn't anywhere nearby," Emma replied, looking out of the back of the ambulance into the growing crowd.

"He'll be long gone by now. Anyone with any sense would be, especially with all these cops around," Truman said, sounding more as if he were trying to convince himself.

"He didn't look like a man with sense when he was trying to break the car window."

Truman leaned the back of his head against the interior of the ambulance. "What the hell do we do about him?" he said, nodding toward Isaac.

"We need to take him with us."

"Hey, I'm all for tryin' to get to the bottom of this, but I don't think that's a smart move."

"We can't just leave him."

"Why not?" Truman said. "Maybe it's better. Get us some real protection from this guy. He's a god-damn psycho."

"No," she said, shaking her head. "I know this is hard, but trust me, I've experienced this before. We need to take him with us. I need you to trust me, Truman."

"Look, don't be sayin' I don't trust you. I've helped you so far haven't I? It's just that things have changed. Shit's got real now. Just look the fuck outside." He glanced out of the door at the police cars parked along the side of the road, beacons flashing in silent warning. "This is serious shit, lady."

"More than you know," Emma fired back. "Now, are you going to help me or do I have to do it all myself?"

"What the hell are we supposed to do?"

"See over there?" she said, nodding toward the side of the road at a silver estate car.

"Yeah?"

"Driver left the keys in the ignition. He's over there being interviewed by the police."

"So?" Truman said, getting a nasty feeling he knew where this was going.

"So, it's only, what, ten, fifteen feet from here to there?"

"No way," Truman said, shaking his head. "Are you out of your fuckin' mind? With all these cops around you want to steal a fuckin' car?"

"Borrow. Just to get us clear of here."

"No way! That's crazy. You know how this will look for us?"

"If you want to stay here you can," Emma said, climbing out of the ambulance. "Good luck explaining who you are. And that Isaac isn't my brother like I told the police."

"Whoa, whoa, wait just a second. You're going anyway?"

"Well I'm not staying here. You said so yourself, we're in serious trouble once they find out we lied about who we are. Once they know we're not the kid's family, it's over for us."

"Goddamn it, it looks like I have no choice."

"Good. Now grab Isaac and let's get out of here."

"What if someone sees us?"

"Nobody is even looking at us. Come on; let's go now before it's too late."

II

He watched them from his place in the trees as they made their escape, the cold in his bones no worse than the black pit of emptiness inside him. The air was crisp and fresh, and he longed for the time when it would be filled with the stink of blood and death.

He asked the voices in his head how he could stop them from leaving, and they responded by telling him that the boy could wait. He grabbed the mobile phone from his pocket. He'd found it in the doctor's car and had taken it along without thinking. Now, he dialed a number, not sure if it was his own doing or if it was the will of those who controlled him. He waited to see if the line would connect, counting the number of rings, prepared to dial for as long as it would take.

"Hello?" the cautious voice said on the other end.

"It's me," he said, speaking to his brother for the first time in over three years.

"Henry? Where are you? Do you know what you've done?"

"If you want to stop it, the death, the killings, the brutality, you know what you have to do."

"Henry, listen to me, I want to help you but I can't unless you let me."

"If you want it to stop, then all you have to do is find me."

"Tell me where you are. Let me help you," Dane said.

"You know where I'll be. You know where to find me."

"Henry please—"

Henry ended the call and tossed the phone into the undergrowth. The voices had spoken, and there was a more pressing matter to attend to. He asked them where they wanted him to go, and they spoke the answer he had longed to hear. They were sending him home.

CHAPTER 23

Police swarmed over the Edgeware Road address where Henry Marshall had massacred Isaacs's adoptive parents. The house had been ringed by yellow police tape, the whole scene illuminated by the revolving red and blue beacons of the half dozen police cars and two ambulances that were on scene. Curious neighbors stood on doorsteps, faces wearing worry and concern at the events in their otherwise quiet neighborhood. Petrov pulled up at the edge of the tape and climbed out of the car, taking in the scene. Warren waved him over and Petrov ducked under the cordon after showing his badge to the officer keeping the public at bay.

"It's a fuckin' mess in there, Alex," Warren said, taking a cigarette offered by Petrov.

"Any sign of the kid yet?"

"No, not yet. Although we have it confirmed that it was Henry Marshall who did this."

"Jesus," Petrov said, looking at the house. "That's bold, really bold. Are we sure?"

"Half a dozen people saw the kid charging down the street and jumping into the car, and Marshall getting into his vehicle and giving chase. It's him."

"How the hell did he slip the roadblocks?"

"Damned if I know, but he did."

"So where are we on this? What's the

timeline?" Petrov asked.

"Come on up to the house, its better you see it for yourself."

Warren led the way, Petrov following behind, avoiding the crime scene officers in paper forensic suits milling around the property. They went around the back, where a white tent had been erected over the door, and ducked inside, Petrov immediately seeing the scale of violence.

"Jesus Christ," he muttered. No matter how many crime scenes like this he saw, the brutality of man never ceased to confuse and depress him.

"So, here's how I'm guessing it goes down," Warren said, who, unlike Petrov, was unaffected by the bloodbath. "Marshall comes around the back of the house. The guy on the ground there opens the door to take out the garbage. Marshall is waiting, slits his throat on the doorstep and gains entry. He shoves the husband down on the ground and puts the knife right there through his skull. The wife, she doesn't move. Marshall drowns her in the sink then goes looking for the kid, who was hiding upstairs. Anyway, the boy escapes through the back door here and Marshall gives chase."

"Not bad," Petrov said. "Almost right, too."

"You think you know better, Alex?"

Petrov nodded. "The husband died later. Probably when the kid was trying to escape. You see the smears in the blood there from his hands? You don't do that if someone plunges a knife in your skull. You go down and stay down. My guess is, Marshall slits his throat when he opens the door and leaves him there bleeding out. He comes in and drowns the wife just like you said, then finds the kid. Chases him back down here. See the shoe print in the blood there?"

"Yeah," Warren said.

"Size seven. My best guess is the kid is cornered here by Marshall, the stepfather has a little fight left in him and tries to help, and that's when he eats the knife in the skull. It gives the kid enough time to run and get out of the house."

"And that's when he got picked up around the corner?"

"Exactly."

"Yeah, I see it now," Warren said. "Marshall chases them. It seems they ended up heading out of town when Marshall runs them off the road. The car is a mess, and—"

"I know. I just came from there. The kid and the people he was with had disappeared before I got to them," Petrov grumbled.

"Shit. Didn't anyone think to stop them?"

"Why would they?" Petrov said, rubbing his temples. "Nobody knows who they are. They were just victims of a car accident waiting to be taken to hospital to be checked over. There was no need to detain them, not at the time anyway."

"Jesus Christ," Warren grunted. "What about Marshall? Any sign of him?"

"More than that. He was right there at the crash site. Apparently he was trying to get into the car. With everything going on, nobody noticed him leave the scene. I had to pull the men stationed in Oakwell away to help with the search.

They're out now looking for him."

"So who are these people who helped the kid?" Warren said, looking at the devastation in the kitchen. "Jesus, it's a real mess, ain't it?" he added as he popped a stick of chewing gum into his mouth.

"We don't know who they are," Petrov sighed. "None of this is adding up, Warren."

"Does it ever?" Warren said.

Petrov didn't respond. He was tired, not just physically, but mentally. Over the last couple of years, he had found himself struggling more and more to switch off at the end of the work day. Of course, some of the things he saw would live with him forever no matter how much he wanted them to go away, but it seemed for some reason, the part of his brain that filtered out the usual shit that made living a normal life possible wasn't working.

"You alright, Alex?" Warren asked, sensing how distracted his partner was.

"Yeah, I'm good, just struggling to process everything. Let's get the hell out of here." Petrov ducked back out of the tent covering the door, inhaling the fresh air, a light sweat forming on his brow. His brain felt as if it were pulsing in his head, a sure sign of a coming migraine.

"Why don't you knock off? I can take it from here," Warren said.

"I'm fine."

"You look like shit."

"Love you too."

"I'm serious, man. You look like you need a break."

"I can't now, Warren, not with this thing unraveling the way it is. We need to find this kid and fast."

"I know. I'll tell you something; I wish we still had the death penalty here for when we catch that prick, Marshall."

"Yeah, well, if he carries on being as bold as this, we stand a decent chance."

"So what do we do now?" Warren asked.

"Stick around here and question the neighbors. You're good at that. See what you can squeeze out of them."

"What about you?" Warren said as Petrov walked toward the front of the house.

"I'm going to tell the Samson woman her kid is missing."

"Why don't you see if local law enforcement can cover it?"

"No, I'd rather do it myself. Besides, I could do with having a little time to think."

"What the hell fuck do you think's going on here, Alex?" Warren said.

Petrov hesitated, unsure what he wanted to say or how to say it. Some things, he reasoned, were better without words, or at least any form of committal answer.

"At this point, I don't know. Let's just play it by ear and see what we can find out."

Petrov skirted around the house before Warren could ask any more questions. He ducked back under the tape, pushed through the crowds and got into his car.

PART THREE:

FULL CIRCLE

CHAPTER 24

Detective Petrov pulled up to the rundown apartment building and gave it a cursory once-over as he shut off the engine. He sat for a moment, composing his thoughts, taking a second to get what he wanted to say clear in his mind. He exited the vehicle, paused to take a look up and down the street and entered the building.

Some places were nicer inside than out, however this wasn't one of them. The hallways were dark and dusty, the wallpaper cheap and a good few years past its best. He took the stairs to the fourth floor, paused outside room 413 and, after popping a stick of chewing gum into his mouth, knocked on the door. When no answer came, he knocked again, and was about to do so a third time when the door to the next apartment opened and a short, dumpy hag of a woman stepped out into the hall.

"Who you looking for?" she asked, looking Petrov up and down.

"I'm here to see Mrs. Samson. Have you seen her?"

"Maybe. Who are you?"

Petrov flashed his badge. "Police. It's important I talk to her."

"She's not in," the old woman said with a shrug of her shoulders.

"Are you certain?"

"Listen, son, I'm neighborhood watch. You and I are on the same side. I keep my eyes and ears open. You have to in a place like this. I was telling my grandson last week that he really ought to—"

"Ma'am? You were saying about Mrs. Samson."

"I was?"

Petrov stared and said nothing.

"She went out earlier. Seemed in a hurry. She normally talks to me in the hall. Her husband died you know, and her kid, well she never talks about him. I think there's something going on there. Nobody has that many secrets."

"Did Mrs. Samson say where she was going?"

"No. She had a bag though, and she seemed upset. Course, she always does. My cousin is the same you know, has that depression. Strange thing if you ask me. I told my grandson—"

"Thank you, ma'am," Petrov said, already striding down the corridor.

"Don't you want to take my name? In case you have questions?" she called after him.

"No, thank you. You were a great help."

Petrov jogged down the steps two at a time and ran out to his car. A man used to trusting his instincts, he had a good idea where she was going.

CHAPTER 25

Getting the woman to stop was easier than he anticipated. Even looking the way he did, he knew it was only a matter of time before someone naïve or trusting enough would pull up to the roadside to ask if he was okay. The woman driver, who was now sitting in the passenger seat, was in her twenties. Henry looked at her, dressed in her business attire, brown hair tied into a bun high on her head, deep blue eyes which would have been sensual if not for the fear that filled them.

The roads had been remarkably free of police, another thing for which he thanked the voices for. He sped past the sign telling them they had reached Oakwell, and he pulled to the side of the road, stopping the car.

He looked at his prisoner, hands bound with duct tape. She was docile and afraid. Beyond, just visible through the trees, were the few white flashes of rooftops of the abandoned town. As confident as he was that there was nobody there waiting for him, he wasn't prepared to take the risk.

He turned to the frightened woman, watching her, eyes hungry, not for her flesh like most men, but for her blood. His eyes flicked to the road behind them, ensuring it was clear, then landed on what was on the back seat. He reached back and brought it to the front.

A half dozen red roses. He pulled the small white card out and read it.

Rachel,

So sorry about everything. I hope you can forgive me and know I still love you.

Billy.

"Is Billy your husband?" he said, watching her, enjoying her fear.

She shook her head.

"Boyfriend?"

She nodded, still terrified, wanting to run but knowing she would never dare.

"What did he do?"

She didn't answer, instead stared out of the window, looking for help.

"Nobody's coming," Henry said, watching as she cried, make-up streaking down her face. "This road only leads here and nobody but us has any cause to come this way. The bulk of traffic will be taking the highway. If you're looking out there for help, it's not coming."

"Please let me go," the woman pleaded, her voice no more than a whisper.

Henry looked at the flowers, then back at her. "What did he do? This Billy. Why did he buy you flowers?"

"Please, just let me go."

She wasn't listening, and Henry was growing angry. It was easier to hear them now, those things in his head, especially now they were so close. He breathed in the flowers, closing his eyes, trying to remember the last time he'd experienced such scents. The only smells that seemed pleasant to him anymore were those of fear and blood. His eyes flicked open.

"What did Billy do?" It wasn't a question but a demand. She sensed it, because this time she answered.

"He forgot my birthday," she said.

"Is it today?"

"Yesterday."

"How old are you?"

"Look, please—"

"How old!"

"Twenty. I'm twenty."

Henry nodded, satisfied. "That's a good age. A whole life ahead of you if you do as I tell you. I don't want to hurt you."

"What do you want?" she asked.

"Do you have tow ropes in the back? A toolbox?"

She wept, a mucus bubble expanding and contracting in one nostril as she breathed.

"Answer me!" He glared at her, hoping she saw, hoping she understood that he wasn't joking around.

"There are ropes, I think," she replied, refusing to look him in the eye. "But I don't have a toolbox."

"You really should carry one," Henry said, stroking her hair with filthy fingers. "You never know when you might need one."

"I only got the car a week ago. It's new," she said, risking a look at him.

"Birthday gift?"

She nodded. "My parents. They… they'll be

missing me."

"I have no doubt," Henry said, opening the car door. "Come on. It's time to go."

"Where are we going?" she asked, looking beyond him into the trees.

Henry walked around to the passenger side door, opened it and led her out by her elbow. He led her around the car, pausing to pop the trunk, then as an afterthought, popped the hood as well. He saw her looking and grinned. "In case somebody comes by and wonders why the car is here. They'll think it was a breakdown."

He led her to the trunk and found the tow ropes where she said they would be.

"Are we coming back?" she asked, trembling.

Henry didn't answer. He ducked back into the car and grabbed the roses, shoving them into her hands.

"No, I'm afraid we're not," Henry said as he led her off the road and into the forest. As dense as it was, he knew the voices would make his passage easy. After all, he had a very important job to do.

CHAPTER 26

Consciousness was slow to come back to Isaac, and for a few precious moments, he had forgotten what happened to him. As he woke, it came to him in pieces. First the pain. The dull throb in his wrist, the ache in his neck and shoulder. Next came sound. Screams, agony. Pain. Or was it? He concentrated his efforts, trying to listen through the fuzzy cloud of near consciousness. Not screams. Singing. Music. It was a radio, the DJ talking around a chart hit that Isaac didn't recognize. He turned to his other senses. Inhaling, mentally reeling at the smell of rotting flesh and decay. Only, it wasn't decay. It was a good smell. Bacon frying. He could hear it sizzling behind the chatter of the radio presenter.

He opened his eyes, squinting at the white light, trying to get a feel for his surroundings. He was on a sofa, head propped up on two pillows, twisted cover over his body. The room was dusty and cluttered with all kinds of objects that seemed to make no stylistic sense. He lifted his head, the headache screaming its arrival the instant he moved. Point taken, he lay back down again, taking in what he could. Trying to make sense of what had happened.

It came back to him without warning. The man from his nightmare. Grant and Tanya. The crash. The people who had helped him. He remembered the footsteps coming toward him as he lay trapped in the car, seeing him at the window, desperate to get in, desperate to get to him like some kind of wild animal, and then… black, and he couldn't remember anything after that.

He risked lifting his head to get a look at the room, this time the headache bearable. He was on a sofa, in a standard sitting room. The window across the room was open, letting in dust-filled bars of sunlight. Ahead of him, beside the overfilled bookshelf, was an open door beyond which he could hear the sounds of the radio and smell the cooking bacon. He could also hear voices speaking in whispers.

"Hey kid, you feelin' alright?"

Isaac turned toward the source of the voice. A man stood framed by the open door, one he recognized from the car. He had his arm bandaged and a large plaster on his head.

"Where am I?" Isaac mumbled. "Who are you?"

"Take it easy, kid, you're safe here. My name's Truman, and if it helps, I don't have a damn clue what's goin' on here either. Hang on, I'll get Emma. She's the person you need to talk to. She seems to know what the hell this is about."

With no means of arguing the point anyway, Isaac lay back on the pillow and waited for someone to come and tell him what was going on.

"You don't remember me, do you?"

Isaac shook his head. "No, I don't know you."

"I'm a friend, okay? You don't need to be scared."

"That man. He wanted to hurt me," Isaac replied, his lip trembling as he recalled the snarling face of Henry Marshall as he tried to get into the car.

"You can relax here. Nobody will hurt you."

"Who are you?"

"My name is Emma. This is my house. How do you feel?"

Issac shrugged. "Okay I guess. I don't remember." He sat up, staring at the window. "What if he followed, that man…"

"He didn't. You're safe here."

"Are you sure?"

Emma nodded, and took a deep breath. "I need to talk to you about something important, Isaac. Something that you might not understand at first and that might be scary for you, but you need to hear it."

"You don't have to talk to me like a baby. I'm ten years old, not four."

Emma smiled. "I'm sorry. I'm not used to talking to kids."

"It's okay," he said, settling back down on the sofa. "What do you need to talk to me about? Is it about that man?"

"No, not him. How much do you know about your mother?"

"She doesn't want me anymore. That's why I had to live with Grant and Tanya. They said she's sick," Isaac said, not making eye contact with Emma.

"Your mother does want you, Isaac. Don't believe otherwise."

"Then why did she send me away?"

"I'm sure she wouldn't have done if she didn't have to. Right now, I need you to focus on this talk, okay?"

He nodded, watching her and waiting.

"What do you know about the place where your parents used to live?"

"The bad place," Isaac replied straight away. "I dream about it, even though I've never been there. Sometimes I hear them in my head, those... things. I don't like them."

It took all of Emma's strength to keep a neutral expression at the simple way he said it. The same thing had plagued Alex until he took his own life, and that was something she was still struggling to come to terms with. She shuffled on her seat, and somehow dug up a smile; a warm expression that said everything was fine with the world, and there was nothing to worry about.

"Yes, the bad place," she repeated. "See, I was there too. I know how bad it is. That's why I need you, Isaac. I need you to help me stop those things, the things that keep talking to you in your head... the things that make that man want to hurt you."

"They scare me. I don't like the things they say to me. I know they control him too, don't they?"

"Yes, they do. When they talk to you, do they ever tell you to do things? Bad things?"

"Sometimes, but I never do it though. They hate that even more. They get angry and swear at me."

"What would you say if I told you I knew how we could get rid of them for good?"

Isaac shrugged. "Good I guess. How though?"

"Wait here a sec, honey. It's easier if I show you."

Emma left the room, disappearing out of sight down the corridor. Isaac thought about making his own move. Getting out of there and running away. Then he considered the sobering thought that he had nowhere else to go, and that the man who tried to kill him was still out there somewhere. It was, in the end, academic, as Emma returned carrying a jar, which she placed on the coffee table between them. The jar was around a third full with dirt. Isaac watched as she took her seat and looked at him.

"That scar on your neck," she said, still staring. "Do you remember how you got it?"

Isaac involuntarily touched the two inch line on his throat. "A bad man did it."

"That's right, he did. Do you remember that night?"

Isaac shrugged. "Not much. Sometimes I remember things, but they always go away when I wake up."

"What do you remember?"

"Being scared, then it was bright and I didn't feel scared anymore." He shuffled and shrugged again. "That's all really."

"The man who chased you today, the one who came to your house. He did that. Or at least he tried to."

"You mean he's not from my dream?"

"No, honey. He's real. He tried to hurt you. Don't you remember?"

Isaac shook his head, then changed his mind and nodded. "I remember a little."

"Okay, that's fine. You see, honey, I know your mother, or at least I knew her for a while. She told me that something happened to you that night. She never explained it, but said it was something to do with your father."

"I don't know. I don't remember any of that stuff," Isaac mumbled.

"See Isaac, ever since that night, I've been determined to find out what happened. I wanted to find a way to stop it. I think now I know. And I need you to help me. How do you feel about that?"

"I don't know. I guess so," he said, his eyes drifting to the jar of dirt.

Emma picked it up. "You want to know what this is, don't you?"

Isaac nodded.

"This is dirt taken from the bad place."

"Why did you want dirt from there?"

"I wanted to have it tested, looking for anything that might help tell us why the bad place is the way it is."

"What did you find?"

"Not as much as I wanted to. The soil's normal. No imbalances. No foreign bodies. There's no reason why plant life shouldn't grow there, and yet, nothing does. That entire patch of earth is a dead-zone."

"I don't understand…"

"Sorry," she said, setting the jar back on the table. "What I'm saying is, the tests on the dirt said there's nothing wrong with it. It's just normal soil."

"So why did you keep it?"

"I'm getting to that," she replied with the faintest glimmer of a smile. "Because I had no answers from the clearing, I started to look into other places that might share similar traits, other bad places that might be the same. One of them was a forest in Japan. Another was in Romania. The point is, these things are more widespread than people think."

Isaac looked at the jar of dirt, then back to Emma.

"I'm getting to the dirt, just give me a second."

"Okay. Sorry."

She hesitated, knowing that the next thing she had to say couldn't be watered down because of Isaacs's age. He needed to know the information and she decided to deliver it to him straight.

"My research found that across all the sites where genuinely weird things happen, there was one common theme. One link between them."

"The dirt?"

"Death."

"Oh…" Isaac said, folding his hands on his lap.

"You know what I'm talking about, don't you, Isaac. Those voices in your head; the ones that talk to you."

He nodded, doing all he could to avoid eye contact.

"It's okay. You can talk about it to me."

"You don't know what it's like," he said, the helplessness in his voice making her feel a tremendous sorrow for him.

"Yes I do."

"No you don't, you don't know anything."

"I hear them too," she said softly. Taking a deep breath, she composed herself. "I hear them all the time. Pretending to be my friends. My *dead* friends. Pretending to be Carrie. Pretending to be Scott and Cody, and now Alex. Trust me, I know what it's like."

"What do we need to do?" he asked.

"Pick up the jar."

"Why?"

"Just pick it up," Emma said.

It took a tremendous effort for him to reach out and pick up the jar. All of his senses were alive as he rotated it in his hands, looking at the dark brown earth inside.

"Remember where I told you that had come from?"

"The bad place. I know."

"Open it."

"Why?"

"Just do it."

Isaac put his hand on the lid, then paused, and held the jar out to Emma. "You do it."

"I can't," she said. "This is your task to do. You need to understand for yourself."

"What's going to happen?"

"Please, just open it."

Isaac did as he was asked and snapped the lid open. He felt it almost immediately, the oozing sick feeling. In the back of his mind he could sense his slumbering passenger begin to rouse.

"I don't like it. I feel sick."

"It's normal. Trust me. I know what I'm doing."

"What do you want me to do?"

"Reach into the jar and touch the dirt."

"I don't want to. It reminds me of the bad man."

"You have to. I need you to do this so I can show you what needs to happen."

"Can't you just tell me?"

"No, you have to do it."

Isaac held the jar close to him, peering inside. Even though there was only a small amount of dirt in it, he could feel the same skin-crawling sensation which had become all too familiar. With a tremendous effort, he reached into the jar, his fingertips hovering just above the earth. He didn't want to touch it, imagining it seeping into his skin, getting under his fingernails, becoming impossible to clean off. He saw microscopic creatures, born from whatever darkness dwelled at the clearing, getting into his body, growing and spreading.

"Isaac, do it," Emma said, watching him intently.

He looked at her, trying to decide if she could be trusted, or if he was being silly. After all, it was just dirt. Just ordinary dirt. He inched his fingertips closer, his nostrils filled with that earthy stench, guts tight and churning. He had never been more afraid. For whatever reason, the jar and the thought of touching its contents filled him with a sense of dread, the likes of which he had never experienced before.

It's only dirt.

It's only dirt.

It's only dirt.

Despite his inner voice's assurances, he couldn't bring himself to move. He was frozen there, fingertips a few inches above the dirt, the nausea inducing feeling coming from within the glass.

"Do you promise it's safe?"

"Of course I do. Touch it."

Isaac took a deep breath, and plunged his hand into the earth. Warm air pushed out of the jar as some of the topsoil was displaced. The jar vibrated, and as Isaac watched in awe, the dark feeling faded. His terror seemed distant and silly. Staring wide-eyed at Emma, he moved his hand around inside the jar. No fear. No sense of foreboding. No icy tightness of the gut.

"What happened?"

"You purged it."

"What does that mean?"

"You took the bad out of it. It's just dirt now."

"How?"

"You can take your hand out now," she said gently.

Isaac did as he was told, putting the jar on the table and wiping his hands on his jeans.

"There's a woman, someone I know. A spiritualist. She's from a long line of her kind. My grandmother went to her family to find a way to protect Hope House just before your mother and father moved in."

"Is she here?"

"No, but you'll meet her soon enough. In fact, she insisted on it. For now though, I want to show you something. Do you feel up to walking? Not far, just outside."

"Yeah, no problem. My neck is a little sore, but I'm okay."

"Good, come on."

Isaac followed Emma down a narrow hallway, one wall recessed and lined with books, and through the kitchen. Truman was sitting at the table, sipping from a mug of coffee and finishing off the remains of a bacon sandwich.

Emma led Isaac through a rear door to a small yard outside. Sunlight warmed half of the yard, the rear masked in the shadow of the wall surrounding it. Wooden shelves lined the perimeter and a white exterior gate stood to the left, leading out into the street.

"Over here."

Isaac took his eyes from the street and joined Emma at the back wall.

On the shelves, evenly spaced, were two jars,

identical to the one he had just placed his hand in. He inspected them, and realized what Emma was trying to show him.

"These are yours and his, aren't they?" he said, looking at her.

"Yes. This is how we know. That one is mine."

The flower inside was vibrant; a purple rose, snaking out of the jar in its quest to reach sunlight.

"That one belongs to Truman," she added, pointing to the second jar, the plant inside thick and full, the flower blood red with yellow at the base.

"Will mine be the same?"

"Yes. We can plant in it now. The dirt is good. Purified."

"Are you saying we just have to touch the dirt and we can get rid of the bad things?"

Emma laughed, and Isaac smiled. "I wish it were that easy. These soil samples all came from the clearing, but they have been blessed by the woman I was telling you about earlier."

"Blessed?"

"Well, maybe blessed is the wrong word. Whatever she does to cleanse the earth, she did to these jars."

"How does she do it?"

"I don't know. She spends time with them, whispering to the dirt, writing things down. It's incredible to see. The problem is, she wasn't born in that place. She isn't tied to it. It needs someone directly involved to finish the purification."

"And that's where we come in?"

Emma nodded.

"Doing something like this to a jar of dirt is one thing. Going to that place and performing it on that scale is completely something else."

"I feel sick," Isaac mumbled as he tried to take it all in.

"I'm sorry. It was never going to be an easy thing to tell you. All I can say is that you are safe here for now. You're welcome to stay until we've done what we need to do."

"What if it doesn't work?"

"It has to," Emma said, staring at the jars. "It just has to."

CHAPTER 27

Petrov had been staring at the card Kimmel gave him, wondering if he should make the call and, if he did, what he would say. He sat in his car, staring at his phone, the number already punched in. His thumb hovered over the dial button but he couldn't bring himself to press it. The fact was, he didn't want to admit to Kimmel or anyone else that he was running out of ideas. He fully expected to have found Marshall by now, and certainly hadn't expected the extra complication of the missing Samson kid and the people who were, for whatever reason, helping him. Although he wasn't initially convinced about Kimmel, it seemed that for better or worse, he was the closest thing they had to an ally.

He stared at the phone number again, checking that it corresponded to the number on the phone display.

He probably won't answer anyway, he thought, then on the heels of that, *why don't you call him then you dumb shit?*

He snorted, wondering why he felt so uncertain, then pressed the dial button and waited to see if the line would connect, simultaneously wondering if he would leave a message if the option was given. The phone was answered on the third ring.

"Hello, Detective Petrov," Kimmel's smooth

voice answered. "I wondered when you might call."

"How did you know it would be me?"

"Nobody else has this number."

"I'm privileged."

"Yes you are. I take it this is about Henry Marshall?"

Petrov hesitated, his lips dry. He looked in the rear-view mirror, and hating the uncertainty he saw there, averted his gaze. "Yeah, it is."

"Did you pull your people from Oakwell like I suggested?"

"I had to. We're spread thin on this. With the roadblocks and the crime scenes, I can't afford to have them standing around."

A few seconds of silence followed, and Petrov was about to ask if Kimmel had heard him when the former general replied. "He'll be heading there now. Might even be there already."

"I don't think so. We have men out looking for him. I doubt he could slip by us again."

"He will," Kimmel said.

"How can you be so sure? What's there for him?"

"It's his home. And they will be calling to him, Detective. Make no mistake."

"I already told you. I don't believe in ghosts."

"No, I know you don't. Just give me a second, Detective. Hold the line if you would."

Petrov waited, listening to the phone click as Kimmel set it down. He heard the distant rustle of paper then Kimmel returned. "I can be there before nightfall. Pick me up at the park where we met last time, will you?"

"You're coming up here?" Petrov said.

"Of course. I have to."

"Why?"

"Because you don't believe. And if you don't have me with you, there's a good chance you might become a victim of this too."

"It sounds like you're trying to spook me, Kimmel."

"Not at all. I'm trying to help you. I'll call you back on this number when I'm close to the park."

"What then?" Petrov asked, genuinely curious.

"Then we go to Oakwell and find your escapee, Detective."

"And what if he doesn't come without a fight?"

Another pause, Kimmel's breathing the only indication he was still there.

"I'll call when I'm close," Kimmel said sharply, then disconnected.

Petrov tossed Kimmel's card and his phone onto the passenger seat and leaned his head back against the headrest. Somehow, despite having every hope of clearing up some of the confusion, he had managed to make more for himself.

CHAPTER 28

Emma had driven them to a quiet, quaint neighborhood with nice houses with nice gardens, and nice people who no doubt had nice jobs to pay for their nice cars and nice furnishings. The house on Sycamore Street was American suburbia at its finest. They pulled up outside number seven. A picket-fenced, white-walled home with trimmed lawn, pruned rose bushes and a 1960's bottle green Mercedes parked in the driveway. Emma, Truman and Isaac climbed out of the car.

"This is it," she said as she stuffed the car keys into her bag. "This is where Mrs. Alma lives."

She led them through the gate and up to the house. Next door, the old woman at number five scowled at them as she raked leaves from her garden, her huge Alsatian panting on the doorstep. Isaac nodded, but she ignored him, watching the three of them with cold indifference.

The lady who answered the door was skinny and dour looking with short blonde hair and cold blue eyes. Once, she might have been good looking, but the years had been unkind, and the deep network of lines set into her skin meant that she could quite easily be an old sixty or young seventy-something.

"Come in," she said, her voice the quiet mumble of someone lacking confidence.

She kept her gaze away from them, either on

the ground or over their shoulders. Emma led them into the sitting room as Mrs. Alma closed the door.

"Take a seat," she mumbled again, taking her own place in an ugly red floral chair. The others sat on the sofa opposite her, Isaac confused and a little afraid, Truman and Emma tense and respectful.

Mrs. Alma offered them no welcome. No drinks or opening conversation. Instead, she lit a cigarette, long bony fingers working with well-practiced ease. When it was done, she inhaled, closed her eyes, then on the outward breath, turned to face them, making eye contact with Emma.

"I wondered when you would bring him. Does he understand the situation?"

"I've explained it to him," Emma said.

Mrs. Alma looked at Isaac, forgetting for a moment that there was anyone else in the room. He looked back, afraid and uncertain.

"The world beyond ours is invisible to those who don't want to see. My question to you, boy, is what will it take to make you believe?"

"I don't understand."

"Your father is here with us."

She said it in such a conversational way it took him a second or two to understand what she meant. There was no channeling, no incantation. Just the words.

"What do you mean?" he asked.

"He's joined us from the light. He's come to see you. He said he'll always be watching. He wishes he could protect you from those who wish you harm."

"The bad man," he said.

She nodded. This time she did close her eyes, inhaling deeply, cigarette hanging from her limp fingers.

"I hear those who speak to you. The ones who want to worm their way into your mind. There's one in particular. A dark one. He wants you to hurt yourself. He wants you to do bad things. Your father, he isn't strong enough to protect you anymore. His light grows dim as the darkness becomes deeper."

"I see him. Sometimes when I'm asleep, sometimes when I'm awake."

"Eto is his name. Your father battles him in the other world. That's why you are so confused. They are both there in your head. Light against dark."

"I don't understand why, though."

"You are the key. The key to bringing their torment to an end. The only child conceived on those lands. Some long for freedom, the innocent souls trapped there. Others will do anything to remain in the space between worlds. Eto and his kin have grown bitter and resentful of humanity. They are afraid of you, boy."

"I'm scared."

"But you will go there," the woman said without hesitation. "They want you to go there. They want you to fear them. This is what feeds them, and they will stop at nothing to harm you."

"They can't hurt me. They're just voices,"

Isaac said, trying to convince himself.

"Words can sometimes be a more powerful weapon than you think. This has been proved on countless occasions during the history of that place. Besides, they have a human vessel to do their work for them. Through him they will get to you. They fear that which fears them. This is how they will be defeated. It will take all of you. You will all have to decide if fear or light will consume you. This is how it is. This cannot be undone."

She blinked, the glassy sheen in her eyes lifting. Isaac exhaled, unaware he had even been holding his breath. Mrs. Alma lifted the cigarette to her mouth, flicking the long snake of ash from its tip into an ashtray, her hand trembling.

"There is a place you must go. A secret place. I do not know where it is, but you can find out."

"How?" Isaac asked.

"You allow them access to your mind."

"No, you can't do that to him," Emma blurted.

Mrs. Alma silenced her with a glare, then turned back to Isaac.

"Through me you will have protection. If you are willing to let Eto in, you can read him as he reads you. You will be able to learn of the source. You will learn where you have to go to end them."

"I don't want to. I'm scared," Isaac said, chewing his thumbnail.

"It doesn't matter. This is the only way."

"Is it safe?"

She didn't answer. Instead, she took a last drag on her cigarette and mashed it out in the ashtray.

"I don't know. They are powerful, and much more malevolent than anything I have dealt with before. This Eto, his light is cold. Unpredictable. By channeling through me, I can dilute his strength, for a while at least. The rest is up to you."

"Can he... harm me?"

"No," she said with a shake of her head. "He can project through me, but he can't cause you physical harm."

"So he can't hurt me?" Isaac said, feeling a touch more positive.

"Not in the sense you're thinking of," Mrs. Alma said as she tapped a spindly finger to her temple. "In there, that's where they will get you. They'll make you do things. They'll make the most frighteningly insane decisions seem like the most sensible choices in the world. You need to be sharp. You need to beware."

"Then I'll do it."

"Isaac, you don't have to. This is insane," Emma said, pleading with Mrs. Alma.

"Do you want to fix this or not?" she replied, speaking to Isaac rather than Emma. "You come to me for help, and this is what I offer. This is the only way. The land can't be purified without locating the source. You are the only one who can find it."

"Mrs. Alma," Emma said, leaning forward on her seat. "Everyone I've ever known has been changed by those things permanently. I've seen what happens when you let them in. Don't do this to him, he's just a boy."

"Alex says you should trust what I do. He says what he did to himself was his choice, and that you should leave the boy to make his."

Emma inhaled sharply, her mind going blank at the words Mrs. Alma had uttered.

"Its fine, I want to do it," Isaac said, bravado overcoming sense.

Mrs. Alma turned toward him, folding her arthritic hands in her lap. "There are no guarantees. It all depends on whether he wants to come. I can't force him, only channel him if he chooses to make himself known."

"He'll come. He's been waiting a long time to speak to me," Isaac said, agitated with a nervous excitement.

Mrs. Alma looked at him, and for the first time appeared uncomfortable.

"Very well. Let us begin."

Truman looked around the sun-bathed room. "Do you want me to close the curtains or somethin'? Set the mood?"

Mrs. Alma shook her head. "No. There can never be enough light if I'm to channel something so inherently dark. We will need the sun."

Truman nodded and glanced at Emma, who was watching Isaac.

"We'll see if he will come." Mrs. Alma managed a half smile. "The rest will play out as it will."

She closed her eyes and took a slow, deep breath. Isaac waited, hovering somewhere between excitement and fear. Without warning,

Mrs. Alma's eyes flicked open. In that instant, Isaac was grateful for the sunlight streaming through the windows, because the thing in the chair, which glared at them as if from behind a semi-transparent human mask, was no longer Mrs. Alma. The entire room took on a new atmosphere; a dark, unwelcoming feeling, impossible to ignore. Emma and Truman felt it too, and shrank back against their seats. The thing in the chair twitched and sneered.

"What do you want with me? Why won't you leave me alone?" Isaac asked, surprised at how calm his voice was.

The thing in the chair screwed up its Mrs. Alma mask features, and flexed its gnarled hands. It began to speak, each word hissed or spat in a language unspoken for centuries. Somehow, Isaac understood everything, its words automatically translated into English in his head.

"Death will come to you. There is no escape. Your father burns and screams for your blood. Death finds all eventually. Soon it will find your mother. Soon it will take you and your friends. The souls of the dead curse you, boy. Only when you join us will they be free. Only when you sacrifice yourself will all be saved. Blood will spill and be on your hands. Let me inside and I shall make it quick and painless. Let me help you do what must be done."

"Isaac…" Emma said, unable to finish her sentence before the thing in the chair snapped its head toward her.

"Shut up, cunt," it hissed in broken English,

flashing a yellow grin.

Emma took a sharp breath and shrank against Truman as Mrs. Alma turned back toward Isaac and reverted to its own language. "Do you understand you cannot escape us? Don't you realize death comes to all eventually? This way is easier. This way is better. Give yourself to us and we will spare your friends. If you do not, then they will suffer the consequences."

"I'm not afraid of you anymore," Isaac said. Or maybe he thought it. Either way, the thing in the chair heard and understood. It threw its head back and laughed a wet, choking gasp. Still it twitched and flexed its hands and fingers in what looked like some kind of constant state of seizure.

"There is no lie you can tell that I cannot see through. I know you, boy. I know everything you feel, everything you think."

"Where is the source?" Isaac asked.

Mrs. Alma said nothing. She glared and twitched, drool spilling out of her mouth and onto her chin.

"Tell me where it is!" Isaac screamed.

Mrs. Alma bucked in her chair, but didn't respond. She stared at Isaac with a wet grin. Isaac looked inward to the thing that, for as long as he could remember, had been trying to get inside his head. Something that now had a name.

Eto.

Instead of following the instinct to repel them, which had been with him for as long as he could remember, he opened his defenses, drawing them into his head, letting them roam among his secrets.

Mrs. Alma lurched, her flat chest thrusting outward, gnarled hands gripping onto her chair. She kicked out a leg, losing a slipper in the process. She screamed, a deep growling baritone, which had no place in such a slender woman. Isaac also screamed as those awful things were left to run amok in his mind, filling it with the extent of their knowledge.

They were more than just a series of images, they were snapshots of people. How they lived, how they loved. How they died. Even the Gogoku's innermost secrets were shown to him. Everything from how they became, to how they descended into madness and turned to the darkness which exists in Oakwell. Such an overload of information would have been too much for anyone to take.

For a ten year old boy like Isaac, there was never any chance. Filled with more information than he could process, Isaac lurched out of his chair and let out a scream from the deepest recesses of his stomach. Eyes screwed closed, veins bulged from his neck. He flexed his hands into claws, grasping at things only he could see.

"You will die like those who came before. I have already shown you this." Mrs. Alma said, her voice like fire and brimstone, the language understood only by Isaac.

"No. I won't let you," Isaac said, horrified to hear his response in the same tongue as the thing in the chair.

Mrs. Alma's eyes rolled back into her head and she gritted her teeth, breathing in snorts. The icy discomfort in the room built to incredible proportions, then just as it seemed something might happen, it faded away. In her chair, Mrs. Alma groaned as her body relaxed. Exhausted and covered in sweat, her eyes would barely open. Isaac froze, mouth open, hands flexed. Time appeared to stand still. Isaac looked to Emma. She saw the change in him and knew that things would never be the same again. As she watched, blood started to drip out of his nose.

"He's gone," Isaac whispered, then collapsed, his head slamming off the floor.

Emma scrambled to him, turning him over. He was unresponsive. Eyes closed.

"Is he alive? Is he breathing?"

Truman put his ear to Isaac's chest. "Yeah, he's breathing. He's just... out cold."

"Jesus, did you hear him? Did you hear the way he was talking?"

"Yeah," Truman said, knowing it was a language he would never be able to forget.

"I don't know what to do. We can't phone an ambulance, we'll be arrested."

"He doesn't need an ambulance," Mrs. Alma croaked, pushing herself up on her elbows. Like Isaac, she too had a bloody nose, and her eyes remained closed as she tried to compose herself.

"What do we do, Mrs. Alma?"

"Kitchen."

"What do you need?" Emma said, starting toward the door. Her mind was filled with concoctions and potions, secret remedies and incantations.

"Tea. I need a cup of tea."

"What about Isaac?"

Mrs. Alma looked at him, almost as if she was seeing him for the first time. "He'll be fine. Go put him in the spare bedroom. Let him sleep it off."

"Sleep it off? You sound so casual. You were speaking—"

"In tongues? Yes, I know."

"Mrs. Alma—"

"Please," she said, holding up a hand. "I need to recover. It always takes a lot out of me."

"And what about him? He's just a boy. You shouldn't have done that to him. We came here for your help."

"And now you have it."

"How?"

Mrs. Alma picked up her cigarettes. "Because he now knows the answer. We just need to wait for him to wake up."

"There's something else isn't there? What is it you're not telling me?"

Mrs. Alma looked at Emma, her face tight and frightened. "Before the end, the boy will die. It's the only way this can be stopped."

"No, there has to be something else."

Mrs. Alma shook her head. "No. I wish there was, truly I do. If this is to end, the boy has to die. It is the only way to close the circle created by his birth."

Emma put her head in her hands and the room fell into silence.

II

He was in a black room. In his dream, Isaac stood, or more accurately existed, floating in perpetual emptiness. He was everywhere and nowhere. Something and nothing. He saw a man. Cheap suit. Blond hair. He was standing by a car talking to two other people. Isaac wished he were closer. The second the thought registered, he was moving, drifting toward them.

As he moved nearer, the scenery around the group started to take form, appearing out of the black, becoming more and more solid until he was floating in the physical world. The blond-haired man in the cheap suit was laughing with the couple, his body language awkward.

Isaac saw the house, the thatched cottage in the woods. He realized two things in quick succession. This was something which took place before he was born. And the people talking to the blond-haired man were his parents.

What's his name?

Isaac didn't say it. He thought the question. Even so, the answer came back to him almost immediately.

Donovan.

Isaac watched his mother. She seemed full of optimism and happiness as she ran around to the back of the house. Isaac stayed with Donovan and his father, eavesdropping on their conversation. Donovan was speaking, leaning close, Jester's grin wide. Too wide.

"Don't worry about the trees. They just take a bit of getting used to," he said, nodding toward where

Steve was staring. "The last owners spent many happy years in this house before they decided to sell up and move to Australia." He flashed his wide, salesman grin.

Only Isaac knew they hadn't moved to Australia. They died horrible painful deaths in the forest. The woman screaming. The man cackling as he strangled her, squealing with delight as her face turned blue. Leaving her there to rot. Leaving her there for Donovan to have his way with again, and again, and again until the smell was too much even for him. Leaving her there to go back to the house. To hang himself in the bedroom, smiling all the while.

Isaac moved through time. He was still at the house, but now there were boxes everywhere. Isaac saw his father, sitting at the bottom of the garden, listening to Melody bark orders at the removal men. He saw his father first notice the path over the river, staring at it without knowing that its discovery would start everything unraveling for them all. He also saw Donovan again, crouching in the trees, watching the house.

Watching Melody.

Watching her shout at the removal men.

Watching her pick up one of the lamps they knocked over.

Watching her come to the front door to get some fresh air, fanning herself with a magazine.

Watching.

Watching.

Watching.

Isaac saw Donovan in his house, Polaroids spread out on the floor. Isaac didn't need to see them to know what they depicted. He could feel the fear of every victim; the cold cut of every savage knife attack.

Donovan staring. Fantasizing. Imagining Melody as part of his collection. Donovan doing things to himself which Isaac knew about but didn't want to see.

Show me something else, he whispered.

Again he moved. Or maybe the scene around him did. He couldn't tell. Either way, he knew time had shifted.

Once more, he floated above the house, watching Donovan drive up to the property.

Danger.

Isaac's mother was home alone. How he knew, he had no idea. He just did. Nothing he saw appeared new to him. It was as if he were recalling vague memories, which was impossible. He hadn't been born yet. Snapshots of what happened next came to him, flashing in and out of his consciousness.

His mother, disturbed from her bath, answering the door in just a towel. Donovan's eyes, hungry with the thought of her becoming part of his collection. Thinking of that more than anything else. More than why they'd sent him.

Donovan inside the house, imposing but still friendly. His mother uncomfortable. Going upstairs to dress. Donovan sitting in the chair, rocking back and forth. Over and over again. Staring at the trees. Listening to the house creaking out its instructions. Telling him to make sure the secret place remains hidden. But Isaac knew Donovan was distracted by his own agenda.

Thinking of his Polaroids. Thinking about adding Melody's image to his gallery.

The house creaked with more urgency, the trees rocked with more bluster.

But Donovan knew they couldn't reveal themselves just yet, and so he ignored them. He ignored why they'd sent him. All he could think about was Melody and her towel. Skin gleaming and wet. She would make a great picture, that much was certain.

Another flash forward.

Donovan unable to resist. Forcing himself on Melody. Her desperate fighting, scrambling to escape. A chase through the forest, the trees thundering in fury, not at Melody, but at Donovan for his defiance. But still he chased, the trees contracting. Not to stop *her*, but to stop *him*.

They guided her, leading her toward the clearing. Toward *that* place. Light as she exploded out of the forest, fear slamming into Donovan as he knew he no longer had the strength to deny them. Enraged, they chastised him, speaking their vile words into his head as he stalked on the edge of the clearing. They wouldn't allow him to enter. Wouldn't allow him to kill her as punishment for his defiance and for not ensuring the secret place under the house remained hidden.

Under the house.

Show me, Isaac said.

He was whisked forward again. This time to Donovan breaking into the house, terrified of the Gogoku, heeding their final warning that they would tolerate no further disobedience. His instructions clear. Tie up loose ends – those who know about the secret place under the house. Kill the Samsons to ensure it stays a secret. Loose ends. The malevolent things are afraid of the seed the woman carries.

For a while Isaac didn't understand they were referring to him.

A simple task, but the woman wakes and leaves the house, lost in a daze, heading across the river in a trance-like state. Donovan's plan to butcher the Samsons while they sleep ruined. Steve Samson waking, hearing the intruder.

A scuffle.

A fall.

A fatal wound.

Donovan unaware he's dead.

The house burning as Steve and Donovan fight, his body worn like a glove by those forces who will stop at nothing to protect their secret.

The Gogoku in the clearing, doing the job Donovan failed at. Like him, pawns to a bigger game. Servants to a darker power. They try to destroy Melody and her unborn child by the will of their masters, but Steve's destruction of Hope House to forces them to stop. The house burns, but the secret place remains.

Under the house.

Suddenly Isaac was moving again, flying at breakneck speed. Down into the ruins. Down into the pantry, through the hatch beneath the rug, into the catacombs, to the place kept secret for centuries, the thing that dwells there as old as the earth itself. An abomination. A sight that defies words.

It was clear to him then. Donovan was the chosen guardian. And when he died, Henry Marshall took his place. Images of the hotel being built in fast forward appeared next. Henry changing plans, arguing with the architect who wanted to bulldoze the remains of Hope House. Telling him he couldn't, knowing the secret couldn't be revealed. Giving specific plans for the building foundations, specifying where they had to go in order to keep the secret safe.

Isaac knew where they had to go, what they had to face to do it. The demons in his brain continued to probe and manipulate, refusing to leave now they'd gained entry. Already they were speaking to him, trying to convince him to join them or suffer. Worse, telling him if he didn't do as they said, everyone he knew would suffer with him.

He opened his eyes, drawing breath. Taking in the room in Mrs. Alma's house, relieved to be back to normality. Back to the world of light and smell and touch. He listened inwardly, trying to feel if anything was different, and realized it wasn't just one thing. Everything had changed. He got out of bed and went downstairs. He needed some air, anything to rid himself of the image of the thing he had just seen.

CHAPTER 29

Rachel sat on the ground, wrists tied behind her. She was pinned to the trunk of a tree by the tow ropes Henry had taken from the car. She could barely breathe, the cord digging into her chest and stomach. Soon after restraining her, he'd disappeared into the forest. She'd screamed of course, screamed until her throat burned and her voice broke. Nobody came. Nobody could hear. Although she knew it was useless, she squirmed against her restraints, her wrists rubbed raw from struggling, the dirt at her feet displaced where her heels dug into the ground in an attempt at leverage.

"That won't help you."

The voice came from over her shoulder, deep and throaty, somewhere out of sight amongst the trees. The crunch of twigs and leaves heralded his arrival. She looked up at him, squinting against the sun. A desperate need to get away overwhelmed Rachel, and she renewed her struggles, violently kicking in a desperate effort to be free. Henry watched, and she noticed that even his smile was devoid of any semblance of human emotion. She waited for death to come, for him to attack her. Instead of doing so, Henry sat cross-legged on the ground a few feet away, staring at her.

"Please, let me go, I promise I won't tell

anyone I saw you," she pleaded, pulling at her restraints.

"I can't do that." He looked into the trees as he said it, then turned back to her, a flicker of a smile on his lips.

"You need help, please let me go."

"Nobody can help me. Only them," he whispered, staring back into the trees.

"Please, there are people that can help if you just let them. I won't tell anyone." She was crying, which seemed to further increase Henry's enjoyment. He leaned close, his face inches from hers.

"You sound just like them. The doctors and the psychiatrists. They didn't understand what lives inside me. That's why the voices told me not to speak to them. Not to share their secrets."

"There are no voices. They're not real. Please, my family has money, they can pay to help you get better."

"No," he said, rearing back and plunging his hands into the earth at her feet, digging furiously, his eyes burning into her as he did. "I'll show you. I'll prove it."

"Please, stop! What are you doing?" she shrieked, pulling away from his furious movements.

He didn't answer, just kept digging deeper, gasping for breath, sweat dripping off the tip of his nose from his exertions, the manic grin never leaving his lips as he tossed handfuls of earth from under him like some kind of rabid dog. He pulled something up, something white and smooth.

Rachel pushed herself back against the tree trunk, whimpering as Henry dragged the human skull out of the earth and tossed it toward her, its sightless eye sockets staring into the sky.

Still not finished, he scrambled a few feet to his left and repeated the process, digging with his fingertips, ignoring the pain and blood as his nails were torn off by the ferocity of his actions. A second skull was uncovered, this one complete with a broken ribcage. Like the first, he threw it at her, the bones breaking up as it hit the tree. Still he went on, moving from spot to spot, digging up fragments of lives that had been extinguished over the centuries. When he was done, he sat back, panting and staring. Around her, bones of the dead littered the ground, some half out of the earth, others just fragments.

"Don't you tell me they don't talk to me," Marshall said between gasps. "I hear them all. Every last one of them."

"What's going to happen to me?" she whispered.

"Do you believe in God?" he asked, eyes cold, observing her with almost childlike curiosity.

"What?"

"God. Do you believe in him?"

She shook her head. "I won't answer that. It's a trick. There's no right answer."

"Do you believe in man?"

"What?" she gasped, confused at his line of questioning.

"Do you believe a man with enough power can *become* a god? If a man could wield the spark of life and the hammer of death, then by default would he not be god-like?" He was smirking now, enjoying her terror. "I can become a god. They told me what they want me to do. They showed me how I can become what I'm destined to be."

"Please, just let me go. It's not too late."

Henry's faraway smile melted. "Oh no. I need you. I need you to greet them for me. I need you to be my messenger."

He scrambled to his feet, kicking bones aside. He started to walk toward her, then paused and picked up the bunch of flowers, leaving bloody smears on the wrapping from his damaged hands. "You will have the flowers Billy meant for you to have," he said, moving closer.

Her screams were muffled by the wind thrashing through the trees.

CHAPTER 30

Garbage littered the floor of the empty building. At some point during the intervening years since its abandonment, it had been stripped by looters and vandals, leaving it a mockery of its former glory. A section of roof had collapsed, exposing joists and leaving a carpet of broken plaster.

Rotten furniture, thick with grime, remained like relics of a different world, while water from broken pipes and years of frequent rain had left the walls covered with a thick carpet of black mold.

Henry Marshall cared about none of these things. He stumbled inside, exhausted from his efforts with the girl, smeared in her fluids, his memory filled with her innards as he'd desecrated her flesh. The offering pleased them, his masters, but still he wasn't finished. He needed tools, things with which to cut and hack. His destination had been unknown to him as he'd walked through the town, keeping to the shadows, using the dead husks of houses and shops that once thrived with life for cover. Now he was here, awaiting the arrival of those he was destined to destroy. The once grand and luxurious hall had suffered badly from its neglect and yet, to him, it still felt like home.

Exhausted, his physical body was in need of

respite. Only his mental strength was keeping him going, or more accurately, the things whispering in his head.

The drip of a pipe.

The creak of a floorboard.

The groan of wind channeled through one of the broken windows.

Message received and understood.

He walked around the room, remembering ghosts of conversations once held there with friends. Colleagues. People who were most likely dead now. Some at his own hand.

The scrape of a radiator thermostat.

The rustle of dead leaves skittering across floorboards.

The squeak of rats in the walls going about their stealthy business.

Yes.

He understood what had to be done. Their instructions were clear. Not yet though. First there was something else that needed to be done. A detour before he went to his beloved voices in the trees.

A hiss of wind, making the old town hall groan on its foundations.

"Yes," he said to the empty room. "I love you too."

He strode out into the deserted streets of Oakwell, and headed back to the place he knew better than any. The place where he would find the tools he needed to finish his work.

Home.

CHAPTER 31

The lack of light didn't hinder Henry Marshall as he picked his way through the dilapidated rooms of his former home. Memories, nothing more than distant echoes of a life that may not even have been his own, lingered somewhere in his psyche, and yet he was completely disconnected from them.

Like the rest of the town, this house was a dying remnant of a world where light once existed. Now, this place in particular was filled with a darkness that could never be banished. Sealed up shortly after Henry's arrest, it was a time capsule of sorts to life before the death. Before the blood.

Henry stood in the entrance to the sitting room, litter strewn across the floor. The chair which had contained his dead wife for so long shoved against a wall, ominous stains in the approximate shape of her body visible even in the gloom; the aroma of death still lingering in the air.

He crossed to his chair, the one in which, many, many years earlier, he'd sat whilst he and his wife watched television of an evening, doors closed against the winter chill, flames licking in the fireplace.

He resumed his position in the chair, springs squeaking, dust billowing up only to settle back onto the fabric once more. He waited to see if any signs of familiarity would come back to him. The mildew smell of rot. The damp cling of fabric against his thighs. He leaned back and set his arms on the wooden rests of the chair, no more than an automatic gesture, a memory of a time before all he knew was death and the desire to cause it. He felt nothing. No emotion, no sorrow. His fingers danced around on the armrests, and he shifted his eyes in the darkness, able to see enough of the word he had carved there.

Donovan.

Henry's fingers traced the name over and over again, and he looked around the room, the gloomy interior lit by a weak moon from where the boards had been pried from the front window. Amid the yellow wallpaper hanging from the walls, loosened by the damp, he could see the name again and again.

On the cabinet in the corner. *Donovan.*

On the back of the door. *Donovan.*

On the fireplace. *Donovan.*

He flicked his eyes toward his wife's chair. Even she hadn't been spared the cut of the blade in order to write that name. He recalled how easily the flesh sliced, and how little blood had escaped compared to when he'd cut her throat. The savagery, the blood. The copper smell mingled with fear in the seconds before it happened, when realization came to her of what he was about to do.

He stood and walked from room to room, that name carved into every surface like a talisman.

Donovan.

Donovan.

Donovan.

Every memory was tarnished by that name. The grandfather clock in the hall, bought for them by the townspeople to celebrate their fifteenth wedding anniversary, scarred by the name of the man he was doing everything he could to live up to.

The banister rail, which he had spent six weeks building with his own hands, lying broken and warped, the name etched into the wood hundreds and hundreds of times.

Those voices, so dark and in control, spoke to him, whispering, communicating only with him. Telling him that he was more of a man than Donovan ever was. Telling him that in time, it would be his name that would be remembered for the great deeds he would accomplish.

"Are you sure?" he said to the empty house.

A gust of wind whistled through the broken door, channeling through the hallway and moving leaves across the ground, the natural sounds providing the answers he sought.

Donovan was flawed, they told him. He was never the vessel they wanted. Too selfish. Too obsessed with his own agenda.

Henry smiled in the dark.

They continued to praise him, sometimes responding though creaks and moans of the house and the wind, sometimes directly into his head.

He, they said, was the true vessel. He had chosen to give himself fully to them, and now it was time to take the final step to complete his mission and make the transition from the living world to the realm of the dead.

"What do you want me to do?" he asked.

More sounds. A flutter of decaying curtains flapping against glass, the slow opening of a door.

They told him where to go, what he must do. He let them lead him, feet padding on the dirty, litter strewn floors, through the dining room, past the shattered kitchen and to the door leading to the garage. He pushed it open and stood at the threshold, nose wrinkling at the stench. Something had died in there, the smell pungent enough to make an ordinary man's eyes water. Henry, however, wasn't an ordinary man. Not anymore. He was guided by something else. He walked forward, crossing the space where his car would have once been parked, to the workbench. A thick film of dust covered its surface, and without realizing, he started to doodle in it with a fingertip.

D

The small lump hammer. He would need that for the task they'd set him.

O

The screwdriver with the flat tip, and the file that was beside it, the ones owned by his father, the wooden handle worn smooth with age. Those would assist with his transition from man to the monster he was to become.

N

Screwdriver to tooth, the scrape of metal against bone, taste of bitter steel in his mouth. Panting now, fearing the pain that was to come, instantly soothed by the blackness in his head. Hand trembling, not wanting to go through with it. Angry now, so angry. Giving him no choice, giving him no option.

O

Picking up the hammer and holding it under the screwdriver. Asking for assurance it wouldn't hurt, that they would protect him from the pain. Promise given. Assurances they would keep the pain away.

V

First strike, and an explosion of agony as a tooth shattered. Blood, thick and hot, spilling onto the workbench, greedily soaked up by the dust. More in his throat, eyes wet with anger at their deceit and the fanged, amused smile he sensed in them. Next tooth. Another hit. More agony. Spitting fragments and blood, tears hot on his cheeks.

A

On it went. Top and bottom. Shattering his teeth, turning them into uneven daggers. Unimaginable agony. So much blood. Hands trembling, black things in his head smiling. Pushing him on.

N

Setting down the hammer, mouth a broken mess. Not done yet though. Not by a long shot. Picking up the file with trembling hand, lifting it to his mouth, sharpening, sharpening. Each scrape of steel unbearable. Those voices, black and cruel, telling him to use his anger on those who were coming. To turn his frenzy on those who sought to capture him. Too delirious with pain to care, he did as they commanded.

Done. Transition from man to monster complete. Henry stood in the dark, testing his shark-like crimson smile. He looked at the name he had written in the dust, finger still poised on the upward stroke of the 'N', blood still dripping onto it.

No.

Not anymore.

Not him.

He wiped his hand across the dust, erasing the name in a bloody smear.

Beside it, he penned a new word, one which held much greater meaning. He had earned it, they said. He deserved it. Taking a last look around the place he used to call home, he spied his old toolbox, a brown film of oil and grime covering the chipped blue metal casing. Inside, there were things he could use for the display he had in mind, so he grabbed it and headed to where they said she would be, waiting for the pawn he would need so that the endgame could begin, and knowing his legacy had begun with that one word. A word that would become legendary.

That word was Henry.

CHAPTER 32

There was no fear when Melody arrived back in Oakwell. All she felt was a neutral sense of foreboding, heightened by the desolation of the town. She wasn't sure if she could go through with what she intended to do. She had gone on a tour of sorts, revisiting places, which until that point, had only lived in memories long buried.

She'd stopped by the boarded-up Old Oak tavern, remembering her last real day of happiness before everything started to unravel. Her intention was to head to the grounds of the hotel next, the place where Hope House once stood. She didn't quite feel ready to face that yet, so walked the streets instead, leaving her car parked on the edge of town, enjoying the cool air as day faded into night. She found herself at Mrs. Briggs' home.

Like everywhere else, it was an abandoned relic, the once pristine garden overgrown and the walls of the house covered in old graffiti.

Devil's mother was sprayed across the wall and front door, along with several pentagrams and other lewd scrawls. The graffiti, she supposed, was apt. After all, this was the home of the woman who'd given birth to the man who became Donovan.

Giving no consideration to any danger it might put her in, Melody opened the gate, the wood scraping along the path on its loose and broken hinges, and up to the front door, or more accurately, the space where the front door should have been. At some point in the past, someone – perhaps a souvenir hunter or someone anxious to see inside the home of the woman who had spawned the devil – had broken the door off, and it lay in the garden, covered in dirt and moss, the grass growing around and over it, its paint cracked and faded.

Melody looked into the darkened home. The hallway beyond, with its stench of mildew and rot, should have made her turn and run, but instead, knowing the end of her existence had already been decided by fate, she stepped inside, letting the shadows envelop her.

She walked into the sitting room, which appeared enormous now it was free of the clutter that had occupied it the last time she was there. She knew Annie Briggs had met her end in this room, and hesitated, trying to get some sense of her, anything left over that might have survived the years of decay. She entered the room, stepping over broken bottles. Like outside, graffiti covered the walls, and evidence of life existed. Empty beer bottles and the blackened remains of a fire scarred the floorboards. She crossed to the fireplace, finding the memories somehow fitting to present themselves now she was back in Oakwell. They belonged here. She ran a finger lightly across the mantel.

"I knew you would come here."

She didn't turn to face the wet, hissing voice

of Henry Marshall. Nor did she react. She sensed him in the doorway, blocking her escape route, and yet she felt no fear.

"I have as much right to be here as you have," she said.

"They know you're here," Henry said, his voice a low growl. "You know what that means."

"I know what it means. I know this is going to end tonight," she replied, keeping calm and crossing to the broken window, staring out into the street. Henry entered the room, closing the distance to stand behind her.

"You're not afraid anymore," he said, his breath hot on her neck.

"No. Things have changed."

"I could kill you. They want me to do it. I could reach out right now and you wouldn't be able to stop it," he said, his broken mouth making his voice sound strange.

"I know."

"You knew I'd be here. Why did you come to find me?"

"I know you want my son. I came here to give myself in his place. He's been through enough."

She sensed him fidget, and flinched as his foot nudged a bottle, sending it spinning across the floorboards. "You don't get to choose," he whispered. "They don't want you."

She hadn't expected that response, and for the first time, felt a little fearful, but she refused to show it. Somehow, she resisted the temptation to try and flee or even to face Henry. Instead, she continued staring out at the moonlit street.

"Death doesn't scare me anymore. Or this place. What you did to me has already broken me. I started this. I was the one who convinced Steve to move out here. If you're here to take revenge for the Gogoku, then take it out on me."

"They never wanted you," Henry replied, the simplicity of his words making her shudder. "They want the boy. He's coming here. When he does, I'll be waiting."

"He's stronger than you think," she said, not even convincing herself. Henry snorted a laugh, his foul breath tickling the hair against her neck.

"He's just a boy."

She half turned her head, seeing him as a shadowy mass at the periphery of her vision. "And what happens when he gets here?"

He laid a bloody, filthy hand on her shoulder. This time she couldn't help but flinch. "You will witness it. They want you to see him suffer before you die."

She nodded, looking out into the street again. "Then I'd better come with you."

"I expected more fight from you."

"Isn't this what you want? This place has already taken everything from me. What's the point in fighting?"

She sensed his smile as he reached around her, arms over her chest, hands on her body, face beside hers. She wanted to scream or fight, but knew that was what they wanted. Instead, she stood there, lips pursed as she tried to resist. His hands moved over her clothes, then reached into her open jacket, pulling out the knife inside it.

"I was saving that to give to you later in person. I think I owe you it," Melody said.

Henry grunted and tossed the knife into the corner, then released her and stood up straight.

"We should go. They're waiting." He led her out of the house, one hand on her shoulder. She didn't fight or resist, even when they walked off the road and into the dense darkness of Oakwell forest.

CHAPTER 33

They neared Oakwell, the atmosphere in the car tense. Emma was driving, Isaac in the passenger seat. Truman and Mrs. Alma were in the back.

"You okay?" Emma asked, glancing across at Isaac. "You've been really quiet since back at the house."

"You sense them don't you?" Mrs. Alma said from behind him. "Waiting for you."

He didn't answer, but continued to stare out of the window at the trees flashing past his field of view.

"Hey, there's someone up ahead," Emma said, easing her foot onto the brake. In front of them, just beyond the broken and faded sign which proclaimed they had entered Oakwell, were two cars parked on the edge of the road. A blue Nissan with the hood open, and a tan colored car parked in front. The respective drivers were standing by the roadside, and upon seeing them approach, waved them down.

"Keep driving," Truman said from the back.

"We can't just leave them, especially out here."

"Why would anyone else even be out here?"

"They might be lost."

"Come on, surely you don't believe that?" Truman said.

"Too often in the past I've let bad things happen by not helping when I could. I promised myself I wouldn't do it again. Now just be quiet while I see if they're okay."

She pulled up ahead of the stranded vehicles, the glow of the brake lights throwing the figures into a deep red hue. One of them jogged to the window, waiting for her to wind it down, as the other looked on.

"Thanks for stopping," he said, flashing a broad grin.

"Is everything okay?" Emma asked.

"All good. Engine trouble. Damn thing broke down on me."

"What are you doing out here?" Truman asked, watching the man carefully.

"Well, as embarrassing as it is to say, I'm lost. I know what you're thinking. Who the hell can get lost nowadays in the age of satnav, right? The irony is, I actually have one of those things. My wife got me it for Christmas. It's in a drawer in the kitchen. Still, I've always been a map kind of guy so—"

"Where were you heading?" Emma asked, feeling her senses bristle. Something felt off about the entire situation, and she was starting to wish she'd sided with Truman and kept driving.

"We were just passing through," the man said, his broad grin faltering for a second. "What about you?"

"Same," Emma said, unable to shake her uneasiness.

"You know, it's not safe out here. Did you

hear about the escape?"

"What escape?" Emma said, hating the way the man's gaze was so piercing, so invasive.

"Some lunatic. He broke out of a secure facility not too far from here. I was getting worried being out here on my own."

"No, we haven't heard anything." Emma said.

The man shrugged. "I'm sure you'll hear about it in the news. As you can imagine, it's not a comfortable feeling being exposed out here alone."

"Creasefield is some way away from here," Emma said, wanting to be on her way. "You'll be fine. Do you want us to make a call for you?"

"No," the man said, his grin still firmly in place below that all-seeing gaze. "I have a phone."

"So... why don't you call for help?" Truman asked.

"I did. I was just waving you down to warn you about the escapee, that's all."

"Thanks, we appreciate it," Emma said as she started to wind up the window.

"Just one more thing," the man said, putting a hand on the glass to stop Emma. "How did you know?"

"Know what?" Emma said, growing agitated.

"That it was Creasefield the escape came from."

"It's the nearest place. Just a guess."

"Not really," the man said, the grin oozing from his face. "Ringwood is closer, and bigger. Then there's Elmshaw before you'd even consider Creasefield."

"I thought you were lost," Truman said from

the back of the car. "You seem to know a lot about the area for someone who says they don't know where they are."

"Caught me," the man said, showing them a flash of white teeth. "I guess I'm not a good liar."

"Well, it was nice to meet you. Good luck getting home. We need to be going," Emma said, slipping the car into gear.

"I wouldn't," the man said, the grin once again fading. "I might have a gun in my jacket."

"And we might call the police," Emma fired back, nowhere near as convincing as she had hoped to sound.

"I'll save you the trouble. I am the police. Detective Petrov," he said, flashing his I.D. "And I've been waiting for you to show up for almost an hour."

"I'm sorry, I think you have us mistaken for—"

"No," Petrov said, swapping I.D for gun. "I know exactly who I have here. You're Emma Barrett. The kid beside you is Isaac Samson, who I was planning on speaking to back at the site of the car crash before you chose to leave the scene. As you can imagine, I would really, really like to know why you felt the need to kidnap a ten year old boy."

"We didn't kidnap him, we were helping him," Emma said, glancing at the steering wheel, then at the road ahead. Petrov saw her and leaned close, the smell of spearmint gum drifting into the car.

"Now, you might be tempted to do something

foolish and make a break for it, which is all well and good. Just know there are a dozen officers in patrol cars waiting just inside town. There's another roadblock being assembled as we speak a half mile behind you. There's nowhere to go. I'm sure you all appreciate how much trouble you're in. My advice is to cooperate and do as I say. If you do, then you have my word I'll do everything I can to prevent any punishment coming from this." The lie came easily, and he delivered it with conviction to minimize the chance of them driving away. Until more help arrived, it was just him and Kimmel, who shouldn't even have been there at all.

"Please, Officer—"

"Detective."

"Please, Detective, we need to go. I know you have a job to do, but we have something to do here, something you wouldn't understand."

"My wife tells me I'm an understanding guy. Try me."

"Trust me, you wouldn't understand this."

"Well, either you tell me now and we can do this nicely, or I arrest you all, drag you down to the station and you tell me there. Either way, I'll find out what's going on here."

"Detective, please—"

"Okay. Let's do it your way. Everyone out of the car. Right now."

"Please…"

"Young lady, don't make me ask you again. I'm a good man and I like to think of myself as fair. The downside is, I don't have a hell of a lot of patience, and I *really* don't like to repeat myself. I could forgive you for not knowing that before. Now, however, there is no excuse. For the last time, get out of the car."

Emma shut off the ignition and sighed.

"Good choice. Keys please."

Emma handed them over, and Petrov put the gun back into the holster under his jacket. "You two in the front, get out. And before you get any ideas, don't do something stupid like running. Got it?"

They both nodded.

"Alright, then let's do this. You two in the back, stay where you are for now."

Emma and Isaac exited the car and stood in the middle of the road with Petrov, his steely eyes probing and assessing.

"Okay, follow me," he instructed, leading them toward his car.

"What's going on?" Kimmel said, approaching Petrov.

"Work. These two are involved in what's happening out here."

"We don't have time for this. We need to move."

"This won't take a second." Petrov opened the back door to his car. "In you go."

Now they were closer, they could see it was a standard police vehicle, boasting the same wire divider between back seats and driver, and doors which could only be opened from outside. Isaac climbed in first, shuffling across the seat, followed by Emma. Petrov didn't close the door, instead he leaned in.

"I appreciate the cooperation. Now let me give you something to think about before I go and speak to your friends. I don't know what the hell is going on here and that isn't something I like. You say you were helping the kid and maybe that's the case. But until I'm satisfied with your story, you're going nowhere. What I want you two to do is just sit tight and wait here until I speak to your friends over there and see where they fit into this whole damn mess." He closed the door and strode across the street to the other vehicle.

"What are we going to do now?" Isaac said, staring at Emma whilst keeping a close eye on the shadowy figure of Petrov.

"I don't know. I'm trying to think."

"Are we in trouble?"

Emma shook her head. "It's me who's in trouble, not you. Don't worry, okay?"

"They won't stop talking," he sighed, then looked out of the window at Kimmel, who was pacing by the verge.

"I had no idea. You should have said something."

"I was scared," he mumbled. He could see her ghostly figure reflected in the glass behind him.

"We're all scared. You know how important this is though, don't you?"

He nodded.

"And you know we have to get to that place you told us about under the house?"

"Yeah, I know," he said, seeing the image of what was down there; the thing he hadn't told them about because he didn't know how to. "I don't think we need to go there now."

"What do you mean?"

"He's not there."

"Who, Isaac?"

"The bad man. We have to go to him."

"No, Isaac. That's not what Mrs. Alma said."

"It's what they say," the boy whispered, looking across at Emma. "He has my mother."

"Your mother is far away from here. I know you're scared, but this isn't right."

"Yes it is," he said, staring past Emma to Petrov, who was leaning into the other car and questioning Truman and Mrs. Alma. It was then the door opened. They assumed it was Kimmel, but both Emma and Isaac glanced at each other in shock as a man, dressed in a dark blue hoodie, peered up at them, the shadows thrown from his gaunt face. Kimmel lay on the ground, moaning and clutching the back of his head where the man had hit him.

"Be quiet and follow me," Dane Marshall said.

Too shocked to argue, Isaac and Emma climbed out of the car and followed Dane off the road and into the forest.

CHAPTER 34

Melody recognized the tree she was tied to. It was the same one she'd almost hanged herself from in her old life, shortly before she wrongly believed her nightmare was at an end. He'd restrained her there, telling her he had preparations to make, a greeting for those who were on their way, then left her alone in the place where she intended never to return to. He'd been gone for some time, and she could only speculate at what he might be doing. She was tied with her head and shoulders in the deep hollow in which she and Steve had first found the protective charm placed there by Mrs. Briggs.

Her arms were wrapped half around the immense tree trunk and tied at the wrists. There was no escape from her damp confines. She could hear Henry moving around and muttering to himself, but couldn't see him. She wondered, as she stared into the black, if that's what death would be like when it found her. When she'd last thought about it, the idea had terrified her. Now, however, when faced with the alternative of existing as another trapped soul in the forest, an eternity of nothing seemed like a good deal. She realized just how tired she'd become; how weak.

The cancer seemed to have redoubled its efforts in recent weeks, and she wasn't sure quite how much longer she would last. Her shoulders burned and her legs trembled. She needed to sit down, or do anything in order to rest.

"It's time."

She yelped, his voice hot in her ear.

"What are you going to do to me?" she whispered.

"Nothing. Not yet at least. First, you need to witness."

"Witness what?"

"I need you to bring them to me. I need you to draw them in so this can be ended."

"I won't do anything to help you."

He moved closer, beard tickling her cheek, his body pressed against hers, foul breath pungent as he grunted in her ear. "You have no choice in this. They are in control now."

"Not of me."

"No, not of you. But they do have your son. Right now, he's on his way here. We need to make sure he finds you."

"Please, don't do this. You can be saved. You can fight this."

"Why would I want to?"

"You're not Donovan. You're Henry Marshall. You have to try and fight them."

"I know who I am. I'm more than he ever was," he said, words slurred and strange sounding.

"He was a monster. You don't have to be that same thing."

"I know what he was. He was flawed. He didn't give himself fully to them."

"He was an animal," Melody whispered.

"You were no better."

"What do you mean?" she said.

"They told me what you did. How you flirted with him and drew him in, then rejected his advances. That hurt him. He didn't like that."

"He tried to rape me!"

"No, that's not how it was. You were the one being provocative. You answered the door to him half undressed. How else do you think something like that would be perceived?"

"Are you trying to justify it?"

"You led him on."

"You're insane."

"You offered yourself then rejected him when he tried to take it. That drove him mad. Clouded his judgement. They couldn't use him anymore after that. They were just waiting for a new vessel to do their work."

"You?" she said.

She felt his sharp smile by her cheek.

"Why are you doing this? Why can't you just leave us alone?"

"You started this. Before you came to Hope House, no child had been conceived on these lands. You changed that. Everything that's happened since is your doing."

"And you don't think I've suffered enough? I lost my husband. My son. My life."

"It's still not enough."

"What more do the Gogoku want?"

"Is that what you think?" Henry said. She could hear the amusement in his voice, which triggered a fresh surge of fear.

"What do you mean?" she asked.

"This is bigger than them."

"What does that mean?"

He didn't answer. They wouldn't let him. The secret must remain. Instead, he pulled away from her and walked around the back of the tree, out of view. She felt him manipulating the rope holding her in place, freeing her. She staggered away from the trunk and fell to the ground. Marshall appeared next to her, filthy and wild-eyed.

"Come on," he said, holding a grubby hand out to her.

"Where are we going?"

"You know where."

Melody nodded and got to her feet, letting Marshall lead her, knowing that one way or the other, it was about to end.

He led her to the clearing, which was bathed in pale moonlight. She paused at the edge, too afraid to commit to stepping inside its boundaries. Memories long repressed reawakened. She remembered Donovan, stalking like a caged beast on its perimeter when she'd escaped his rape attempt. Even now, she could feel the malevolence emanating from the area. It almost seemed to hum with a power far more amplified than when she'd last been here.

Marshall shoved her forward, sending her stumbling into the clearing. Immediately, the trees on the edges began to sway and hiss, the wind building, further reminding her of the horrors of the past.

"Do you feel them?" Henry asked as he stood in the center of the clearing.

Melody nodded. It was true. She could sense them probing at her; dark, formless things. Gooseflesh raised on her arms.

"They want to know if you can feel how strong they've become."

"Why did you bring me here?" she asked, doing all she could to ignore the supercharged energy surrounding them.

"You need to see. To appreciate how many there are, you need to see like I saw."

She shook her head, eyes flicking between Marshall and the trees. "I don't want to see."

Henry grinned, his mouth a sharp, bloody, hellish thing.

A shark's grin, she thought, and a wave of nausea surged through her.

"They want me to show you. They want me to show you what will happen to your son."

He put a hand on her shoulder. There was no way to stop the images being fired into her brain. Sent by the dark things that surrounded her and channeled by Henry Marshall, they were incredibly graphic. Nothing could stop the scream ejecting itself from the pit of her stomach. Fed by her terror, the trees swayed in appreciation.

II

Petrov heard the scream rolling to him

through the trees. He glanced in the direction from where it came, then to his car, noticing the rear door was open and Emma and Isaac missing.

"You two stay here. Don't move!" he grunted.

"Wait, what's happening?" Truman called to him through the window.

"Stay there!" Petrov snapped as he sprinted toward his car. Kimmel was on his knees, the back of his head bloody.

"What happened? Where the hell are they?" Petrov said as he helped the General to his feet.

"How the hell would I know? Someone hit me on the back of the head. When I came to, they were gone."

"Goddamn it! Get in the car!" Petrov snapped, running to the driver's side. Kimmel climbed in beside him, pausing to close the rear door.

"You know he's going to be waiting for us up there, don't you?" Kimmel said as he carefully touched his wound then examined his bloody fingers.

"I know. That's why we need to find the kid first." Petrov gunned the engine, flooring the accelerator and snaking away down the dirt road toward town.

Truman and Mrs. Alma sat and watched as the twin red taillights disappeared around the bend.

"Screw this," Truman said, climbing out of the back and into the driver's side.

"The officer took the keys."

"Don't worry about that, Mrs. A. It's

covered." He flipped open the glove box and pulled off the spare key taped to the underside of the door. Starting the engine, he set off after Petrov.

CHAPTER 35

Emma and Isaac plunged through the trees, quite unable to believe that Dane Marshall was with them. He'd said little as they made their way through the underbrush.

"Why are you here? Why did you help us?" Emma asked as the ground started to slope upwards, slowing their progress.

"I have my reasons," he replied, looking over his shoulder.

"That's not good enough."

"This isn't the time to talk about it."

"They know we're here," Isaac said, feeling a rush of nausea.

Whispered voices, disjointed snatches of words surrounded them, calling to them.

Emma yelped and stopped.

"What is it?" Dane said, pulling his hood back and turning toward her.

"My arm." She rolled up her sleeve to show four scratches welling up on her forearm, one already seeping blood.

"What the fuck?" Dane said, nervously glancing around him.

"They're trying to scare us," Isaac said, subconsciously reaching out to hold Emma's hand.

"I'd say it's working." Dane fell back in line with the others. "We have to get out of the trees."

"Agreed. This is taking way too long," Emma said.

"We should meet the road somewhere up ahead."

"How can you be so sure?"

"I know this area. I was going to shoot my show here, remember?"

"Yeah, I see that worked out well for you," Emma snapped.

He stopped and faced her. "Look, let me get something straight. What happened then, back at the hotel, wasn't my fault. I was as much a victim as you were."

"Don't give me that shit. You think you can buy forgiveness by helping us?"

"No," Dane said, shaking his head. "I don't. I just want you to understand things from my side. You think it's easy living with what my brother did? He destroyed the lives of so many people and left my family to deal with the consequences. We lost everything."

"You still have your life. Your brother still has his. My friends lost theirs. Isaac lost his father."

"I know. But I can't do anything about that now."

"You sound just as cold as your brother."

"I'm not him. Don't you dare say I am."

"Both of you, stop it!" Isaac shouted. "It's them. The things in the trees, they're making my head hurt."

"You alright kid? You don't look so good," Dane said.

He was right. Emma could see it too. Isaac

was pale, his hair sticking to his forehead with sweat.

"He's fine. Just scared like the rest of us," Emma said. "Come on, we need to keep moving."

They went on in silence. The voices in the wind were easy to ignore after a while. Harder not to acknowledge were the shapes; the shadowy figures that flitted in their peripheral vision, darting between branches. The scratching continued, increasing in ferocity, only Isaac remaining untouched. Their journey felt as if it would last forever, the woods never ending.

"I see the road," Emma said, lurching ahead, eyes wide and afraid. She'd been stretched to breaking point. Crashing through the undergrowth, she was desperate to put some distance between herself and the torment the trees had inflicted upon her. She escaped the stifling canopy, stumbling and falling onto the hard surface of the road, knocking the wind out of lungs. Isaac and Dane arrived seconds later and helped her up.

"Are you alright?" Isaac asked.

She started to cry. Years of repressed grief had finally found its way to the surface, cracking the cold exterior she'd built for herself. Dane stood awkwardly at the side of the road, kicking his feet in the dirt. He was the first to notice the light approaching them.

"Hey, heads up," he warned.

The light grew brighter and more intense, banishing the dark. Under ordinary circumstances, they would have run, yet in this case, none of them had any inclination to go back into the trees and subject themselves to the horrors that waited for them in there. It was then they heard the engine piercing the wind.

"Shit, I bet it's that cop," Dane said, turning toward the woods but unable to commit himself to entering them. Either way it was too late; they knew they'd been seen. The vehicle skidded to a halt, leaving a great cloud of dust in its wake. Petrov climbed out of the vehicle, gun drawn.

"I wondered if I might stumble across you two. I take it your friend here helped you escape?"

"Detective, please, you have to let us go," Emma said.

"I don't think so. If there was any doubt before, let me make this clear. You're all under arrest. Now get in the car."

"Detective, please…"

"I wouldn't test my patience any more than you have already. In case you didn't know, there's a madman on the loose and I don't want any more deaths. You people might think it's safe to run around in the woods, but I'm not prepared to let you get yourselves killed. Now get in the damn car."

He pointed the gun at them for emphasis as he opened the door with his free hand.

Emma and Isaac got in, heads hanging low. Dane went to follow, when Petrov closed the door.

"Not you. We've met before, haven't we? Back here when the massacre happened. Dane, isn't it?"

"Yeah."

"This day just keeps on giving. Lose one Marshall brother and find another. Hands on the roof of the car please."

Dane did as he was told, placing his palms on the roof and spreading his feet.

"I see you know the drill. That's good. Makes things easier. Now, if I search you, am I going to find any weapons?"

"I have a gun in my jacket," Dane said.

"Alright, I like the honesty. I'm going to reach in and take it. I don't want you to make any sudden moves that might make me shoot you. Got it?"

"Understood."

Petrov took the gun then stepped back.

"Okay, now turn around."

Dane complied, staring at the ground.

"You'd better start talking. What the hell are you doing out here?"

"My brother called me. He told me if I wanted to stop the killings, I had to come here."

"When did this happen?"

"Last night."

"And you didn't think to report it?"

"No. He didn't stay on the line long enough for me to talk to him. He just said I had to come here. I reacted."

"So what took you so long to get here?" Petrov asked.

"I got here as quick as I could. I was out of town."

"You haven't visited your brother since he was first locked up in Creasefield. Why would he decide to make contact with you now?"

"Because my brother is a manipulative asshole. He thrives on this. On being the center of attention. Whatever he has planned, he wants me to see it."

"Alright, say I buy that. Why did you free these two from custody?" Petrov said, nodding toward Isaac and Emma.

"He told me I had to. He said he knew you would have them and that I had to bring them. I was trying to do the right thing and save a life."

"That's not your job. It's mine."

"You sure about that?" Dane said, sneering at Petrov. "The way I see it, my brother might well slaughter you or any of these other people without a second thought. He might not be so quick to do that to me, which I think gives me an advantage."

Kimmel rolled the window down. "Detective, we don't have time for this."

"Come on, all of you. In the car." Petrov opened the door and waited for Dane to get in, shutting it after him. He turned the key in the ignition, and swung back onto the dirt road, the car bouncing and jostling in the ruts.

"Here's the deal. When we get to the hotel I'm going to call this in and get some officers up here. You all stay in the car. No exceptions."

"I thought you said you already had people in the area?" Emma said.

"I don't have backup, I moved them off to search for Marshall after the car accident. I lied so you wouldn't run. Right now it's just me."

"Are you fucking kidding me?" Dane said.

"I was about to call it in when you helped these two escape," Petrov replied. "Trust me, this place will be swarming before you know it."

"This is crazy," Dane muttered. "You know how dangerous my brother is."

"He's still just a man," Petrov fired back.

"No he isn't," Isaac said from the back. "He's one of them now."

"Detective, look out!" Kimmel yelled.

Petrov slammed on the brakes, the car struggling to decelerate on the loose surface.

The scene ahead of them was thrown into harsh light by the car's headlights. Emma pulled Isaac close to her, shielding him as best she could, but it was too late. He'd already seen it.

Either by design or at the hands of nature, two trees had fallen from opposite sides of the narrow dirt road, meeting in the middle above the car, forming an A-frame of sorts.

Hanging from the upper branches in a sick display was a woman, or more accurately, what was left of her. It was tied there with bungee ropes, obviously left for them to find.

Only the upper torso remained, skin sheared back to expose white shafts of ribs, stomach cavity hollowed out. Her arms were outstretched on the branches, her intestines wrapped around her like a gruesome scarf, the slick innards glistening in the moonlight. Her head hung to one side, mouth agape in a silent scream. Worst of all were her eyes. They were nothing but bloodied sockets, each containing a single red rose. Around her neck was a cardboard sign, the writing on the front penned in bloody finger smears.

Find me.

The wind pushed the disgusting display back and forth, swaying it provocatively. Emma screamed then, releasing the pent up terror she'd held on to successfully up to that point. The wind rose in a mocking scream of its own, one much louder than hers.

Petrov and Kimmel exchanged glances. Both of them knew who was responsible for the display. If there was any doubt, Dane vocalized it, breaking the silence.

"Henry."

Petrov put the car into gear, inching forward.

"Nobody look," he said as they passed under the bloody, broken corpse. Nobody spoke, even as Petrov picked up speed and headed toward the hotel.

CHAPTER 36

The hotel grounds were deserted. Petrov got out of the car, drew his weapon and scanned the landscape. Kimmel followed after him, staring into the trees, aware that in the dark, there were almost limitless places where Henry Marshall could be hiding. Petrov ducked back into the car. "You wait here. I have to go and find the source of that scream."

"It was my mother," Isaac said. He was drenched in sweat now, and his eyes were lidded and heavy.

"How do you know that?" Petrov asked.

Isaac shrugged. "I just know."

"Are you alright, kid?" Dane asked.

"My head hurts. They're close," Isaac mumbled.

"Look, just wait here. I'll be back soon."

"We need some form of protection," Dane said. "Let me have my gun back, just in case we need it."

"No. I can't do that," Petrov said.

"Well you can't just leave us here without any protection at all," Emma added.

Petrov hesitated, torn as to what to do. "Damn it," he grunted, opening the car door. "Come with me and stay close. Keep behind me at all times, got it?"

Emma had to help Isaac out of the car. He was

holding his head and muttering under his breath.

"What's wrong with him?" Kimmel asked.

"It's this place," Emma replied. "He's sensitive to it."

Petrov was on the radio, trying to call in backup. "Goddamn it. Reception is awful up here."

He eventually managed to get through, and although weak, he was able to call in the backup they urgently needed. He tossed the radio handset on the seat and turned to them. "They're on their way. As soon as they arrive you'll be safe."

"What about my brother?" Dane asked.

"We'll find him."

"Detective," Kimmel said quietly.

Petrov looked in the direction in which Kimmel was staring. The steel shutter covering the door to the hotel had been pried away, exposing the black maw and whatever secrets lay beyond. Penned on the shutter was the same message as was on the sign around the girl's neck.

Find me.

"Wait here," Petrov said as he unchecked the safety on his weapon.

"You're not going in there?" Emma said, hugging Isaac against her.

"I'm not giving him a chance to escape. Not again."

"You know where he'll be, don't you, Detective?" Kimmel said, his face tense and, for the first time, showing signs of fear.

"Yeah, I have a pretty good idea."

"And what about the rest of us?" Dane asked, walking toward Petrov. "You go in there and leave us out here without any protection?"

"There are officers on the way."

"And until then? What if my brother isn't even in there?" Dane said. "What if he's watching from the trees waiting for you to go inside so he can attack us?"

"I thought you said you'd be safe because he's your brother."

"I thought you said I wasn't," Dane fired back.

"He's in there alright," Kimmel said. "Waiting for us."

"I don't know who you are old man, and I don't care. I sure as shit ain't gonna take your word for that. Especially after what we just saw on the road."

Petrov hesitated, before handing Dane the gun he'd confiscated earlier. "Ok, just for protection. Don't follow us in there."

Petrov and Kimmel strode over to the hotel's entrance and looked into the absolute darkness beyond.

"Here," Kimmel said, handing Petrov a small flashlight from his pocket.

"Thanks." Petrov shone the beam into the hollowed out foyer, illuminating the dirty floors and boarded up windows.

"Alright," he said, looking at Kimmel. "Let's do this."

He ducked under the steel sheet, closely followed by Kimmel, the two instantly swallowed by the darkness.

Emma and Dane stood outside, unsure of what to do, when they heard a vehicle approaching. They turned toward the road, the dim illumination of headlights piercing the dark, growing brighter by the second.

"I hope that's the police," Emma said, glancing at Dane. "You might want to put the gun out of sight just in case."

Dane looked at it as if he'd forgotten it was there, and tucked it into the back of his waistband before covering it with his hoodie.

Emma's excitement faded when she saw that the new arrival wasn't the police after all, but her own car. Truman parked up, and he and Mrs. Alma got out. His eyes were wide and disbelieving. They didn't have to discuss why. They knew it was because of the awful display hanging above the road.

"Where's the cop?" Truman said, eying Dane mistrustfully. "And who's this?"

"It's a long story. Are you both ok?" Emma said.

"Yeah, we're okay apart from… coming in here."

Emma nodded. "We saw. The detective is going after Henry now. He's in the hotel."

"Hey, kid, come back!" Dane shouted, but Isaac was already moving. At first, it looked as if he were going to follow Petrov and Kimmel into the hotel, but instead he skirted around it, keeping close to the building before disappearing out of sight around the corner.

"Isaac, come back!" Emma shouted, giving chase.

Dane and the others followed, heading into the night and whatever waited there.

II

Isaac headed for the bridge, sprinting in the effortless way children could. He knew it had been wrong to fake his headache, but it was something he'd needed to do so that he could make his escape.

The voices were there of course, probing and thrashing around his head, but more pressing was the need to go to what he knew as 'the bad place'. He charged into the trees, the moonlight snuffed out by the canopy. Even the dark didn't stop him. He knew where every root and every rock was, even though he'd never been there before. Emma and the others trailed behind, tripping and stumbling, branches whipping into their faces.

The wind howled, sending the trees into a never ending tango of moving leaves. The voices, which now lived inside his head, were screaming at him, using words he didn't understand. When that happened, they showed him visually explicit images of what would be done to him and those with him if he didn't follow their instructions. Pale and frightened, he pushed on.

Emma and the others were close behind, and as before, were being plagued in a more physical manner. Emma continued to be scratched, her arms a crisscross of bloody welts. Dane was also suffering the same fate. He grunted and stumbled, watching as a perfectly formed bite mark appeared on his forearm. The most affected was Truman. As a man who still didn't believe in anything to do with the paranormal, and had mostly taken Emma's words on faith, he struggled to understand the inexplicable assault he was under. Shadows danced on the edge of his vision, only to be gone when he turned toward them. Nonexistent fingers poked and prodded him. Worse were the words. Screams delivered with fury right next to his ear. He became detached from the group, falling further behind as he was tormented. Mrs. Alma was also troubled, her lips pursed as she endured her own similar horrors. She stumbled, her hands and knees hitting the ground, and Truman helped her to her feet, the two falling even further behind.

CHAPTER 37

Petrov stood at the entrance to the tunnel. "Looks like he's expecting us," he said, glancing at Kimmel. He had led them through the deserted first floor of the hotel, senses on full alert, waiting for the attack. He'd known of course, that the attack wouldn't come, that it was just his way of avoiding the prospect of descending into the tunnels beneath Hope House, forcing himself to go on. Climbing down the ladder again after what had happened before had been one of the most difficult things he'd ever had to do.

Torches had been placed down the length of the hall, showing them the way forward, flames flickering and making shadows dance on the low ceilings and uneven walls. They might have stood there forever if not for Kimmel, who took the first step forward.

"Wait," Petrov whispered, showing him his gun. "Me first. Just in case." The General nodded and let Petrov take the lead.

Petrov hesitated. The red fuel can Henry used to light the torches was sitting against the wall. "Grab that," he said to Kimmel.

"Why?"

"We don't know when the light will run out."

"What about the torches? Should I bring one?"

"No. I don't want him to see us coming,"

Petrov said as he led the way.

Even though the air was frigid, Petrov was drenched in sweat.

"You realize how crazy this is, don't you?" Kimmel whispered as they cautiously made their way down the passage. "Marshall could be anywhere, just waiting to pounce on us."

"I'm trying not to think about it too much."

They moved on, aware as they went deeper of that awful feeling growing stronger. The hostile malevolence was much worse down here near its source. Now, it was able to manifest itself in a physical way. Shadows flitting across in front of them.

Disembodied screams and cackling laughter came from all sides. Subconsciously, they drew together as they entered the altar room, its stone altar devoid of decoration. It was here that Petrov had seen the part human, part animal tribute, but it had since been removed, leaving only the faint smell of death behind.

Kimmel looked at the four chambers leading off the main room. "Which one is it?"

"I don't know. I never made it past here."

"He could be in any one of them," Kimmel said, eying the four entrances.

"Didn't the army map this place out?"

"Our technology malfunctioned every time we attempted to do so. After what happened up in the clearing, we were never going to send people down here."

"Alright, then I guess it's down to us."

Petrov led them to the first entrance, noting

that the tunnel beyond had collapsed some time ago, the space filled with dirt up to the roof.

"That leaves three," Petrov whispered, his breath fogging in the cold air.

The second door opened onto a square room. Kimmel drew a sharp breath as he took it all in. The room was filled with bones, or more accurately, skeletons. They sat in perfect formation, leaning against the walls. Many had long since collapsed and were now littering the floor, while others had retained some of their ancient flesh, the dry, leathery covering barely holding the bones in place.

"Jesus, what the hell is this?" Kimmel swore. "These bodies must have been down here for hundreds of years."

"I don't know. Look at how they line up, it's like they were deliberately placed this way."

"We should move on," Kimmel said. "I don't like how exposed we are here."

"I couldn't agree more." They walked to the two remaining tunnels, neither betraying any hint of which they should choose. Unlike the other tunnel, there were no torches to light their way, the black secrets beyond remaining shrouded in mystery and darkness.

"Kimmel, give me that flashlight."

Petrov switched it on, swinging its beam into the first chamber. A corridor, low and narrow, delved deeper into the earth, the torch beam barely penetrating the stifling void. As desperate as he was to find Henry, he wasn't quite in the right place to venture into those black depths yet.

He moved toward the other chamber, gun held at arm's length with the torch beside it. He followed his training, keeping close attention to his angles as he shone the beam into the space beyond. Like the room filled with human remains, it was square, a concrete chamber around ten feet by twenty.

"Jesus Christ, what the hell is that?"

"Graffiti, although it's pretty spectacular," Petrov muttered as he stood in silence, staring at the artwork adorning the entire length of the wall. Even though the concrete canvas had cracked and the paintwork had faded with age and exposure, it didn't hide how talented, and possibly deranged, its creator was.

It was, at first glance, a nature scene. Towering trees grew around what was plainly Hope House, which dominated the center of the piece. The artist had daubed sunlight in diffused patterns across half of the property, which was expertly painted in yellows, browns and greens. At first sight it was perfectly natural until the text daubed in sharp red font across the top encouraged the viewer to look deeper.

The trees curved toward the house, seeming to reach out for it with talon-like branches. The house itself also appeared off somehow, as if the angles didn't quite fit together properly. It could have been forgiven as the artist not possessing a full grasp of perspective, if not for the flawless creation of the rest of the work.

It seemed that, for whatever reason, the decision had been taken to give the walls of the property the kind of nauseating angles which made the viewer uncomfortable.

A thin mist covered the ground in the scene, clinging to the trunks of the trees. Upon closer inspection, countless faces could be seen in the mist, some no more than vague forms painted into the curls and tendrils. Every one of the ethereal faces was screaming. Between the trees were animals. There was a lifelessness to the way they had been painted, eyes dead, slivers of red visible in the shadows under the beasts necks.

Most disturbing of all, however, was the bedroom window of the house. A light was on, casting its yellow glow out into the dusk, and a vague figure of a faceless man holding a baby under one arm could be seen in the room.

It appeared at first glance that he was holding up the curtain with the other, perhaps to look out at the night.

Either by design or some kind of optical trick, the scratchy way the curtain had been brushed made it resemble not cloth, but a sharp bladed knife being held above the child, perhaps ready to sacrifice it to whatever waited out in the dark. The writing above the piece fitted the image perfectly. It read:

'The truth is no words.'

"I don't like this," Kimmel said. "I mean, who the hell would paint something like this? How? This place has been sealed up since our people left."

"Unless there's another way in," Petrov replied as he stepped further into the room. He wanted to take a closer look, to examine the sometimes delicate, sometimes aggressive brushstrokes up close.

His initial reaction had been one of repulsion, but now, the more he looked and saw the sheer depth of the work, the more he thought it was beautiful. He stepped closer, casting the torch beam fully onto it and was now able to see the artistry. It resonated with an energy of its own, as if it were something created just for him, something that had waited in the silence under the abandoned house for him to discover, and was only now showing itself in all its glory.

He took another step closer, lowering his gun. He had a bizarre impulse to touch it, to press his hand or perhaps his face to that cold concrete wall, to breathe in the paint.

He wondered if he would smell the scents of the things that had been painted: the deep richness of earth, the sweetness of grass and leaves, the copper tang of blood.

Petrov reached out, tentative, unsure why he felt so compelled to put his hand on the mural. Palm flat, he touched it to the cold concrete. As soon as he did so, it was like he'd set off a trigger. A surge of information, an influx of knowledge, fired into his brain. He squeezed his eyes closed as it took on a more visual feel. Instantly, he understood exactly where he was and what the place they were in was used for.

CHAPTER 38

The Gogoku boy comes of age between his fifteenth and seventeenth year. It is at this time that their people hold an initiation ceremony, usually performed by the village Elder, the one who garners the most respect from his people. Such a group of boys now stand in the center of the village, huddled together and afraid.

They know of course that many of them will not return from the ceremony. The village is small, its simple huts constructed of wood and dry grasses, the buildings arranged in a circular formation around the outer perimeter of the clearing in tribute to the god eye Rakh-Mon.

Eto, the village Elder, strides out from his hut. He has been in power for three seasons, and is feared by all. A broad man with powerful arms and legs, he is wearing his full initiation apparel: white paint on his face representing the passing of the dead, a red streak on his forehead drawn in the blood of a chicken.

He stands before the five boys, looking at them. He speaks, the dialect of their language short, his teeth deliberately broken and filed into points, terrifying the children as he addresses them.

They, of course, know what is to come. The initiation ceremony takes place twice yearly, and this particular group have watched it take place enough times for their fears to be justified. The rest of the Gogoku come to the center of the village: older men, teens who had already been initiated, women, some with young children who would one day have to endure the same process. They stand and watch, even the mothers of those set to be initiated look on with curiosity more than love, wondering if their child will be strong enough to be deemed worthy of taking their place in the community.

Silence falls on the clearing. The Elder looks at the children, cold eyes on the fearful.

He speaks to them, telling them that not all will survive, and that some had already seen their last sunrise. He leads them away from the village, into the cool shade of the forest.

The children follow, trying to hide their nerves as best they can. Eto leads them through the trees, moving silently. They reach the river and he takes them across, wading through the cold waters to the opposite bank. More trees slope up a steady incline, the peak of which is their destination. The children's fear grows as they see the clearing made by the Gogoku men. Eto leads them into it. There, in the ground, is the hole.

The children stand around it in silent awe. The trees around them hiss and groan, leaves shuddering even though there's no breeze. Eto stares at the boys, eyes burning into each of them. He, of course, has already endured what they are about to. He points to the hole, offering no words, no encouragement. The children obediently descend, lowering themselves down by ropes tied to the surrounding trees. Eto watches as the last of them reaches the floor. He goes to each rope in turn, pulling them back to the surface, removing any means of escape. Elder and children look at each other, and then Eto turns and leaves them to their fate.

The children walk down the tunnel, close to each other, the dim torchlight their only company. The smell is pungent, a sickly stench of rot. They inspect the markings on the earthen walls, the clawing desperation to escape of those who had come before.

A rumble is heard through the dark. They know what has caused it, and some are already being changed, their eyes glazing. The others do nothing to help them. They know the more of their kind that die, the better their own chances of survival are.

The group enters the altar room, the walls adorned with crude paintings left by the Gogoku men in tribute to the thing that lies below. On the altar is a boy of their age, or more accurately, what's left of him. White ribs poke from rotten flesh; milky eyes are turned to the heavens as if in prayer. He has been hacked into a pulpy mess and left for them to see.

The group huddles closer, or at least those who haven't begun to feel the chamber's strange effects do. The others stare blankly, eyes glassy, mouths agape. Those are the weak, the ones already infected by the things that speak to them.

They file into one of the sub-chambers, an annex of the main one, and line up along both walls. As one they sit, shoulder to shoulder, arms touching. This is where they will wait and either live or die.

The room vibrates, and the thing living deep in the darkness below calls to them. The weak, those already affected, go first.

Two of them stand, wordlessly leaving their companions. They stumble to the tunnel entrance and descend into the void, called by the thing they are already slaves to.

It goes on. Hours blend into days. The tributes continue as the voices whisper and scheme, corrupt and cast doubts. Each of them has brought only a small amount of food, and as the mental and physical toll of their torture begins to wear them down, more lose the battle of wills and venture into the tunnels below.

Four days pass, and of the original fifteen, only seven now remain in the holding room. Weak and exhausted, drained and close to death, they wait to see if they will be called.

One by one, they begin to die, too broken and weak to fight. The last of them, a boy of fourteen, desperately fights the coming death, fights the voices that even now try to corrupt and convince him to go into the dark. He resists, his shallow breathing becoming labored. He can't fight anymore. He inhales.

Silence.

Death brings serenity to the chamber. Soon, the eight who went into the dark emerge. They are no longer afraid. They have become one with the thing below, and have earned their right to live. Silently, they begin to remove the bodies, taking them to feed their new master. When it is done, they return to the chamber, pausing at the tribute. They understand its purpose now. Sometimes, one of the chosen attempts to flee, refusing to give themselves completely. This is what they become. This is what no boy wants to become. They file back toward the entrance, squinting as the first sunlight they have seen for five days touches them. Eto is waiting; watching. He lowers the ropes and they climb, no longer boys, but men.

Eto says nothing to them as they ascend, weak and exhausted, but alive. Later, the villagers will host a feast in their honor. The last of them clambers onto the surface and begins the short walk back to the village. Eto hesitates for a second, then follows, knowing that for now, their master is satisfied and peace will exist until it demands sacrifice once more.

Petrov inhaled, staggering back from the painting, dropping both weapon and torch. The glass lens of the torch smashed on the ground, plunging them into darkness for a second before the light flickered back on.

"What was that? What the hell just happened to you?"

"I know what this place is. I know what happened here," Petrov gasped, senses reeling. Now that he knew what the purpose of the place was, the voices swirling around in his head took on a whole new meaning.

Kimmel grabbed him by the arm. "What is it? What's got you so spooked?"

Petrov tried to explain, to give Kimmel some kind of answer, but his throat was dry and the words wouldn't come out.

"The room with the bodies," he managed at last. "None of them were suitable, Kimmel. None of them fitted the bill. That's why it made them attack their own. That's why the village burned. That's why they were cursed."

"What people? What the hell are you talking about?"

Petrov ignored him. The voices in his head filled in the blanks and missing spaces that making contact with the painting had missed.

"They tried to make amends. That's why they

raided the neighboring villages. That's why they took the children, so they could feed it. So they could satisfy it and stop it torturing their minds."

Kimmel backed away, cautious of the wild look in Petrov's eyes.

"It was never enough. Never enough to make them stop. In the end, Eto burned them all. Every last one of them, then threw himself into the flames. But it still wasn't enough." He laughed; a short bark, which had no place in such a hostile environment. "It demanded more. Always more. Always more. That's why that animal was down there when I first came here. The cat with the wings. Donovan and Annie Briggs… They tried to please it. Tried to make it an offering."

He laughed again. "It was never going to be enough. Not some cobbled together animal. Not for its needs. Not by a long shot."

"Goddamn it, pull yourself together!" Kimmel shouted, shaking Petrov by the shoulder, but his words came without conviction. There was no denying it. Here in the dim, flickering light of the torch beam, he was as afraid of Petrov as he was of the environment they were in.

"They built the house in the wrong place. Too close to this thing. Too close," Petrov muttered, glancing back at the painting. "Jones knew. He thought filling the hole in would be enough."

"Jones? Are you talking about Michael Jones?"

Petrov nodded. "He never told anyone what he'd found. He wanted this place. Had already committed to building here."

A noise came out of Petrov then, a pained whine. "If he'd just let the forest take this place back, it could all have been avoided. All of it. Why did you have to build here?"

He glared at Kimmel and shoved him. "Why did you have to build it here!" he screamed.

Kimmel backed away, holding his hands up. "Just relax, take it easy. This place is doing something to you. You're not used to it."

"Even when it was sealed it could still get to them… in here." He tapped his temple. "It was only when Donovan dug it out and opened the tunnels that it was able to reach out. That it could further its influence away from the clearing."

"Detective, I think we need to get out of here."

"You started this," Petrov said, eyes glazed as he turned toward Kimmel, seeing what the voices told him to see. "This is all your fault, Michael."

"I'm Kimmel, goddamn it, pull yourself together."

Petrov grinned and picked up his weapon, firing off three shots at Kimmel.

CHAPTER 39

Isaac was first to reach the clearing. He stood at its edge, unsurprised by what awaited him. The others caught up and stared in fear, while Isaac simply waited, completely calm.

Henry Marshall stood in the center, lit by a pale moon. Melody stood in front of him, his filthy hand on her shoulder. Isaac began to walk toward him, but Emma pulled him back, throwing a protective arm around him. Henry showed them the nearest thing to a smile his broken mouth would allow.

"I knew you would find me," he said, staring at Isaac before letting his eyes drift to those behind. The grin slid off his face. "I don't know why you brought these people with you."

Dane stepped forward, but wasn't quite brave enough to venture into the clearing.

"I've come to help you, Henry. To take you out of here. Nobody else needs to get hurt."

"I don't need your help. For once, I'm doing something on my own. Something you can't do better, or quicker. Something for me. Something that's mine."

"Henry, you can't escape. The police are on their way. If you don't want them to shoot you, then you need me."

"I don't care if they shoot me," Henry snapped.

"Henry, please—"

"This doesn't concern you. This is about the boy and me."

"You're alone here, Henry. You can't stop us all."

Henry looked at Melody, head down and crying, and then at the group by the clearing. "What makes you think I'm alone?"

Sounds came from behind them; chattering, heavy whispers and grunts. The group stared down the path as gravel crunched, branches broke, and the echo of disembodied footsteps lurched toward them. It was an involuntary action.

The weight and hostility of the atmosphere forced them into the clearing. The instant they were within its perimeter, the sounds stopped, plunging them into an absolute silence which was somehow even worse. They huddled together, frightened and unsure of which was worse: Henry, or the things that surrounded them.

"What do you want?" Emma said, breath fogging in the cold air.

"He wants me," Isaac muttered, pulling free of Emma's hand.

Emma and Mrs. Alma glanced at each other, the older woman giving a barely perceptible shake of the head.

"No," she said, putting a hand on his shoulder. "That's not happening."

"How about an exchange?" Henry said, enjoying the unfolding events. "One Samson for another. Mother for son."

"No," Emma said more firmly. The trees around them hissed in defiance, pushing them closer together.

"You know what they'll do to you if you refuse?" Henry said, looking at each of them in turn. "Did you really think you would be able to stop them? A confused lesbian slut, an old spiritualist whore and the descendant of a nigger slave. What a joke." Henry leaned over Melody's shoulder, bringing his other hand up toward her throat. "She came here thinking she could stop them until I showed her. Look at her now."

Melody flinched away from him, head down, trembling.

"You might think it's me she fears, but it's not." He looked to the trees, enjoying the theatrics. "It's them."

Dane reached back, going for the gun tucked into his jeans. Mrs. Alma touched his arm, stopping him. Dane let his hand fall back to his side as his brother went on.

"None of you will be allowed to leave here alive unless you hand over the boy."

"That isn't happening, Henry," Dane said, taking a cautious step forward. "I know you better than anyone. You don't want to do this."

Henry grinned, a monstrous image which caused his brother to flinch. "You knew the man I was. You don't know the monster I am now."

"So what do we do? The boy stays with us, Henry. Nothing is going to change that."

Henry considered it for a moment, licking his tongue against his broken teeth. "Maybe you're right. Maybe I misjudged you all. Maybe, if an exchange is off the cards, I don't need the boy's mother. Maybe I'll tear out her throat right here in front of him. How would that be? Both parents killed by the same hand."

"No!" Isaac screamed, pulling free of Emma and running toward the center of the clearing. Emma tried to follow but was pulled back. At first, she thought it was Truman, or maybe even Mrs. Alma, but as she was thrown to the floor, she realized whoever had grabbed her had no earthly presence. She sat in the dirt, still able to feel the pinch of the invisible fingers gripping her, holding her fast. The rest looked on as Isaac sprinted forward, standing just ten feet from his mother and her demonic captor.

"Please... don't hurt her," he pleaded as he stared at the man who'd plagued his dreams for so long. He tried to look at his mother, but she had her head down, silently sobbing and shaking as she dealt with the trauma of whatever Henry had shown her.

"They don't want her. They want you," Henry said, leaning his chin on Melody's shoulder. "Walk to me and I'll send her toward you. An exchange." He whispered.

"You promise you won't hurt her?" Isaac said, forcing himself to look Henry in the eye.

"Oh I promise," Henry said, stifling a smile. "I won't hurt her at all."

"Okay, I'll do it," Isaac said, glancing back to the others at the edge of the clearing. Their mouths moved as they gesticulated and shouted, yet he could hear nothing. He turned back toward Henry. "I'm coming over," he said, taking a step toward him. He wanted to run, of course, but felt like he had no choice but to comply. The probing things in his head were in a frenzy now, screeching and wailing as they urged him on, warning him that those he was with would suffer slow, painful deaths unless he did as they said.

He walked closer, his feet acting independently. Henry shoved Melody toward him, barking at her to walk. She flinched at the sound of his voice, but did as he asked. Mother and son crossed, and for a second locked eyes. Isaac took a sharp breath. Something in his mother had broken. He could see it even in the pale light of the moon. Her eyes were unfocused, indifferent. Her face pale, mouth slightly agape. He wasn't even sure she recognized him as she moved past, trudging toward the opposite end of the clearing as Isaac took the last few steps toward whatever awaited him.

He reached Henry, standing in front of him, a bloody, filthy, living nightmare that towered over his slight frame. Henry grinned, and with the moon at his back, Isaac finally felt absolute deep-seated fear. His stomach rolled violently, and he turned to run, snapping out of whatever spell had entranced him, but it was too late. Henry clamped a hand on his shoulder, pulling him close.

The clearing exploded in noise.

The sounds, which to him had been muted, thundered back: The screams of Emma and the others pleading with him not to go, the incessant howl of the wind as it shook the trees with a violence that was terrifying in its own right, and finally, Henry. Henry laughing.

On the edge of the clearing, the same spell that bound Melody was also broken. She collapsed in front of Emma, letting out a scream of her own, trying to scramble back to Isaac. Truman and Dane held her back, letting her grieve, letting her screams feed the things in the trees, which increased their activity, sending a rain of leaves into the clearing.

"What do we do now?" Emma shouted to Mrs. Alma, who, of them all, seemed the calmest.

"Nothing," the old woman said.

"What do you mean? What about the reason we came? What we talked about?"

Mrs. Alma turned to Emma, the defeat in her face clear. "Without the boy, we can't cleanse this place."

"Then we have to get him back," Emma screamed. "We have to."

"No," Mrs. Alma said, shaking her head. "His fate is decided. Death is coming to him. And coming to him soon."

"I can't accept that. I won't accept it!" Emma screamed, now struggling to be heard above the bluster.

"You have to," Mrs. Alma replied coldly. "It's over. They've won."

CHAPTER 40

Kimmel moved down the tunnel in the pitch dark, the bullet wound in his shoulder burning with a fiery intensity. He stumbled and almost fell, pausing to listen.

He could hear Petrov following him some distance behind, still talking, still rambling. Kimmel pushed on, unsure where he was going. Unlike before, there was no light to guide him, his torch left behind in the painting room when he'd run from Petrov.

Instead, he had been forced to inch through a thick sea of claustrophobic black. Even those terrible voices that had plagued them since they'd arrived grew silent. Feeling his way across the wall, he was aware of the ground dropping away, taking him deeper underground. Time seemed to stop entirely. There was no sense of direction, no sense that he existed in the world as he knew it. The opacity of his surroundings made it easier to see those faceless entities as they flashed in and out of the ether. Mouthless elongated things with sunken holes for eyes. The torture went on, but still he went deeper, Petrov's taunting forcing him to go where his instinct screamed at him not to.

The tunnel began to grow lighter, a soft glow ahead giving definition to the walls and enabling him to at least see where he was going. With sight came other senses. A stench beyond description, a putrid, rotten ammonia-like smell that burned his nostrils. The tunnel opened into a wider room, another chamber supported by ancient wooden beams. Kimmel could finally see the deep red staining on the arm of his jacket. Lights were placed intermittently down the length of the chamber, flickering and spluttering. Kimmel saw a wooden torch discarded in the middle of the room, its end black from recent use. He suspected Marshall had done this, showing them where he was. Kimmel was painfully aware that he was running away from one threat and straight into another. Something caught his eye, a flash of metal from down the hall.

"Goddamn," he muttered, heading toward it.

The GT16 lay on its side where it had been left, devoid of power, a relic destined to remain there forever. Kimmel paused, not recognizing the particular model but knowing it was military hardware. No doubt some fancy new prototype brought in by Fisher to remotely explore the tunnels.

Petrov's voice came to him, uncomfortably close, pushing him to move on. He hurried past the abandoned unit, hoping to put some distance between himself and the detective, then paused, staring at the floor. Bones littered the ground: skulls and ribcages, arms and legs. All broken and discarded. He tried to mentally guess how many there were, but the more he looked, the more he could see. As he gazed at them, the voices returned.

They caught him unawares, assaulting his

senses, clambering into his brain and filling it with vile imagery. Kimmel fought back, pushing them out and gritting his teeth as he pressed on, wading through the human boneyard, trying not to think about what he was stepping on or how strong the stench was.

He hesitated; the torches ahead were unlit, the tunnel beyond opaque and oppressive. It was the fear of Petrov catching up to him that forced him on into the darkness. He stumbled on, bones displaced under his feet, hissing, chattering voices in his ears, unseen hands clawing at his clothes. All of it horrifying enough, but not as much as the thoughts being placed into his mind; ideas and images he was no longer able to fight. Not here, not so close to the source. Familiar voices spoke to him like they always used to. The voices of the dead.

His sister – killed in a car crash back in the summer of eighty-six.

His mother – in her grave for almost twenty years.

His best friend, Joe Davies – killed by an IED in Baghdad years earlier.

All of them vying to advise him, their poisonous words clinging to his mind like intertwined, overgrown thorns. They alternated between soothing, friendly tones and sneering, barked commands and insults. Worse still were the images, fragmented pictures placed in his head by his tormentors.

Plunging his wife's head into the flames of a roaring fire, holding her there as she kicked, thrashed and tried to scream through melting lips.

Dismembering his daughter. Hacking her body into a pulpy mess. Eating her flesh. The chew of sinew. The copper taste of blood.

Tearing his son's stomach open, guts steaming in the cold night air.

Next he recalled the names of the men he'd lost under his command. Men with wives, girlfriends and families, who'd survived some of the most brutal and violent warzones on the planet only to lose their lives in the shithole of a town above his head. He recited their names in his mind as he continued to wrestle against those mental demons and stumble further toward whatever awaited him.

Reynolds.
Layfield.
Shaw.
Landro.
Levas.
Blanchard.
Drench.
Cook.
Williams.
Brook.
Frederick.

With each name, the black things in his brain showed him how each had died. How each had been tortured, and how, in the end, each had begged for death. Kimmel let out a low groan, one which seemed to delight the things in the dark.

Reynolds. *Skewered on a spike he'd carved from a branch in the night.*

Layfield. *In his body bag and then gone. Gone, gone, gone.*

Shaw. *Hanging from a tree, face bloated and covered with flies.*

Landro. *In the clearing. Disemboweled, entrails between his teeth.*

Levas. *Floating in the river. Fish feasting on his bulging eyes.*

Blanchard. *Bullet hole in his head, brains splashed all over the forest.*

Drench. *Disappeared without a trace. Sounds of screaming, screaming, screaming.*

Cook. *Throat slit with hunting knife, gargled bloody laughter.*

Williams. *Slit wrists and rock in hand, standing over Brook's body.*

Brook. *Head a pulpy mess without shape.*

Frederick. *Gone like Drench. Into the woods never to return.*

He was sure he was about to break. It was inevitable. He wondered if, years from now, they would find him, just another skeleton on the floor with the rest. A forgotten, nameless victim of a horror unlike anything ever seen before. He looked at his hands trembling in the gloom and realized he shouldn't be able to see them at all. He looked around him, surprised to find he could see the walls, bathed in a soft red hue.

The tunnel curved away to the right, the light source coming from whatever lay beyond it. Petrov whistled behind him, and Kimmel had no choice but to exit the tunnel and into the room, somehow managing to stifle a scream as he saw what lay beyond.

CHAPTER 41

They came through the trees; wispy forms melting through the branches, white mist forming into human shapes. Men, women, children. All who had lost their lives on the land over the centuries. They lined the edge of the clearing, bodies materializing and dematerializing, weaving between semi-transparent and solid.

Their arrival brought with it silence. Emma and the others edged away from them, moving further into the clearing. The ghosts watched; black voids where their eyes should be. Silent. Waiting. Two of them came forward, appearing like some cheap magician's illusion at either side of Henry. Melody whined, grabbing Emma's hand and squeezing it, feeling a fear she had almost learned to forget.

The pale form of Donovan stared at her, hungry lust on his face. Beside him was Eto, clad in full tribute paint, white skull daubed on his face, pointed teeth exposed, symbols on his body in honor of those he worshiped.

The group stared, unable to comprehend. The atmosphere was so heavy, so charged, it was hard to breathe. They had transcended reality to a place beyond fear, beyond any known capacity to deal with what was happening to them. They knew they were a part of whatever was about to happen, and were completely powerless to stop it.

Henry spoke, Eto and Donovan's mouths mirroring his as he addressed those who had come to witness the death of the boy.

"They want you all to witness the end. To witness their eternal existence."

"You can't get out of this, Henry," Dane said, thinking about the gun and if he would be able to use it if he had to. "They'll shoot you where you stand, you have to know that. You don't have any chances left. You can't talk your way out of this like you used to."

"They won't be here in time. Not now."

Dane pulled the gun from his jeans, hands shaking as he aimed it at his brother. "I'll do it myself if I have to."

Henry smiled; an expression more of pity than amusement. Dane faltered, realizing he had made a mistake.

"No, you won't," Henry said.

It was then they came, those on the edge of the circle. They rushed the group, exploding from their positions; a swirling, screaming mass of formless things.

"It's time," Mrs. Alma said. "Form a circle, just like we practiced."

Truman, Emma, and Mrs. Alma linked hands as Dane stared open mouthed at the rushing, ducking, diving spirits.

"You too," Mrs. Alma said to Melody, holding a hand out toward her.

"Me? I don't understand…"

"You're part of this too. Join us."

"My son…" was all she could manage as she

watched Henry and Isaac.

"Quickly!" Mrs. Alma snapped.

Melody grasped Truman's hand and pulled herself up.

Gunshots echoed around the clearing as Dane fired at the translucent forms of the dead, his bullets passing through them and into the forest.

Mrs. Alma blocked everything out. She closed her eyes and began to chant, mouthing secret words in a language long forgotten. "Close the circle," she said, finally opening her eyes.

"What about Isaac?" Emma screamed above the noise.

"You know his fate. We can't stop it now but we might be able to save ourselves."

"There must be something we can do."

Mrs. Alma looked at Emma, the answer evident in her eyes.

"Please, close the circle," the older woman said.

Sobbing and trembling, the group joined hands. As their link was made, the ground began to rumble and the trees swaying furiously, shedding branches as they were violently pushed by the spirits of the dead.

In the middle of the clearing, Henry leaned close to Isaac, whispering in his ear. "Every night in my cell I dreamt about this moment. Now, it's finally a reality."

Isaac was about to ask what he meant, but Henry's hands were already on his throat, squeezing, blocking his airway. Isaac kicked and choked, clawing desperately at Henry's hands as the life was squeezed out of him. Henry roared in ecstasy, and the trees roared back.

CHAPTER 42

The room was located directly underneath the clearing in the woods, and was the same size. What existed within it could only be described as an abomination. It was organic, and clearly alive, its gelatinous mass pulsing and flexing, its skin glowing a dull red. It was an unholy amalgamation of humanity. Legs and torsos, heads and arms. Countless in number. Some of the corpses were putrid and rotten, yet remained alive.

Sightless, maggot-infested eyes stared out at their eternal torturer, and the air was filled with screams of everlasting agony. The thing was part of the walls, part of the floor, fused within them, embedded within the very makeup of the chamber. From the top of the giant mass, large tubes fed up into the ceiling.

The pulsing thing quivered, unleashing a furious roar from its thousand dead mouths.

"We've been waiting for you," Petrov said as he exited the tunnel, blocking Kimmel's only means of escape.

The General wasn't listening. He couldn't help but stare at the unimaginable mass that dominated the chamber.

Putrescent fluid from the decomposing corpses flowed across the floor as the creature withdrew from the center of the room, giving them space. Small tentacles snaked from the mass and sucked the fluid up, reabsorbing what it had lost.

He turned toward Petrov, who was also watching the creature as it pulsed and quivered. The detective was plainly under the influence of the monstrous thing. His eyes were glazed, mouth open in slack awe.

"Amazing, isn't it?" Petrov whispered.

"You need to snap out of it, Detective. You need to fight it," Kimmel mumbled, struggling to resist its insistent probing.

"I wonder if it was always here. Before man even existed? I wonder if it was always waiting in the dirt, growing stronger, waiting to be discovered."

Kimmel headed over to Petrov. The creature quivered, and the detective raised his gun. "Can you hear them? I can hear them."

"It's not real. Don't you know it's not real?"

Petrov leveled the weapon at Kimmel. "Yes. It is."

Kimmel flinched a split second before Petrov fired.

CHAPTER 43

Melody screamed. She thought she knew fear, thought she understood how far a person could be stretched by despair and horror, but it was nothing compared to what she saw now. Her son, eyes bugging out of his head, the tip of his tongue protruding from between his lips as Henry choked him. She knew she had to get to him, to do something.

"Don't break the circle," Mrs. Alma screamed, glaring at her.

"I need to help him!" Melody sobbed.

"This is the only way to help him. By keeping this circle closed."

Emma glared at her as she said it, unable to believe the ease of Mrs. Alma's lie.

"Promise me he won't die," Melody fired back, fighting to get the words out.

"The circle must remain closed no matter what happens, Mrs. Samson. It's the only way to survive."

The wind was a thunderous gale, and the enraged wails of the Gogoku were clear within it as they probed at them, entering their minds, trying to break their bond.

Each of them began to see visions, things designed to terrify them and break the link. Truman saw his ancestor, noose around his neck, tongue purple and bloated, eyes milky and white.

In Truman's head, he heard it telling him he needed to stop, that by continuing he was condemning his family to Hell.

"Ignore their poisonous lies," Mrs. Alma said, still calm, still in control. "They can't harm us while we're bonded."

Emma saw Annie Briggs, glaring and bloody from the knife wounds that killed her. She mocked and chastised, demanding Emma break the circle. Her friends were there too, bodies ravaged from where they'd been nailed to the tree. Carrie mocked, teased and whispered directly into Emma's head, but she squeezed her eyes closed and blocked it out. Melody saw Donovan, leering with his crocodile grin. His words were eerily familiar, bringing back memories of her ordeal at his hands.

Teasing cunt bitch.

Her grip faltered, but Emma was there to maintain it.

Even Mrs. Alma wasn't spared. She saw her demons too, her own connection to the clearing. She saw Michael Jones, his bloated, water-damaged face glaring as he gurgled at his last living descendent not to damn him to an eternity of suffering. She knew well enough that the words came from the darkness that resided there, and easily blocked it out, banishing both sight and sound while concentrating on the task at hand.

Dane was troubled by none of the same horrors inflicted on those within the circle. He was no threat to them or their task. Instead, he glared at his brother as he continued to choke Isaac's limp body.

Dane searched for anything, any semblance of the man Henry used to be, but saw only a monster; a foul, vile creature. There was no redeeming him. No stopping him. Dane's hope of protecting his brother from death in a hail of bullets was gone. He knew now that death was the only release that could bring any kind of peace to his sibling. There was nothing else for him. Gritting his teeth, he strode across the clearing, flinching as the spirits darted around and through him.

He pointed the gun at his brother, hand trembling, and Henry laughed, throwing his head back. The wind echoed him, skittering leaves across the clearing.

"Let him go, Henry. This is over."

Henry threw Isaac's limp body to the floor. "It doesn't matter now. It's done," he said, staring triumphantly at his brother.

"Don't kill him, his part in this isn't over yet!" Mrs. Alma screamed above the roar of the wind.

"He's a murderer. He's killed people. Destroyed lives. Yours. Your families. Mine," Dane said, the anger inside him growing and swelling with each passing second.

"Harming him would be a mistake. You'll go

to prison," Alma yelled. The others in the clearing were still battling with their demons.

Dane looked down at Isaac. Skin so pale, eyes open and unseeing, ugly purple bruises on his neck. "The mistake would be letting him live," Dane said, striding toward his brother and pressing the barrel of the gun into his forehead hard enough to turn the skin white around its edge. "I'd be doing the world a favor by splashing his brains across the ground right here and now."

"Don't harm him," she repeated. "Not now. It isn't time."

"Look, lady. I don't buy into all this witchcraft shit. This is between me and him."

"Not witchcraft," she said, eyes glittering in the darkness. "Forces. Forces most people don't or can't understand, but real nonetheless. Your brother still has a part to play before the end."

"They speak louder than you, whore!" Henry spat. "They are already inside him. Nothing can stop them. Not now."

Dane wondered if it were true. His intention hadn't been to harm Henry when he first arrived. Now, however, the idea of killing him seemed like not only a good idea, but a natural one. It was as if something inside his head was encouraging him, spurring him on. He pressed the barrel harder into his brother's forehead.

"Enough talk," he barked.

"Don't harm him. I'm warning you!" Mrs. Alma shrieked.

"And I'm warning you to keep your damn mouth shut!"

"They want you to kill me," Henry whispered. "They want you to take my place. Do it. Finish it. My work here is done. The boy is dead. This can't be stopped. Soon, I go to them. I take my place at their side."

"Shut up!" Dane screamed. It felt as if there was a chalkboard in the center of his head with a thousand fingernails scraping down it. "Just be quiet!"

"Sacrifice me. You know you want to. You *need* to. They demand it."

Henry pushed his forehead into the barrel, eyes glaring at his brother. "Do it. Do it. Do it. Do it," he repeated over and over again.

In Dane's head, the screech of the chalkboard intensified, building until it was all he could hear.

"I can't!" Dane said, hitting Henry in the temple with the gun and knocking him to the ground. "I won't let you manipulate me, Henry. Not again. You're going back to the hospital."

III

Silence.

The spirits of the dead faded into the ether and the trees stopped their violent commotion. Exhausted, those forming the protective circle collapsed, the mental energy required to resist the spirits draining them. Dane stood, blinking, ears ringing as he tried to figure out what to do.

A cry broke the silence. However, it wasn't

from one of the demonic things that had surrounded them, but from Melody when she saw her son. Dane dropped to his knees, checked the boy's pulse and, finding none, started performing CPR. He compressed Isaacs's chest, counting along as he went, doing everything he could to avoid staring into those lifeless eyes that told him they had failed to protect him. Slowly, the others approached, standing around Dane as he battled to save Isaac's life. Emma and Mrs. Alma were with Melody, holding her upright so she didn't collapse. Time in the clearing seemed to slow as Dane continued to work, alternating his rhythmic compressions with blowing air into Isaac's lungs.

Two minutes passed. Then three.

They all knew the seriousness of the situation, however, none were willing to speak, not whilst Dane was still willing to work. He paused, looking into Isaac's eyes. Isaac's lifeless eyes. He knew it was over. There was nothing else that could be done. He turned, putting his back to Isaac, unable to look at the boy any longer. He cradled his head in his hands and stared at the floor, breathing heavily.

"It's too late," he gasped. "He's gone."

Melody did fall this time, landing hard on her knees, unable to breathe, unable to comprehend. All she could do was scream; an anguished sound that reverberated around the forest.

Isaac Samson was dead.

CHAPTER 44

As Isaac Samson lost his life above ground, the creature below quivered. The tentacles sprouting from its body thrust toward the roof of the chamber, burrowing into the earthen ceiling, ready to claim its prize.

With its energy focused on the world above, its grip on Petrov faltered. He blinked, unable to remember what had happened to him since touching the painting. He blinked again, his eyes growing wide at the beast in front of him, as if seeing it for the first time. He screamed, firing off the remaining bullets from his weapon and then, when it was empty, throwing the weapon itself.

The creature carried on burrowing, unharmed by the ammunition. It was then, when he looked around the room, that he saw Kimmel, lying on his side, bullet wound in his stomach staining his shirt.

Petrov ran to him, dragging him away from the smaller tentacles near the base of the creature that were already reaching out for him. Kimmel groaned as Petrov dragged him toward the tunnel they had entered by.

"Stop," Kimmel grunted. "Stop, it hurts too much."

Petrov set him down, still unable to keep from staring at the creature. "I have to get you out of here. God, what have I done?"

"You have to kill it," Kimmel mumbled, a bubble of blood expanding in and out of his mouth as he spoke. "Kill it."

"How do you kill something like that? It's impossible."

"Light," Kimmel muttered. "Use the light."

Petrov thought about it for a second, unsure if Kimmel was delirious or not. "I'm sorry," he said, then stood and ran from the chamber, leaving Kimmel screaming as the creature's appendages began reaching out for him once more.

Petrov ran up the tunnel, feeling his way, struggling to understand what was happening or what he was dealing with. Breathing was becoming difficult, the air thick, the taste of rot making him gag. He would go for help, he reasoned, trying to convince himself. He would go, and come back with more men, more firepower. More lights. Definitely more lights. He moved through the altar room, remembering how the effigy had first spooked him, something which seemed almost laughable now after the horror he had seen back there. He knew the surface was just ahead, the blessed relief of freedom.

Then he paused.

He stood in the gloom, trying to catch his breath, torn between leaving and staying. He knew that if he ran, he wouldn't come back, despite telling himself otherwise. He had to end it. Petrov tried to focus, relying on his training, on the analytical mind that had seen him rise through the ranks so quickly. An idea, or at least the basis of one, came to him. Something that may or may not work but was worth trying. Although it took a supreme effort of will, he turned away from the tantalizing taste of freedom and headed back toward the awful thing lurking below.

II

Back on the surface, Melody was inconsolable. Her screams had died away, but her sobs and shaking persisted. Even Dane, a man who had no emotional attachment to any of them, could feel her anguish, and it cut him deeper than he expected. A low rumble emanated from the ground, shaking the topsoil. Dane lurched to his feet, staring at the earth along with the others, wondering what was coming next.

Something pushed through the ground by Isaac's foot; something wet and pink. It hesitated, tasting the air, and continued to push upwards. Another joined it, then a third and a fourth, all of them emerging around Isaac's body.

"What's that? What the fuck is that?" Dane said, his voice too high, too shrill.

"It's come for him," Mrs. Alma said. "It wants its prize."

"Don't let it take him. Don't you let it take my baby," Melody screamed, eyes wide, somewhere in a place far beyond fear.

The tentacles were already on Isaac, wrapping around his arms and legs. They watched in horror as a larger one joined them, this one thick and strong. It began to clamber over Isaac's stomach, pulling him down into the soft earth.

"Re-form the circle, quickly!" Mrs. Alma said.

The others began linking hands, and she shook her head. "No. around the boy."

Dane was about to join them when Mrs. Alma held up a hand. "Not you."

"Why not?"

"You're not part of this. You need to go to your brother. Ensure he doesn't interfere. Even now, he wakes."

Dane saw that she was right. Henry was on his hands and knees, blood streaming down his face from where Dane had hit him. Nodding to Mrs. Alma, he went to his brother, grabbing him by the arm and pulling him to his feet. It was the move Henry had been waiting for. He tackled Dane to the ground, snarling and snapping, biting at his brother with his lethal dagger teeth.

"You won't deny them, you won't deny me!" he roared, blood and drool spilling from his mouth. Caught off guard by both the ferocity of the attack and the feral look in his brother's eyes, Dane froze, not reacting until Henry bit his forearm, shredding flesh and exposing fatty muscle. Dane fought back then, his eyes frantically searching for his gun while he tried to hold his brother at bay.

III

Mrs. Alma closed the circle, the four of them linking hands around Isaac's body. As the link was made, the tentacles seemed to flex, as if in pain, then doubled their efforts, pulling Isaac deeper into the dirt. Melody stared at her son, guilt and rage surging in equal measure.

I failed him.

It was an idea she couldn't escape from.

Isaac was pulled lower, his midriff now almost under the dirt. His head lolled to one side, and his dead eyes landed on her. She was certain she could feel the accusation within them; the pain. The lack of understanding of why they'd been separated.

"I won't let you take him!" she screamed, breaking the bond and falling to her knees. She pulled at his arm and grabbed around his chest, wrestling to keep him above ground.

"You mustn't break the circle," Mrs. Alma said, trying to yank Melody to her feet.

"I won't let it take him. I have nothing left!"

"He's already gone."

"I won't accept that. I won't."

"We need you, Mrs. Samson. We can end it, but not this way."

Melody stopped pulling at her son, the fight knocked out of her. Mrs. Alma took her hand and pulled her to her feet, and Emma grasped her other hand and reformed the link around the boy. Once again, the tentacles shuddered and flinched.

Across the clearing, the Marshall brothers continued to fight. Henry snapped and snarled at

Dane, who in turn was still looking for his weapon. Dane rolled, getting Henry underneath him, and from his new vantage point, he saw his gun in the dirt nearby. He scrambled for it, risking putting his back to Henry for the few seconds it would take to retrieve it, and reached out, snatched it up and turned it on Henry.

"Stay where you are, Henry. I don't want to do this, but I will if I have to."

Henry glared at Dane, and then at the others grouping around Isaac's body. "I won't let them stop me, nor you," he growled, slowly getting to his feet.

"I told you not to move. Don't think I won't use this just because you're my brother."

Henry grinned maliciously, closing the distance between himself and Dane. "Then why don't you stop me?"

"Henry."

"Do it, Dane. Shoot me. You know what I intend to do." He showed Dane what was in his hand. A palm-sized rock he'd picked up from the ground. "I'm going to use this to beat your brains in, Dane. Then I'm going to use it on them and stop them taking our prize."

"I swear, I'll do it," Dane said, hands trembling, the pain from the bite Henry had inflicted excruciating.

"No you won't. If you'd intended to, you would have done it already."

There was no distance between them now. Henry walked right up to the gun, pushing his chest into the barrel. When he spoke, it was in a whisper. "If you don't shoot me right now, I'm going to kill you."

"I'm not bluffing, Henry."

"Neither am I."

Henry swung the rock, the smooth surface smashing into the side of Dane's head. He went down hard, gun skittering across the ground, and lay there motionless as Henry stood above him. "I'm going to make you suffer for all the times you made me suffer when we were young. But first, I have to kill your friends."

Henry turned and started to walk toward the group as the chanting from the trees began again.

CHAPTER 45

Petrov reentered the chamber where the gelatinous creature dwelled, once again reeling at both the sight and stench of it. His hope had been to save Kimmel, but he saw that it was already too late. The lower half of him had been taken in by the creature, numerous small tentacles further feeding him into the mass. He was considering how relieved he was that Kimmel wasn't suffering anymore when the General moaned, and blinked, wide eyed and pleading.

Petrov set down the fuel can and torch, ran to him and grabbed him under the arms, trying to pull him free. Kimmel attempted to speak, blood welling up in his mouth.

"Shut up and let me help you," Petrov screamed, planting his feet on the ground and pulling with every ounce of strength he could muster.

There was a sound; a brittle, wet crunch as Kimmel's upper torso came free, intestines snaking. An impossible quantity of blood gushed out across the floor and was quickly set upon by the smaller tendrils at the creature's base. Petrov fell back, dragging the upper half of Kimmel on top of him, at first unsure of what had happened.

He scrambled aside, pushing Kimmel's body away and watching in morbid fascination as the jelly-like creature flexed and stretched toward him, keen not to lose the rest of its meal.

Petrov turned back to the task at hand and his eyes focused on the fuel can he'd retrieved from the upper tunnel. He picked it up, unscrewed the cap and tossed it aside before splashing the contents on the creature.

When the liquid made contact, the creature convulsed and rolled. It began to flatten its mass, extending around the walls, inching toward the exit. Petrov glanced over his shoulder, seeing what it intended to do. He set the remainder of the fuel down by Kimmel's upper torso, sparing another glance at the exit, hoping that when he put flame to the creature it would retract, allowing him time to escape.

He searched his pockets, hands trembling as he looked for his matches. He found them with his cigarettes in his jacket, distantly thinking how much he wanted to smoke, how he would love to just be somewhere outside in the fresh air where he could lie down and stare at the sky and smoke in peace and quiet.

Later. He could smoke later. Right now, he had a different purpose. He pulled out a match and struck it, the head fizzling briefly into life and then dying, its blackened head leaving a wispy trail of smoke. His panic was starting to increase, and he flicked another quick glance towards the exit. The creature had almost completely sealed the way out, its slick flesh meeting as it closed off the top third of the door.

Petrov took another match, placed the head against the phosphorous strip on the side of the box and dragged it across. This time the flame held, and he almost screamed in excitement. The creature quivered, closing the gap around the door even more. He touched the live match to the others in the pack, each igniting its neighbor until they were all ablaze. The flames licked higher, sending orange shadows dancing along the walls. Petrov drew his arm back and threw the fiery box at the creature, a guttural scream escaping from his lips as he did.

He wasn't sure what happened next. A sound, like the distant echo of laughter, filled the air, and Petrov watched in horror as the matchbox lifted above the creature on a motionless breeze. The flames fought for life for a few moments before ebbing away to nothing more than an orange glow. He stood there, eyes fixed on the box as the glow faded and it slowly dropped to the ground, its contents withered and cold.

It was over.

Petrov fell to the floor, staring at the creature as it continued to burrow into the roof. There was no escape. Not anymore. He wondered how long it had been down here, if it was older than humanity itself. He thought Kimmel might have known, and he glanced over to the general's body, staring at the remains, wishing there was more he could have done to help him at the end.

Something caught his eye. He scrambled over to Kimmel's butchered upper half, stomping on the few tentacles that were already probing against the hollow where his stomach had once been. There was something in his hand, something catching the dim light generated by the creature.

Petrov peeled back Kimmel's fingers and felt a moment of such elation he almost forgot how much danger he was in. He snatched the gold lighter out of the general's hand and hoped it would be as lucky for him.

With renewed hope, Petrov stood, took a step toward the torch, and fell, pitching over and landing on his knees. He stared at the tentacle wrapped around his ankle and the sense of elation faded. The torch was hopelessly out of reach, but he stretched for it anyway, pulling against his restraint, unable to believe just how strong the creature was. It was no good. Even at full stretch, he was still at least four feet from the torch. He scrambled back, staring at the tentacle, barely reacting as others inched forward.

The fuel can at his side mocked him; half the solution to the problem, but a meaningless half without the torch. At least that would withstand any attempt to extinguish it, unlike the lighter. He could feel the tentacle pulling him, dragging him toward the larger mass of the creature. He stared at it and wondered how it would feel to be digested, how long he would suffer. He glanced at Kimmel again and was suddenly jealous that his suffering was over.

You know what you need to do.

It was the rational voice, the one he relied on when investigating homicides. It hadn't had much call to be used during the horrors he'd endured so far. Now though, it had something to say.

Do what needs to be done. You know the answer.

He did. He had known from the second it grabbed him; it was just that the idea of it terrified him.

It has to be better. The voice in his head told him. *Has to be better than the alternative.*

He stared at the convulsing mass, knowing the suffering he would endure by it would be far worse than the relatively quick end he could provide for himself.

And quick it would have to be because he could feel the creature pulling him closer, drawing him in. Petrov tucked the lighter into his pocket and stood up, pulling on the creature, using it as leverage. After all, it didn't matter now. He grabbed the fuel can and lifted it above his head, dousing himself and the creature with the rest of the can's contents. With the fumes burning his nostrils, the reality of what he was about to do became clear. He thought of his wife. How she would be expecting him home later. How she would wait by the window when he didn't return, desperate for news. How that news would never come.

Not now.

He took the lighter from his pocket, shaking and afraid. The simple gold lighter was old, its case scuffed. Petrov flicked it open, thumb poised over the roller. He glanced at the creature and hoped it would work, hoped it would burn and die. He, of course, would never get to find out. He put the lighter to his fuel-soaked shirt, took a deep breath, closed his eyes, and thumbed the flint.

The flame took immediately, greedily eating its way through the fuel. Petrov didn't feel anything for a few seconds, then was consumed with an impossible agony as his flesh seared. He threw himself onto the creature, the flame passing between them. It sizzled and withdrew, its skin splitting and spewing its foul contents, releasing gasses which further fed the fire.

It was a spectacular display as the creature burned and withered. Petrov held on tight, the pain easing as his nerve endings died. He gazed at the display of multicolored flames erupting from its skin, their seductive dance the last thing he would ever see.

His blackened corpse fell to its knees and bent back toward the floor as the chamber filled with smoke and fire. Quivering and rumbling, the creature was powerless against its fate, its weakness in the end, the humans it had manipulated into being its protector.

CHAPTER 46

Even as it burned, the creature was determined not to give up on its prize. More tentacles shot out of the earth and tried to pull Isaac down. Smoke began billowing out of the ground as the creature's movements became more erratic.

Mrs. Alma broke the contact with the others and dropped to her knees. "Pull him clear. Now's the time. Pull him clear!" the others complied, dropping to the ground and grabbing onto any remaining part of Isaac they could. An arm, a leg. Melody went to his head, holding it up, brushing the dirt away from his face as he was dragged deeper.

"You won't deny it!" Henry screamed. He lurched toward them, bloody rock in hand.

"Ignore him," Mrs. Alma said. "Pull the boy clear."

"I'll kill you all. Every last one of you. Starting with you," he said stumbling toward Melody. She glanced over her shoulder, eyes wide as he reared back with the rock, his face a filthy mask of hatred.

A gunshot, crisp and loud.

Henry's forehead disappeared in a red spray, taking his eye with it, the devastating impact of the bullet deforming what remained of his face. He stood for a second, framed with the moon at his back, and then fell forward at the exact same time Isaac was pulled free of the creature's grasp.

The group dragged Isaac's limp body aside, the void where he'd been now filled with Henry. The creature grabbed at him, tentacles wrapping around his body, pulling him down, the blood from his head wound sending it into a feeding frenzy despite its own death throes. Dane looked on, gun still in shaking hand, cheeks wet with tears.

"His part is played," Mrs. Alma whispered as Henry was dragged under, his spine snapping under the pressure.

The ground began to vibrate, and then the trees followed suit, swaying and hissing. Truman picked up Isaac's body and followed the others to the outer edge of the clearing, watching as the creature withdrew with its trophy, an orange flicker of flame now visible as smoke continued to billow upward.

The wispy spirits of the dead came from the trees, circling the clearing; a screaming, thousand-faced cyclone. One by one they faded, freed from their bindings to the creature below.

Emma put a hand on Melody's arm, drawing her attention to the clearing.

Steve and Isaac stood in front of them, father and son together.

Melody couldn't breathe, overwhelmed with emotion as her senses were flooded with forgotten memories. The smell of Steve's aftershave, the way his cheeks dimpled when he smiled. There was so much she wanted to say, so much she wanted to explain, but now he was there, the words wouldn't come. Just a jumble of feelings and emotions which conflicted with each other. She wanted to be with them, couldn't wait to die so they could be together at last.

No.

It was him, his voice, his presence injected directly into her head.

It's not your time yet. Nor is it his time.

She watched as Steve took his hands off Isaac's shoulders and gave him a gentle push. His spirit form drifted toward Melody, moving through her and back into his body.

He inhaled, gasping and blinking, coughing and putting his hands to his throat. Melody dropped to her knees and pulled him close to her, kissing his head, hugging him as tightly as she could.

There were no words she could say, nothing she could express to the spirit of her husband that could possibly articulate the gratitude she felt. She turned back to him, hoping to find some words that would mean something. The smile on her lips faltered. He was gone.

They all were. All that remained was the clearing, the ground smoldering and spewing out smoke.

"Do you feel that?" Emma said quietly, turning to the others.

"What?" Truman said.

"Nothing. It feels… safe."

Mrs. Alma nodded, looking at the trees. "This place is cleansed now. The dead can rest." She began walking toward the dirt path leading away from the clearing.

"What do we do now?" Melody asked, still hugging Isaac.

"We go home. It's over," she said simply.

"What about you?"

Mrs. Alma paused, considering the question. "Tea," she said. "I could really use a cup of tea."

Without saying anything else, she headed off down the dirt road toward the hotel.

EPILOGUE

Two Years Later.

Melody Samson was tired. She looked at the world in a different way now, changed by the things she'd experienced. Gaunt, and missing most of her hair, she pulled the hat down further over her ears.

"You'd never know, would you?" Isaac said, leaning on the handles of the wheelchair.

"No, you wouldn't," she replied. "Not at all."

He crouched by the chair, taking her bony hands in his. "Are you okay?"

"I'm fine. It's just taking a little bit of getting used to."

"I know what you mean. It still feels weird."

"You know, I'm glad we got to spend some time together before the end."

"Hey, don't talk like that. We still have plenty of time together."

She smiled; a wistful gesture that was almost sad. "We both know that's not true, although I wish it was. Either way, we had more time than I was supposed to. That's something I'm grateful for."

Isaac lowered his head, staring at his feet. "Are you scared?" he asked, looking up at her.

"No," she said, smiling at him warmly.

"Not even a little?"

"I'm tired, Isaac. Weak. This isn't going to be a life for much longer. I don't want to get to the point where I'm just… existing. Do you understand what I mean?"

"I think so," he said, trying not to show how upset he was.

"Besides, I miss your father. I'm looking forward to seeing him again."

Isaac nodded and looked out over the clearing, the ground already flush with shoots and juvenile plant life where nature had started the long process of reclamation.

"Emma will be good to me, won't she?"

Melody nodded. "When my time comes, she will be your legal guardian. She'll look after you. She'll help you. More importantly, she understands what you went through."

"I like her," Isaac said, then cocked his head.

"Listen." He stood and placed a hand on her shoulder.

She followed his gaze, staring out into the trees, her eyes tracing the perimeter of the clearing. Birds sang in a great multi-species chorus, bees drifted lazily around the flowers and plant life that had already taken a foothold in the fresh earth.

"It sounds… peaceful," Melody said, still scanning the trees.

"I know. That's a good thing, isn't it?"

Melody laughed. "I suppose it is."

"Is it really safe? That thing underneath the ground…" He let his words drift away and kicked his feet in the dirt.

"You know, Dane Marshall tells me the hotel is being demolished next month; the remains of the house with it. That place underneath has already been filled with concrete," Melody said, smiling at him and squeezing his hands. "You don't need to be scared."

"How is Mr. Marshall?"

"He's fine. He's moved back out to California."

"Oh," Isaac said, staring out at the greenery.

"So that's it then. It really is done." Her smile grew as she said it, almost unable to believe it was true.

"There was one more thing I wanted to do since we're up here," Isaac said.

"Like what?"

He shrugged out of his backpack and set it on the ground, then crouched and unzipped it. "I have something for you. Well, something for us. It was something I wanted to share with you."

He took the jar out of his bag and handed it to Melody. She turned it in her hand, the sunlight diffusing in the glass. Inside was a plant; a thick green shoot already beginning to flower. Melody looked at her son and frowned.

"I don't understand."

"Emma gave me this before everything happened. Now this is all over, I had this idea, but now I'm here, it doesn't sound as good as it did in my head."

"No, go on. I'm interested to hear it," she said, smiling at her son.

"Well, it seems to me that we, our family I

mean, have been a part of this place for so long that maybe we should continue to be a part of it."

"What did you have in mind?" Melody asked.

"I thought maybe we could plant this. The two of us together; right in the middle there. What I'm thinking is, that in ten, twenty, even a hundred years, when this place is just another part of the forest, our plant will still be here. I just thought it was something we could do… if you want to."

"I think it's a wonderful idea," she replied, smiling broadly.

For a moment, Isaac could see beyond her illness, the radiance of her smile countering her weakened state.

"Do you feel up to a walk to help me?" he asked.

"Absolutely."

He helped her out of the chair, hooked her arm through his and led her into the clearing. They walked to its center, a place that in the past had brought fear and dread, but was now no different to the rest of the forest.

"Here?" he asked as they reached the middle of the clearing.

"Yes, this is good."

He helped her to her knees and knelt beside her.

"I don't suppose you brought anything to dig with?" she asked, still grinning.

"Oh, I forgot."

"Well, hands it is then."

"Yeah?"

"Yeah," she repeated.

They dug together, scooping out a depression in the soft earth. When it was ready, Isaac removed the plant from the jar, roots and all, and set it in the hole before packing the earth back in around it. He couldn't help but notice how such a simple task had exhausted her. She caught him staring, and smiled.

"What is it?" she asked.

"Nothing," he replied. "I was just looking at you."

She knew why of course, as it was harder to hide how drained she was these days, but she didn't want to ruin such a special moment. She grinned again and turned back to the plant. "It looks good there. It should thrive quite nicely."

"Do you think you'll come back here again?" Isaac asked, watching for her answer.

She considered the question, face half in shadow. She looked at the plant, then at Isaac. "I don't think so. I've seen what I wanted to see. What I *needed* to see. I had to be sure it was over. Thank you for agreeing to bring me."

"No problem."

"Right now, I'm hungry. How about we go find some food?"

"Now you're talking. Come on, let me help you up and get you back to the car. Emma will be wondering where we are."

They reached the outer edge of the clearing, and he helped her into the wheelchair before putting the empty jar back in the bag. He was about to toss it over his shoulder when Melody grabbed him by the arm.

"Look over there," she whispered.

He turned back toward the clearing, a small part of him expecting to see something terrifying, then smiled.

At the edge of the clearing, a small deer gingerly stepped out, nose twitching as it sniffed the air. It regarded them from afar, lifting one foot then lowering it again. It stepped into the sunlight, nosing around the young shoots and keeping a wary eye on them. Isaac shifted position, which was enough to startle it, sending it crashing back into the undergrowth.

"Come on, let's get out of here," Melody said, giving Isaac's hand a gentle squeeze. "This is no place for people anymore."

Isaac turned the wheelchair and pushed Melody away from the clearing, toward where Emma waited on the other side of the bridge. The wind rocked the trees, birds sang, and nature flourished where death had dominated for so long. Neither Melody nor Isaac looked back at the clearing, nor would either of them visit it ever again.

AUTHOR NOTES

Back when the idea for Whisper first presented itself, there was never any intention for it to be any longer than a short story for inclusion in Dark Corners. The initial idea was a story about a newly married couple who move into a house which backed onto a cemetery, and chronicle the weird things that happened to them. I had no idea that the story would go on to not only become a full blown novel, but would also spawn two sequels. I think the inevitable question which might be asked now is about a fourth entry in the series, and if one will ever rear its ugly head.

The answer to that is a resounding no.

I feel like I have told the story for these characters as well as I can, and feel that this particular world can be left alone whilst I move on to other things. I'll be the first to admit, however, that knowing I will never write stories for these characters again leaves something of a bittersweet taste. On the one hand, I'm happy to have resolved the story and given it a conclusion which ties up the loose ends (or at least I hope so).

On the other, it will be with a little sadness that I close the door on this cast of characters for the final time and leave them to their own devices. I look back across the trilogy as a whole story, and like to feel I have done a decent job of telling the tale I wanted to. Sure enough, there were some changes along the way which I didn't expect. In the first book, Donovan was only ever intended as a minor character to appear in the opening exchange with Steve and Melody as he showed them around Hope House. However, I liked the sleazy prick so much and enjoyed writing him enough to work the storyline to incorporate him more. In hindsight, I think I made a huge mistake in killing him off at the end of the first book. There is an existing draft which is vastly different to the final published version, where the roles are switched, and it's Donovan who survives and Steve who is killed. (That particular draft also has a much darker ending which would have made any sequels impossible.)

In Henry, I looked to create a Donovan 2.0. He's essentially the same character with a few minor tweaks.

I hope those of you who have stayed with the books for the long haul have enjoyed the ride. I have received criticism for some of the decisions I have made along the way which comes with the territory. One was making Melody a little bit whiny and intolerable in the first book (unintentional). I also took some flak for making the town of Oakwell a hybrid of English countryside and American small town (deliberate), and for offing poor Steve at the end of the second book (sorry, but he had to go!).

I accept this and take it on the chin. This business is one in which it's impossible to please everyone, and I, as the author, have to be prepared to accept the backlash if it comes. The flipside of that is that the praise is quite nice when it comes and the calls I made in the plot are validated.

As for the story you just read, I really, really hope you enjoyed it. I wanted to do something different again to the last two books, and had no desire or intention of creating a cookie cutter sequel. Lastly, I want to thank everyone who is reading, has read or intends to read (after all we need all the readers we can get) my books, and of course my long suffering family who tolerate the hour upon hour that I spend with my nose buried in my laptop.

This then, is the end for the Whisper story. Oakwell is far behind us and fading into the dark. That shape up ahead is a different world where I might just have something new to show you. I'll see you all when you get there.

7/11/14, Leeds, England.

www.ingramcontent.com/pod-product-compliance
Lightning Source LLC
LaVergne TN
LVHW020811020825
817671LV00001B/80